WHO SHOT
WILD BILL

ALEX
GORDON

THE CRIME LAB

This edition published 2016

by Ringwood Publishing

Copyright © 2016 Alex Gordon

All Rights Reserved

ISBN 978-1-901514-31-5

A CIP record for this book is available from the British Library

Typeset by Park Productions

Cover design by James Hutcheson

To Mary and John, the parents who introduced me to a wonderful wee island when I was seven years old. Also, to my sister Betty who was forced into taking penalty-kicks against me at the West Bay football pitch before she was allowed to go dancing at the Garrison in the sixties.

And, of course, my wife Gerda for being a constant source of inspiration. Millport's got the Crocodile Rock...I've got my wee rock.

ACKNOWLEDGEMENTS

Eddie and Margaret Hughes, John and Jeanette, Kirsty, Tom and Kath, James and Helen, Arthur and Trish, Graham and Ann, Gerry and Mrs Gerry, Jim, Martin and Joan, Tom Nellis, Big Stevie, Shirley, Tracey and the two Johns, Bobby and Jean and their John, Alasdair, Colin, Yildrum, Tony and Sarah, Alex, Bob and Margaret Caldwell, Billy, Stuart, Kath, Liz, Sandra, Janice, Lesley, Robert, Ian, Pete and Kathy, Wee Willie.

Also, the good patrons and owners of the following establishments: The Kelburne Bar, The Tavern, Frasers, Newton, Mintrels and the George Hotel. Not forgetting the Deep Sea Chippy!

Last, and certainly not least, Bob Smith, the publisher who literally got on his bike to give this book a push. Respect!

My apologies if I have overlooked anyone.

PROLOGUE

Wild Bill Hickok was smiling. Which was odd considering there was a bullet hole between his eyes.

The cowboy was lying flat out, sprawling on the grass, blue eyes open wide, staring towards the pale overhead clouds drifting in a dark grey sky; eyes searching for an answer that would never come. His arms and legs were spread apart, the toes of his boots pointing towards heaven.

His jet-black, wax ankle-length coat was wide open, acting as a sheet underneath his prone body. His black wide-brimmed Stetson was perched at a crazy angle, balancing backwards on his head. His long, lank grey hair cascaded down onto his shoulders. His moustache was neatly trimmed round his lips before taking on a life of its own as it rampaged its unruly way down and over his chin. His faded black denims were tucked neatly into his tan knee-high boots. A gaudily embroidered scarlet waistcoat enveloped a green and black plaid shirt. A yellow neckerchief was haphazardly and loosely strewn around his neck. His dark brown gun belt, with both ivory-handled revolvers still snugly in place in their holsters, was tightly drawn around his waist. The ostentatious brass buckle was adorned with the American symbol of the Bald Eagle.

He was quite dead. The giveaway sign, besides the bullet hole between his eyes, was the fact he had ceased to breathe. Yet, he still looked incredibly pleased to be placed in this rather awkward position.

'Aw, Jeez.' Constable Fiona Anderson was not in a happy place. 'Aw, Jeez,' she repeated. The cop gazed at the body. 'Could you not have waited another fortnight?' In the gathering late-evening gloom, she thought the bundle on the ground at the dimly-lit West Bay playing fields was a dog when it attracted her attention. She was on her way back after checking out the Millerston Hotel,

1

part of her nightly grind on the graveyard shift, a hitherto dull routine that had never presented the unexpected. Until now. 'No, you had to be a fuckin' cowboy, didn't you?'

PC Anderson, her plumpish figure squeezed into the jacket and trousers of her uniform, felt the urgent need to scream, piercing the stillness of a murky evening. She had been the only police presence on the tranquil North Ayrshire island of Great Cumbrae for two years and was about to be transferred back to the mainland to Greenock. Two weeks and counting. And now there was a corpse lying at her feet. With a bullet hole between his eyes.

'Fuckin' Country and Western Festival,' she observed, her expression a mixture of puzzlement and anger. 'All these lunatics dressed up like John Wayne, shooting at each other with their stupid toy guns.' Wearily, she shook her head. 'Why me?'

Strathclyde Police had actually doubled the constable head count to deal with the demands of the Country and Western Festival. Fiona had a partner out there somewhere. A partner who wasn't answering his mobile phone. Into the bargain, the battery on her walkie-talkie was kaput. Her new short-term colleague's name was Steven Murphy, a spotty youth recruited from the Largs cop shop on the mainland and he didn't look old enough to cross the road on his own. 'Where's that little prick?' Fiona, understandably in the circumstances, was growing more than slightly agitated. 'Probably fuckin' blotto. Or trying to shag Annie Oakley.'

Hand in hand, the chill and the darkness had already sneaked onto the island as she tried to collect her thoughts.

'What the fuck happens next?'

CHAPTER ONE

Charlie Brock arrived at the Cumbrae slip on the 10.15am ferry. The crossing from the North Ayrshire coastal resort of Largs to the Isle of Great Cumbrae embraced all of ten minutes. The Firth of Clyde had been known to be spiteful in late August and early September, but the old lady put away her snarl that morning. The rolling swells had agreed to take the day off. It was a pleasant voyage that whisked Brock from humdrum to heaven.

Even after all these years, there was still something magical and wondrous about this small island for Brock as he prepared to disembark and be greeted with the sign, Failte gu EILEAN CHUMBRUAICH - Welcome to the ISLAND OF CUMBRAE. One step off the ferry and there was the uplifting feeling that the mainland, and the world's problems, were well in the distance, light years away. To him, it was a tiny part of God's good earth. The island that time, thankfully, chose to forget.

Brock could see sunshine settling on the surrounding hills, vividly green at this time of year, a few sheep going about their business. Beyond were the mountains of Arran, also bathed in beautiful light. A few puffs of scattered clouds wandered serenely across the bright azure skies, as if posed by an artist to create this hypnotic image. There was the merest hint of a breeze to remind Brock he was still, in fact, in Scotland. His father had been fond of saying, 'Money couldn't buy this, son.' And, many years later, Brock still acknowledged the insight and wisdom of his father.

After the calm crossing, it was onto the sixty-seater bus to be driven four miles south to the town of Millport, the beating heart of the island, which was prepared once more for the swarming rabble that descended on the island for the annual Country and Western Festival. Brock shared the ten-minute coach journey with a varied array of garishly-attired fellow-passengers. Politely, he had given up his seat to a fifty something female who bore more than a passing resemblance to Miss Kitty, the owner of the Long Branch Saloon in Gunsmoke, the western TV series from another era.

'Thanks, y'al,' she drawled and winked suggestively. Brock real-ised she was already in character for what lay ahead. Among the passengers, there was the usual assortment of individuals adorned in what they earnestly believed Wyatt Earp, Doc Holliday, Billy The Kid and Co wore back in the day. Most, labouring under the impression that cowboys were obliged to sport some embel-lishment of facial hair, wore beards, some neat and square, some long and straggly. Apparently a fair percentage of the weekend gunslingers were in agreement that hair gathered back in ponytails was de rigueur for any self-respecting Jesse James.

Idly, Brock couldn't help wondering about the six Elvis Presleys on the packed coach. They weren't the Elvis of the 'Love-Me-Tender' era. They were more the Elvis of 'Who-ate-all-the-burgers?' era, or the 'Elvis-bursting-out-of-his-white-sequined-jumpsuit-while-making-a-complete-arse-of-himself-in-Las-Vegas' era. The six had invested in foot-high black wigs with extended cow licks that could have doubled as diving boards. They had wild side breezers plung-ing towards their Adam's apple. Brock wondered what his brief travelling companions did for a living in the real world.

Brock, a sports journalist, was now freelance after working for what seemed a hundred years for the Daily News, Scotland's national newspaper. Great and interesting times, but he knew it was time to go after yet another cost-cutting exercise the faceless fat cats in London persisted in calling 'streamlining'. What that actually translated to, in Brock's mind, was the end of the road for a lot of good, experienced newspaper operators. They would be 'getting a tap on the shoulder' to be replaced by an excitable group of computer-literate graduates who, to be fair, were dab hands with new technology. The kids were all smartly turned out. Hair combed, teeth brushed, shirt and tie, freshly-pressed trousers with needle-sharp creases, well-polished shoes. Coming in with their own sandwiches and never going anywhere near that 'bad place' Brock called the pub. Their mammies would be proud of them. One small snag, though. They knew bugger all about being newspapermen. And Brock realised it was time he had to go before he was up on a murder charge.

'Last week I couldn't spell journalist. Now I are one.' That was the joke, but it was too close to the truth for Brock. He overheard one prospective giant of the written word talking on the editorial floor one day. 'Everything in modernisation is my motto,' he said. 'Yes, everything in modernisation.' Brock sighed. He knew the budding Carl Bernstein wouldn't have known the Fourth Estate from the Four Tops, or the difference between a menagerie and a ménage-a-trois.

This was the same editorial floor where Big Fitz, a marvellous character and a damn fine Features Sub-Editor, came back from a liquid lunch one afternoon and promptly stood in a metal waste-paper bucket and didn't seem to notice. He clanked and clunked his way along the entire length of the editorial, about one hundred yards long, clattering the bin off desks, chairs and anything else that got in his way. Eventually, he arrived at his desk which, unfortunately for him, was at the opposite end of the door through which he had entered the editorial. He left a trek of chaos and carnage behind him. Norman Adam, a very prim and very proper Features Editor, stood up, his full five foot four inches, and said, 'Fitz, have you been drinking?'

Big Fitz, totally dishevelled, his shirt-tail hanging out of his trousers, his jacket struggling to remain on his shoulders, his tie knot down to his navel, his bright red eyes popping out of their sockets and with his right foot stuck in a bin, attempted to focus on his Editor and mumbled, 'Who cliped?'

Brock, sadly, realised this was a situation that would never be re-enacted any time in the future. Newspaper offices, once vibrant, frantic, hectic, busy workplaces with demanding, shrieking telephones sounding an endless background cacophony, had become sterile, neat and orderly areas that could have been those of a Building Society. He didn't want any part of it. He may have been a dinosaur, but he had been a happy dinosaur. The redundancy deal was too good to knock back. And, so, he was about to embark on another journalistic adventure, coming at newspapers from an entirely different angle, from the outside looking in. Magazine work was also a possibility. He may even get round to writing that book he had been promising to knock out for a couple of decades. One thing was certain in his brave new world. 'They can take my job, but they'll never take my freedom,' he smiled. No more working with or for semi-literate nincompoops.

As ever, Brock was looking forward to the annual Country and Western Festival on what was known to him as Fantasy Island. He laughed to himself. He was well aware that Millport was the biggest open-air lunatic asylum outside of Fife. Maybe that's why he fitted right in and had invested in the island. Maybe 'invested' was a bit too grand. No, he had purchased a holiday flat, on the top floor at Quayhead Street beside the old harbour.

It was the ideal hideaway for whiling away the hours, watching the world roll by. Not for the next few days, though. This was the Country and Western Festival and that meant mayhem and madness. And, if he got lucky, some curvaceous wench might share his bed. When he bought the one-bedroomed flat, a rare intelligent purchase, he must have been in a rampantly optimistic mood. He could have settled for a single bed, but, in an instant, had decided on a double. It had been a wise choice, even if it hadn't been needed as often as he'd have hoped.

He had just turned fifty-five and had been flying solo after the breakdown of his second marriage eleven years earlier. When asked if he was married, he would normally answer, 'On and off.' First time around, he had wed at twenty-one and his older newspaper colleagues insisted he was too young and told him he should wait. No, he would do his own thing. He got married to a lovely secretary called Irene. And got divorced three years later. 'My fault,' he would always tell himself. 'Booze and birds, lethal combination. A stiff cock knows no conscience.' He tried again five years later, a barmaid this time. Wendy. That crashed and burned after fifteen rarely-dull years. He laughed as he recalled telling a pal, 'Wendy always wanted a walk-in closet. Now I've got one. I live in it.' Home, in fact, was a small unfussy, two-bedroomed flat in Glasgow's Merchant City that suited his needs more than adequately. Handy for pubs, restaurants and takeaways. What more could a man want?

Brock hadn't totally ruled out getting hitched again. 'Well, two's not a bad start,' he would tell himself. In his head, he still felt quite youthful. The birth certificate told a different story, of course, and you couldn't argue with that little document. However, Brock was happy enough in himself. He was two inches over six foot, had blue eyes, still possessed his own teeth, had body-swerved baldness, even that annoying little monk circle on the crown, although his once fair hair was now greying rapidly. He felt in reasonable nick, although there were now disturbing signs of a slight paunch. He would work on that, he promised himself. Maybe next week.

A few years ago, Brock remembered, a drunken American tourist on holiday in the west coast of Scotland, who'd spoken to every Campbell in town as he searched for long lost cousins, was convinced Brock was Kirk Douglas. Brock, who possessed the Douglas chin and dimple, put up an argument at first, making the point that he was at least five inches taller and a couple of decades younger. But when he realised Li'l Abner was having none of it, he settled down in The Oban Inn and was fed booze all night. 'Tell me about Spartacus,' urged Li'l Abner. 'What about the Vikings? Was Tony Curtis a poof? Gee, I've heard all sorts of things about Burt Lancaster. Eh, Kirk? Was Burt a bender? Man, I thought you were brilliant in The Detective Story. Hey, what about The Heroes of Telemark? Was Richard Harris a booze bag? What was it like to kiss Lana Turner? Gee whizz, you lucky, lucky man. The hooters on that dame! I don't mind telling you, Kirk, I've frictioned off at least forty sets of fingerprints over that gal. Hey, Kirk, did you slip her a crippler? Bet you did, ya dirty, lucky bastard.'

Brock nodded, smiled, said yes and no at regular intervals as the brandies kept coming and his companion for the night - 'all the way from Kentucky, yeehaaah!' - got out his face on Southern Comfort. Brock had a fair idea that Li'l Abner would wake up the following morning convinced that Lana Turner was a drunken, lesbian Viking. And Richard Harris was a Norwegian gladiator with a swell pair of hooters.

As the coach took off from the Cumbrae slip, Brock looked out to his right as it passed the National Watersports Centre which always seemed busy, no matter the time of year. 'Hardy souls, these water worshippers,' thought Brock. 'Good drinkers, too.' Then there was the Lion Rock, perched at an angle on the mountain-side, which might actually have looked like a lion if you indulged in the Class A drug of your choice. The islanders, always on the look-out for any sort of financial funding, asked Rowntree, manu-facturers of the Lion Bar, if they wanted to sponsor the rock. The chocolate people actually sent a representative to view what the locals insisted on calling the 'world famous Lion Rock'. The guy returned to London and reported back to his bosses, 'I couldn't see any bleedin' lion.' Maybe someone should have slipped some LSD in his porridge. The Marine Research Station was up next, again on the right. Brock went in once and saw a squid. And another squid. And then another squid. Possibly he had chosen the wrong day to visit the island's 'world famous museum and aquarium'. Five minutes into the journey, Millport beckoned.

To Brock it was always a thrill to get his first look at the town that had somehow escaped the transformation from the thirties to the twenty-first century. It stubbornly refused to bow to the demands of time. The front - Brock could never call it a promenade - of the town was a stretch of roughly one mile. On the right was a row of extremely fine Victorian and Edwardian buildings propped up by all sorts of shops and the grand Garrison House which had been magnificently restored, at the cost of £5million, after the old one, constructed originally in1745, had been burned down by some half-wit who, as drunk as a skunk, climbed through a window one night and fell asleep with a lit cigarette still in his mouth. It didn't take the island's solitary cop long to track down the culprit the following day with it not being too easy to disguise a face that looked as though it had had a recent conversation with a blowtorch. Maybe it had been a blessing in disguise, the original place, once owned by the Earl of Glasgow, had been looking just a wee bit tired.

On the left, the waters of the Firth of Clyde benignly lapped the shell-riddled, seaweed-strewn, pebble-festooned beach. Apparently, there was some sand down there, too. It was rather reassuring, to Brock, and about another 12,000 weekend cowboys, that there were so many pubs on such a small island, ten miles in circumference, that boasted a population of around twelve hundred.

To set the tone for what lay ahead, as Millport was transformed to Dodge City, the pub owners had changed the name of their establishments. Hand-painted wooden signs replaced the usual legends. Robbie's Tavern had been magically transported back to the 1850s. It was now Cactus Jack's. The Mitre was the Kentuckian. Hugh's Bar was the Nashville. The Georgics Hotel was the Confederate HQ. McCabe's Bar was the Stagecoach Inn and McIntosh's Bar was renamed, not too enticingly, the Varmint Inn.

The only supermarket had been reinvented as The Chow Stop and the newsagents' shop was The Oklahoma Chronicle. There was a time when bales of hay were neatly arranged and stacked outside the pubs. Unfortunately, the pyromaniacs among the visiting cowboys soon put an end to that little affectation. The Nixe snack bar, where Brock first sampled the delights of hot peas and vinegar, was renamed Katy's Cantena. Jimmy's Amusement Arcade was now The Golden Nugget.

There were Stars and Stripes and Confederate flags, mixed with Union Jacks and Saltires, fluttering from lampposts and the overhead cables that strung the multi-coloured lights from the harbour at Quayhead all the way along the promenade to Kames Bay. To keep the flavour going, some of the locals had erected wooden crosses on their very own Boothill cemetery beside the Garrison. Brock noticed one that proclaimed 'Billy The Kid Is Buried Here'. Below it, someone had scrawled in chalk, 'Naw he's no'.'

As the bus neared its destination, Brock looked out at the painted Crocodile Rock and wondered for the umpteenth time how many kids over the many years had had their photographs taken on this interesting rock formation. He smiled at the story he'd been told that many years ago the local GP, a fellow named Doctor Eric Redford, had imbibed his way along the front, stopping at each and every pub. He pictured the scene as images came to mind.

Robbie's Tavern had been the sixth inn of drunkenness on Doctor Redford's way back to the two-storey grey sandstone building just past Kames Bay he shared with his adoring wife Ethel, with its neat, little surgery attached at the back. After yet another couple of swift snifters, Doctor Redford, much respected fellow and prized member of this parish, slurred his goodbyes, took his leave and blundered out the doors of Robbie's Tavern. Suddenly, he jerked back on his heels, coming close to somersaulting through the plate glass door behind him. He tried to focus as he squinted across the road. 'Is it my imagination?' He rubbed his tired eyes. 'Or is that a crocodile?' He had walked past the rock on countless occasions during his ten years on the island, but this was the first time he had seen the image of a crocodile. A bulb lit up above his befuddled head. He must capture the moment. He staggered at pace in the direction of home.

'Ethel, where's the paint buckets?' he shouted to his dutiful wife of twenty-six years as he practically collapsed through the front door into the hallway, looking more excited than he had done for years. 'I need paint. And brushes. Now.' Ethel didn't want to ask.

'They're in the garage, darling, where you always keep them,' she replied.

'Garage, oh, yes, of course. Thanks, dear. Back soon.' He tumbled in the general direction of the back door.

'Mad as a cowpat,' thought Ethel.

The road sweepers were first on the scene the following day. 'Whit the fuck's that supposed to be?' One asked the other. They both looked at the newly-painted rock and tilted their heads simultaneously to the right.

'Is that supposed to be an eye?' one asked, completely puzzled.

'Naw, that's an ear, I think,' answered the other.

'Is that teeth?'

'That no' a foot?'

'That a hand?'

'That no' a nose?'

'Is that red thing a cock?'

'Could be. Aye, that looks like a cock, right enough. A big red cock.'

'Somebody's gone a bit mad, I think. Will we take away these paint pots? Or will we just leave them?'

'Och, toss them in the back. Just in case some arsehole comes back to try and paint a dug or something.'

From the kitchen of their two-storeyed grey sandstone building, Ethel could hear her husband shouting down from the upstairs' bedroom.

'Ethel, dearest, why is my suit covered in paint?'

'Stupid old bastard,' thought the GP's wife.

Brock smiled broadly as the coach pulled in it at its destination. 'What has Millport got to throw at me this time?' he thought.

CHAPTER TWO

LATE SATURDAY EVENING, SEPTEMBER 1

'A pint of lager, please, Hughie,' ordered Boring Brian, adding as a casual aside, 'See they've found a deid body over at West Bay.' He could have been discussing the weather. 'A cowboy. Shot. Just lying there. Wee Fi's going off her nut.'

'What are you talking about?' asked Hughie Edwards, owner of Hugh's Bar, renamed the Nashville for the next four or five days of the Country and Western Festival. He started to pour the pint. 'A dead body? In Millport? Shot? No chance. We don't do murder here. Probably some punter just steaming and sleeping it off. Happens all the time.'

'Not this time,' said Boring Brian, a tired, sorry-looking individual with a tired, sorry-looking straggly moustache. 'There's a bloke over at West Bay lying deid, I'm telling ye. Pan breid. Wee Fi says he's got a bullet hole in the heid. Away and have a look if you don't believe me.'

'Where is he?'

'Swing park, beside the weans' slide. I'll bet you a pint he's deid.' Intrigued,

Hughie couldn't help himself. 'Maggie, hold the fort for a minute, will you?' His wife was out on the floor in the narrow confines of the pub collecting drained glasses while jostling with the would-be cowpokes, in various states of good-natured drunkenness.

'Christ, Hughie, you're not leaving me with this lot and Calamity Jane, are you? Where the hell are you going?'

'I'm just popping over to West Bay. Back in a minute,' he attempted to calm his wife. 'This I've got to see.' He turned to Boring Brian, 'If you're lying, Brian, I'll bar you for life.'

'Go and have a look. He's pan breid. Deid. Shot in the heid.'

It had just passed ten fifty in the evening and the pub was knee deep in thirsty cowboys, one of the craziest and most lucrative days of the year. But, undaunted and for once forgetting about the cash register known lovingly to him as the Jewish Piano, Hughie practically ran round the bar, dodged a couple of unsteady John

11

Waynes and made for the door. He looked back to see if his pal Charlie Brock wanted to accompany him. He couldn't see him through the rabble. He turned again to Boring Brian, 'See if you're lying ...'

Boring Brian lifted his frothing pint to his lips. 'Go and see for yourself. You owe me a pint. I can taste it already.'

'Hurry back,' shouted a harassed Maggie. Calamity Jane, the makeshift barmaid who did her best to live up to her nickname by creating havoc behind the bar, seemed oblivious to anything that was going on around about her. She certainly wasn't paying any attention to the Man in Black at the corner of the bar, an obvious admirer of Johnny Cash.

'A murder in Millport? That's got to be a first. This I must see,' mused a clearly excited Hughie. He was a sprightly fifty-six-year-old who thought he had been through it all on the island. He walked at a brisk pace along Clyde Street, taking the short cut to West Bay a couple of minutes away. Sure enough, he could see PC Fiona Anderson standing over something, but, in the faded light, he couldn't quite make out what it was lying at her feet.

As he moved closer, he shouted over to Fiona. 'What's this about a murder?' Fiona, with her back to him, was holding her mobile phone to her ear.

'Shhh,' she said as she turned and put her forefinger to her lips. Hughie could now see clearly what was at her feet. A man's body. Dressed in cowboy gear. With a bullet hole between his eyes. Lying there. Dead.

'Fuck's sake,' he said.

Fiona was nodding her head as she listened intently to the voice on the other end of her mobile. 'Right, fine, I've got that. Okay, right. No, I've checked, there's no pulse. Apart from that, no, I haven't touched the body. No, I won't touch the body. No, of course, I won't move the body. Yes, I'll stay with the body. Right, fine. Secure the scene? Okay. Generator? No, I don't think we've got one. Tape? Yes, plenty of it. Never used it.' Pause. Even in the rapidly deteriorating light, Hughie could see colour draining from the policewoman's face. 'What? How do I do that, sir? What? All of them?' And then she ended the conversation. 'Right, sir, I'll wait here. I won't move. Thank you, sir.'

She looked at Hughie and pointed to the body at her feet. 'Jeezus Christ, Hughie. What a fuckin' mess, eh? Somebody's gone and killed this arsehole.'

'So much for not talking ill of the dead,' Hughie observed.

'They only want me to cordon off the entire fuckin' island! How the fuck do I do that? Nobody's to get off. Nobody's to get on. The entire fuckin' island, Hughie.'

'You could start by searching for a particularly long rope,' offered Hughie, rather callously considering there was a corpse at his feet.

'This is no laughing matter. I checked with Cal-Mac at eight tonight and they reckon they've already dropped off around 12,000 punters. TWELVE FUCKIN' THOUSAND!'

Hughie looked at his wristwatch. 'Well, at least, the last ferry's gone. Unless they've got a boat, they're stuck on the island, anyway, until the first sailing tomorrow. That's due in at seven. I suppose you could get Cal-Mac to call a halt to all the crossings. Christ, the island will be in chaos. People will be wanting to get home for work on Monday.'

Fiona said nothing. Hughie added, 'No-one hear anything? A car backfire? Loud bang? Anything like that?'

The cop sighed. 'Haven't had a chance to knock on a door, but with all the fireworks going off all over the place I wouldn't be holding my breath, would you?'

Hughie shook his head before asking, 'I take it reinforcements are on the way?'

'They're sending over a couple from Largs right now. The lifeboat people will ferry them over. Saltcoats will organise a helicopter for a few of the CID lads. They're sending forensics, as well. A wooden top like me can't be trusted with this.'

'Do we know who he is?' Hughie asked the cop, one of his best customers who could see off more than a few of his regulars when she went into overdrive on the large gins and tonic. He knew his profit margin would drop alarmingly when she left the island. The Jewish Piano would get an unwanted rest in a fortnight's time.

'Haven't a clue. I'm not supposed to touch him. Can't check for a wallet for ID. Have you seen him before?'

Hughie squinted at the body, taking off his spectacles and bending over for a better look. 'Christ,' he said, 'he was in the pub yesterday. Had a few beers and bored the shit out of me and Charlie. That's Wild Bill Hickok.'

'Wild Bill Hickok? What the fuck are you talking about?'

'He came in, ordered a drink and I called him "mate". He told me to call him Wild Bill. He told me he was Wild Bill Hickok.'

'Oh, great. I'll phone my bosses back and tell them we've identified the body. It's Wild Bill Hickok. That'll go down a treat.'

She stood and looked again at the body. 'I can't just leave him here, Hughie.'

'And you can't touch him, either.'

'Stay here, will you, Hughie? I'm going to nip over to the station and get a blanket or something to cover him. I've got to get tape. Watch him for me, will you?' Hughie looked at the body. 'It's not like he's going anywhere.' She started to race in the direction of the police station, a converted whitewashed bungalow, which, conveniently, was situated at the corner of Millburn Street and Crawford Street, a two-minute sprint away. She paused, 'Hey, Hughie, how did you know about this?'

'Oh, Boring Brian came into the pub and told me.'

'Aw, fuck. That means the entire island will know in half-an-hour. That's all we'll need. Maybe we should sell tickets.' With a fair turn of pace, she continued on her way to the station.

West Bay was deserted at that time of night. Everyone with a brain was getting out of theirs. The pubs were bulging, bursting at the seams as the cowboys went doolally. The first of the Wild West wannabes had started to arrive on Friday morning. Their numbers increased with every crossing from Largs. Caledonian MacBrayne, the ferry company, was also laying on late-night ferries. There had been the usual avalanche of gun-totin', buckskin-adorned guys and gals and more would arrive tomorrow to survey the debris and wreckage and willingly join in with the lunacy. Now Hughie found himself taking on sentry duties with Wild Bill Hickok, rather disconcertingly, smiling up at him from under his walrus moustache. With a bullet hole between his eyes. Hughie had never actually seen a bullet hole before. It certainly looked like a bullet hole.

CHAPTER THREE

FRIDAY MORNING, AUGUST 31

When the coach pulled in at the harbour side, Charlie Brock disembarked along with the Wyatt Earps, the Doc Hollidays, the Billy the Kids and the Elvis Presleys. His travelling companions hung around waiting for the first pub to open its doors at 11am. The drinking would start in earnest in roughly fifteen minutes' time and only the Good Lord knew when it would end.

Brock paused to have a quick look at the billboard pinned to the side of the bus shelter. 'What has Millport lined up, then, by way of entertainment this weekend?' he wondered. The Country and Western Festival was the island's answer to the Rio Carnival. Mardi Gras. Notting Hill. Most of the islanders, in particular the pub owners, made a genuine effort to make it memorable. Well, as memorable as possible when most of the visitors had every intention of going swimming in a vat of alcohol every day.

Brock looked at the board and recognised some of the names who had been performing since the Festival came to life back in 1994. It was the brainchild of an extrovert cowboy fan called James Wishart who seemed to be on every committee on the island. Remarkably, for such a small island with such a small population, there seemed to be an awful lot of committees. But Wishart was to be commended for putting together the Country and Western Festival. The island had to fight back when cheap overseas holidays battered hell out of its economy. The Country and Western jamboree went a long way to attempting to redress the financial imbalance.

Brock noted that the High Plains Drifters were still on the go, five guys with banjos who actually sounded okay after about ten pints of strong ale. After THEY had about ten pints of strong ale. It was a similar tale with the High-Falutin'-Rootin'-Tootin' combo, three chartered accountants from Troon. Brock continued to peruse the list. There were six lawyers who assembled themselves as The Legals, a tribute band to The Eagles. He smiled. There was someone called Hooch Cassidy, who billed himself as the 'Dean

Martin of C&W'. Then there was a husband and wife double-act called 'Larry'N'Me' who, apparently, had come all the way from Laramie to perform at Millport. 'Probably from Govan,' thought Brock. Underneath them on the card was the 'Billhillies.' 'Maybe someone just can't spell. Maybe he's a young journalist.' Rusty Springtrap, he was informed, would be performing the songs of Dusty Springfield.

There was the tried and trusted 'Ponderosa', who were a father and three sons team just like the Cartwrights in TV's Bonanza. Brock's eye fell on 'Guns'N'Poses' and wondered what sort of music they would serve up. There was the 'Six-Shooters' who, funnily enough, consisted of only four musicians. 'Maybe they should rename themselves the Four Skins,' mused Brock. The billboard made more interesting reading than that day's newspapers. And Brock should know; he had been in that industry since God was a boy. 'Oh, this is brilliant,' he said out loud to no-one in particular. 'Brawhide!' 'I've got to see them just to buy them a drink for coming up with that name.'

But, on the supporting cast, was the character who won the ultimate accolade. 'Ladeeez and gennnlemen, drumroll, please, I give you...Hugh Chapperal!'

Brock's input to the sartorial elegance of the weekend was a red and black checked shirt, a pair of stone-washed blue Levi's jeans and a brown pair of Chelsea boots. No Stetson. No waistcoat. No spurs. No bandanas. No guns. He was there for the madness and the mayhem. And for what passed as music. But he had no intention of looking like a poor man's Hopalong Cassidy. 'Let's have a right good time,' he said to a passing golden Labrador who ignored him and seemed more interested in sniffing a lamppost. Brock lifted his holdall with his change of clothes, two more checked shirts, a couple of T-shirts, another pair of Levi's, a couple of pairs of black socks and a change of underwear. A two-pint carton of milk and a scattering of teabags completed his weekend requirements. 'The lumpy stuff - food to everyone else - 'will come later.' That was way down his list of priorities for the next four or five days.

He made his way across from the bus stop to the front door of the tenement close, sandwiched between the Georgics Hotel and the Deep Blue Plaice. The fish and chip shop had been taken over recently by a wild-haired punter from London, who looked as though he had just made his way home from Woodstock. Or Glastonbury, as the younger folk may have corrected. The locals immediately renamed the takeaway 'The Hippy Chippy'. Who said islanders lacked a sense of humour?

Brock hadn't realised it at the time, but his flat was located in what was known as the Millport Triangle. People tended to disappear around that part of the island. As he faced the front door of the tenement, there was the Georgics on his immediate left, McCabe's Bar was just over to his right, McIntosh's was a one-minute walk up Cardiff Street and Hugh's Bar was across the road on Stuart Street, about a two-minute stagger away. Brock would have paid extra for that location.

He picked up his holdall, opened the front door and climbed his way upstairs to the top floor flat. He had named his bolt hole the 'Schloss Adler' which translated from German to the 'Castle of the Eagle.' Goodness only knows how many times he had read the book and watched Alistair MacLean's war movie 'Where Eagles Dare' where Richard Burton leads a crack team to infiltrate the German High Command in the so-called impregnable castle, the Schloss Adler, set high in the snow-capped Bavarian mountains. That was the film where Clint Eastwood shot about five hundred Nazis without stopping to reload.

Brock was so impressed by Burton, always one of his favourites, in the movie that he purchased what he thought looked like a replica white parka coat with a giant hood. He would walk along the promenade, running parallel to the beach, in the morning, sucking in God's fresh air and getting rid of the cobwebs, and believed he was doing a reasonable portrayal of Burton's character, the fearless British Major Smith, in MacLean's film. The locals thought he resembled a tall Womble.

Brock looked out of his top floor hideaway and, as ever, was impressed by the panoramic views presented before his very eyes. He was on the third floor and his vantage point was by far the best at the harbour. From the back of the flat, Brock could look towards Largs over the Firth of Clyde, beautiful and peaceful on this day. He had seen it on other occasions when the angry waves battered against the rocks down below, sending a steady stream of spectacular showers all the way up to his back room window. A

17

sight to behold. Who needed Krakatoa? The old grey Hunterston B Nuclear Power Plant was a carbuncle, as Prince Charles would have said, on the landscape. As the current Duke of Rothesay, Brock wondered what His Highness would have said if they tried to build a power station anywhere near that particular Ayrshire island.

To his right, he could see the mysterious Little Cumbrae, a rugged, isolated island that had been home to very few people over the years. It possessed a small castle that had been a retreat for Scottish kings in the dark and distant. The island, all 680 acres, had been up for sale for £3million for years without any takers. Then it was sold for a 'bargain' £2million with the land owner, an Earl of Something-or-other, cutting his losses. Now it belonged to some strange sect. Brock wasn't sure exactly what their mission was in life. Save the Baboon or something like that. Brock had seen one of the Little Cumbrae inhabitants wearing a T-shirt that proclaimed, 'SAVE A TREE...EAT A BEAVER.' Perhaps that's what they were up to. Eating beavers. The secretive sect were yoga enthusiasts who, for a lot of money, ferried keep-fit numpties to and from their little island on a daily basis. Brock wondered what really went on at Little Cumbrae away from prying eyes. Maybe best not to know.

From the front, Brock could see the small pier down to his right. On the harbour front was the public clock tower, about thirty feet tall and christened Wee Ben by the locals. Across the main road, running along the face of the town, he could see as far as Kames Bay before the road turned right along Marine Parade towards Farlands Point, a spot where the crafty locals knew was the best location for fishing for mackerel. Directly in front of him, he could see up towards Cardiff Street and some more wonderful Victorian buildings on either side. Heading upwards and taking the right at the junction onto Golf Road would lead you past the Bowling Club and towards the caravan park, a reasonable ten-minute walk away. Just up from that was the marvellous golf club with its immaculate eighteen-hole course. Veering left, before Golf Road, would take you towards West Bay and the swing park and the football pitch where Brock played as a boy, pestering his big sister Betty, six years his senior, to take penalty-kicks at him. He dreamed of playing in goal for Scotland. Early in life, around about his sixteenth birthday, he found himself better equipped to handle an Olivetti portable typewriter than keep a flying football out of the net behind him. Occupation sorted.

A brisk walk past another row of assorted houses on the right, the original Victorian buildings mixed in with newer bungalows, would take you in the direction of Fintry Bay. 'Stuff your Malibu, your Copacabana and your Bondi,' thought Brock often enough. 'Give me Fintry any day.' A leisurely forty-minute stroll - you could walk everywhere on this island - would take you straight to the McKenzie tearooms where the only snag was they did not sell alcohol. You can't have everything.

Once again, Brock reassured himself, everything is where it should be.

'Nothing ever changes in Millport.'

CHAPTER FOUR

LATE SATURDAY EVENING, SEPTEMBER 1

Wild Bill Hickok was still smiling. 'Pity that's not an arrow sticking out of your head, mate,' said Hughie Edwards to the dead body. 'That would narrow the list of suspects down to one. Sitting Bull's wigwam would be getting raided right now.'

There were around 12,000 cowboys on the island and one Indian, a stockbroker from plush Morningside in Edinburgh, called John Harris. Every year for the past decade he had looked out his buckskins, brightly-coloured feather headdress, bow and arrow, rubber tomahawk and suede moccasins. He stopped short at war paint. Then he mingled with the cowboys. Sitting Bull had a decidedly dodgy sense of humour. But there was no arrow in Wild Bill's head. Hughie pondered for a moment. 'Did you come off second best in a gunfight, Wild Bill? You couldn't just have waited till High Noon?'

Hughie wondered what the hell was delaying Constable Fiona. He had a pub to run. The money from this weekend would go a long way to paying for his annual cruise around the Med with Maggie. Another look at his wristwatch. It had just gone beyond 11.20pm. There was still another two hours' worth of drinking to be done, with the possibility of a few extras thrown in after time. He had to get back to the pub. 'Maggie will be having a flakey,' he thought. His barmaid wife didn't do busy. Calamity Jane didn't do much.

He phoned the landline at Hugh's Bar. 'You owe me a pint,' answered Boring Brian before Hughie could say a word.

'Right, don't worry about that just now. Jump the bar and give Maggie and Calamity a hand, will you? Help yourself to a couple of beers.'

'No problem,' said Boring Brian, who *was* boring but could also be helpful.

'Can you see Charlie in the bar?' asked Hughie.

'Aye, just a minute.' The absent landlord could hear a shout above the din and clamour with the karaoke at full belt. 'New York

New York' was being tortured for about the tenth time that night. Sinatra was in as much trouble as Wild Bill. 'Charlie! It's Hughie!'

Charlie held the phone to his right ear, his left forefinger in the other. 'Hi, Hughie. What's all this about a dead cowboy? Shot, says Brian. He's joking, right?'

'Stiff as a board, Charlie. It's fuckin' Wild Bill Hickok! You want to get over here yourself. There's a story on your doorstep.'

Brock looked at his full pint, swithered for a moment, shrugged and said, 'I'll be there in a minute. Don't go away.'

'Where the fuck am I going to go? I'm babysitting a dead body. I think Fiona's fucked off. Probably firing a couple of large G and Ts down her gullet. Lucky bitch!'

Within a couple of minutes Charlie Brock was at the crime scene. 'Sorry, I took so long, but I didn't want to spill this. I thought you might need it.' Brock handed his pal a tall glass containing a large brandy and port.

'Christ, thanks, Charlie. I do need this.' It was gone in seconds.

'Don't throw away the glass, Hughie. Your fingerprints are all over it. They'll be searching this area with a fine tooth comb for anything that might give them a clue. Don't want you "helping the police with their enquiries", do we?'

'Aye, good shout,' said Hughie, pocketing the glass.

Brock looked down at Wild Bill, a drinking companion only a day ago. 'Christ,' he said. 'Either someone's a very good shot. Or someone's very lucky. What a shot. I take it suicide has already been ruled out?'

'Suppose so. I don't know. Better ask Fiona. No sign of a gun around here, is there? Couldn't have shot himself and then thrown the gun away or put it back in a holster. Where the fuck's Fiona?'

Car lights shone about two hundred yards away. Fiona was driving back from the police station, mounting the pavement and driving onto the playfield, weaving the patrol car between the obstacles in the kids' playground. It didn't dawn on her that she might be making a bit of a mess of a crime scene. She got out of the car, leaving the lights on. 'Sorry, Hughie, it took me ages to find the tape. Never thought I would have any use for it,' she offered by way of explanation. 'Hi, Charlie, enjoying the view?' She was carrying a blanket which she spread over Wild Bill Hickok. 'Don't suppose this will do any harm,' she said.

'You could hit him over the head with the Crocodile Rock and it wouldn't do him any harm,' said Brock.

'Don't be a fuckin' smart arse all your life, Charlie,' snapped the cop. 'Take a day off.'

Charlie Brock pulled out his mobile phone from his back pocket. 'I'll give R.I.P. a quick call on this one, okay?' he asked.

'R.I.P? Oh, your newspaper pal. Great. Now the place is going to be swarming with fuckin' newspapermen,' said Fiona. 'Aye, go ahead. It'll be all over the news tomorrow, anyway.'

Brock made the call. One ring and the receiver at the other end was picked up. 'R.I.P. How's it going? I've got a good one for you. I'm in Millport and I'm standing over the dead body of a bloke who goes by the name of, wait for it, Wild Bill Hickok. And he's got a bullet hole right between his eyes.' Pause. 'Yes, I've been drinking. No, I'm not pissed. Seriously. We've got a dead guy and, you'll love this, about 12,000 suspects. It's the Country and Western Festival. The island is packed with guys all wandering around with guns strapped to their thighs, rifles on their shoulders. How's that for a story? Brilliant, eh? Listen, do you want to talk to the cop? She's right here.'

R.I.P. was actually Griff Stewart, one of the best news reporters Charlie Brock had met and worked with at the News. He was also a good drinking buddy. 'Brandy. Gentleman's measure, thank you,' was his order. Brock had also given him his R.I.P. nickname. Griff was often sent to the home of the recently deceased to inform someone a loved one had been shot, stabbed, fallen off a bridge, stepped in front of a train, been bludgeoned, hit by a bus, overdosed, beaten to a pulp. Not the most pleasant side to his role as a Chief News Reporter. Often, he would get there before the police which was a constant source of annoyance to the law. And, once he had broken the sad news and commiserated with someone's sudden loss, he would ask for what was known as a 'collect'. A photograph, preferably a head shot of the deceased that saw them flashing their best smile at a wedding function, birthday party or some other celebration. And this radiant, happy snap would then be placed alongside the story that informed the reader they had been mutilated by some mad axeman.

R.I.P. trusted Brock, but knew his pal possessed a kooky sense of humour after he had allowed a few to glide behind his necktie. He thought it better to talk to the cop.

'This isn't my mate at the wind-up, is it?' he asked Fiona.

She sighed. 'Afraid not. Remember me? It's Fiona Anderson. We met about a year ago in Hughie's. For my many sins, I'm still the beat cop in Cumbrae. And, sadly, there is a dead body lying here at my feet. And, yes, he's dressed up as a cowboy and, yes, even to my untrained eye, it looks as though he has been shot.'

'A hole between the eyes?' asked R.I.P.

'Aye.'

'A bullet hole?'

'It's certainly not a pin prick.'

'Wonderful!' exclaimed the newspaperman. 'Suspicious circumstances?'

'What do you think? Listen, don't bother quoting me. I'm waiting for the cavalry to arrive. I've nothing to say.' Fiona was getting increasingly tetchy.

R.I.P. looked at the clock on the newsroom wall. It told him it was just approaching midnight. He was five minutes away from finishing his shift. He wouldn't touch the story that night. It would have been lucky if it was even used as a short. 'An unidentified body was found dead in Cumbrae, North Ayrshire, last night.' Who cares? Junkies were getting fished out of the Clyde every five minutes. He needed much more information before he would put his name to this tale. 'Thanks,' he said, 'Fiona? Yes, I remember you. Large G and Ts, right?'

'Got it in one. I'll pass you back to Charlie.'

'You got room for one more in your castle in the sky, pal?' asked the newsman.

'Always got time for you, R.I.P. You're not getting the bed. You can have the sofa.'

'What time is the first ferry in the morning?'

Brock checked with Hughie. 'Aye, there's one due out of Largs at 6.45am getting you in for just before seven. If they're sailing, that is. Cops might have something to say about that. See you then?'

'Sure thing,' said R.I.P. 'Don't start the party without me.'

'Too late, mate. It's already up and running. And we've got a dead body to prove it. This is one cowpoke who won't be farting all the way through his beans at breakfast tomorrow.'

CHAPTER FIVE

LATE SATURDAY EVENING, SEPTEMBER 1

Charlie Brock and Hughie Edwards propped up the bar at The Nashville. Drunken cowboys were bouncing off each other in their usual stampede for even more alcohol. Most of them needed another drink in much the same way a drowning man required a glass of water. Hughie surveyed the human wreckage, observing, 'The Alamo probably looked in better nick after the Mexicans had kicked the shit out of Davy Crockett and his mates.'

'It still doesn't feel right. Leaving Fiona out there, alone in the dark,' said Brock, suffering unlikely pangs of conscience.

'That's what she gets for not sticking in at school,' answered Hughie, laughing. 'Anyway, we helped her with the tape, didn't we? It's now a proper crime scene. Just like on the telly.' He couldn't help smiling. 'CSI Cumbrae.'

'Or Millport Vice,' threw in Brock.

'By the way, have you seen her sidekick? The Jelly Tot Kid?' Hughie was serious for a moment.

'Aye, I saw him a few hours or so ago. He was heading for Robbie's, I think. That direction, anyway.'

'Fiona is going to need his help. If he's in Robbie's he better get his arse out of there and over to West Bay. I'll give Robbie a buzz.' He dialed the number.

'Aye, he's here, alright,' answered Robbie. 'He's no' looking too bad. Mind you, he's been at the bar most of the night. Still in uniform. Here Hughie, I heard there was a dead cowboy over at the West End. What's that all about?'

Hughie grinned. Robbie's Bar was about a mere twenty minutes' walk away from his pub, but the locals still called his part of the island the West End like it was miles away on another planet. 'Looks like it, Robbie. Can you tell Fiona's little helper to get his backside over to West Bay before Fiona comes down there and kicks his balls round his neck?'

'Ouch! I felt that. I'll see if I can point him in your general direction.' Robbie hung up.

'This should be fun,' said Hughie to his pal. 'Fiona will tear this wee guy's head off. Remember, "Hell hath no fury like a woman's corns!" Wild Bill Hickok will be in better shape than him by the time Fiona gets finished. Oh, well. Just a minute, Charlie.' Hughie looked at his wristwatch. It had just gone beyond 1 am. 'Time, gentleman, PULEEEEEZE!' No-one took a blind bit of notice. Including Brock, who ordered up another couple of large brandies and port. Maggie was still taking orders for the karaoke from those who could still mumble or slur. 'Don't suppose Fiona will be bothering about late drinkers tonight,' said Hughie. 'Stick a large G and T on that, Charlie, she's bound to get over here at some point.'

The Man in Black, all on his own at the other end of the bar, drained his pint and placed the empty glass on the surface before walking out of the pub without a farewell to anyone.

'Where have you been, you little fuckwit?' screeched constable Fiona Anderson as her colleague finally arrived at crime scene, as it now was. 'We've got a dead body here in case you haven't noticed. I've been phoning you, you little wanker. Where the fuck have you been?'

PC Steven Murphy hadn't signed up for this. When they asked for a volunteer from Largs to help out over the Country and Western Festival he immediately put his hand up. 'A wee holiday,' he thought. 'Nothing exciting ever happens in Millport. That'll do for me.' Now there was a sheet on the ground with a dead cowboy under it. Someone Fiona identified as Wild Bill Hickok. And he had a bullet hole between his eyes.

'Sorry, I lost track of the time. I'm no' drunk. I'm sober. Honest,' was all he could say. As a matter of fact, someone had mentioned something about a body being found at West Bay, but he assumed the locals were having a bit of fun at his expense. He ignored it and ordered another pint of Guinness. Bad judgment call.

'Ach, I'll sort you out later. Make yourself useful and go and get a tent!'

'A tent? At this time?'

'Aye, a fuckin' tent. Go to the Fuckin'-Twenty-Four-Hour-Tent Shop if you have to, but go and get a tent. There's hundreds of them up at Jack's Farm.'

'But they're for the cowboys.'

'Fuck the cowboys. Go and get a tent. Now!'

'Eh, what for?'

'So, we can have a little party by the camp fire before retiring for the evening. This looks like such a nice spot, don't you think? Maybe a bit whiffy with a dead body lying there. Maybe we could throw him on the barbeque. Go and get a fuckin' tent! Steal it, borrow it. But get it. And don't forget the fuckin' pegs!'

PC Steven Murphy didn't completely discount the stomach flu for his partner's erratic behaviour. He headed off for Jack's Farm.

'What do we need a tent for?' he wondered to himself.

Fiona's mobile phone shrilled. She responded quickly. 'Half-an-hour? Fine. See you.' The guys with the white hats were on their way.

'Hey, you, whatever-your-fuckin'-name-is, come back here!' she barked towards The Jelly Tot Kid. 'Can I trust you to stay here for thirty minutes and make sure Wild Bill Hickok doesn't disappear? You got that? Stay here. And then you can go and get a fuckin' tent when I get back.'

'Can I ask where you are going?'

'Aye, you can fuckin' ask,' answered Fiona as she moved off at pace on her way to Hugh's Bar.

CHAPTER SIX

EARLY FRIDAY AFTERNOON, AUGUST 31

Wild Bill Hickok lurched from the bar and threw a right-fisted haymaker punch at Two-Gun Jake. He missed his jaw by at least a foot. Two-Gun Jake toppled backwards, his Stetson flying off, and collapsed in a heap, his head narrowly missing a spittoon, as he sprawled on the sawdust-strewn floor of the Kentuckian. He rubbed his chin and fixed Wild Bill in his gaze. 'You'll pay for that,' he growled.

His assailant nonchalantly picked a bottle off the bar, secured it by its neck, walked across to the vulnerable cowboy, hovered above him for a moment and then smashed it to smithereens on his unprotected head. 'That's for messin' with my lady, you filthy, no-good critter,' he rasped menacingly. Two-Gun Jake remained motionless on the floor.

'Yahoo! Yippee!' There was a round of applause as Wild Bill took a bow.

'That was brilliant,' said bar owner Hamish McNulty. 'The best yet. Did you get all that on film, Jimmy? Excellent! Hollywood beckons!'

Two-Gun Jake got to his feet and once more there were loud cheers from an appreciative pub audience. Wild Bill shook him by the hand and patted him on the head. No sign of blood. Not too likely as the bottle was made of iced candy.

'Do we have to go through this every fuckin' year?' asked a clearly irritated Simon Thomas, the island's bad-tempered butcher and regular in the Mitre. 'When will these arseholes grow up? I drink in here all year round and then we have a few bastardin' days of absolute nonsense with these bampots staging these daft fights. Give me a chance to get up there and I'll use a real fuckin' bottle.'

It meant little to the butcher that the pub owners could earn as much during the Country and Western Festival as they could for the next three months. And if that meant tolerating grown men acting like kids, then they were only too happy to accommodate them. Just so long as the cash register kept busy.

'Drink?' asked Wild Bill.

'Don't mind if I do, purdner,' replied Two-Gun Jake. They hitched up their gunbelts, acknowledged their fleeting moment of celebrity, took a joint bow with a flourish of their Stetsons and moved back to the bar.

'What'll it be?' asked Wild Bill, hoping to sound something close to an authentic thirsty cowboy.

'Two fingers of Red Eye, my good man,' replied his new drinking companion, a man he met only fifteen minutes ago, still picking pieces of candy out of his hair.

Neither would be in line for the red-carpet treatment at the Oscars any time soon.

Wild Bill ordered two large Macallans, chinked his glass against that of his partner and said, 'James Hitchcock's the name.'

'Hickok?' asked Two-Gun Jake, sipping from his full glass.

'No, Hitchcock as in Alfred Hitchcock. H-I-T-C-H-C-O-C-K. You know, the movie director? Psycho? The Birds? Vertigo? Rebecca? Rear Window? That guy.'

'Oh, right, Alfred Hitchcock. Not Hickok. H-I-C-K-O-K. Hey, that's pretty clever. I like that. I'm Andy Boone. Pleased to meet you.'

They shook hands again. 'Why don't you call yourself Daniel Boone?' enquired Wild Bill.

'Jeez, I never thought of that,' said Two-Gun Jake.

'What job are you in, Bill?'

'It's WILD Bill. This weekend I am Wild Bill Hickok and I'll go back to being James Hitchcock when I go home. What do I do for a living? Go on, take a guess.'

'I don't think you're a hairdresser, no offence. Mind you, all that mess, crazy moustache and stuff could be groovy these days, for all I know. No offence. Give us a clue.'

Wild Bill paused, cleared his throat and burst into song,

'*Rollin, rollin', rollin'*,

Though the streams are swollen, Keep those doggies rollin', Rawhide, Rain and wind and weather, Hell bent for leather, Wishin' my gal was by my side.'

Two-Gun Jake pondered and scratched his chin. 'You're a farmer?'

'Not even close. Do you want another clue?'

'Go on,' Two-Gun Jake nodded, warming to the theme.

'Here we go,' smiled Wild Bill. He knew he was no James Taylor, but he gave it a try.

'*There is a young cowboy he lives on the range, His horse and his cattle are his only companions, He works in the saddle, And he sleeps in the canyons, Just waiting for the summer, His pastures to change...*'

Two-Gun Jake interrupted. 'You sure you're not a farmer? Something to do with coos?' Pause. You could almost hear the rattle of Two-Gun Jake's lonely little grey cell rolling around inside an empty cranium. And then, 'You work in a slaughterhouse, right? You kill coos.'

'No,' he laughed. 'I might murder songs, but I'm not a coo killer. Want another clue?'

'Right, I'll try harder.'

Wild Bill thought he would give his mate a helping hand. He strummed an invisible guitar. 'Take me back to the Black Hills, the Black Hills of Dakota,

'*To the beautiful country that I love, Lost my heart in the Black Hills...*'

'Got it,' exclaimed Two-Gun Jake. 'Got it. You're no' a farmer and you're no' a killer of coos. Something to do with grass. You're a landscape gardener. Right?'

'Wrong,' Wild Bill's lips curled up in sharp contrast to the unruly downward trek of his erupting moustache. 'We could be here until the new millennium. One last chance?'

Wild Bill started to hum. 'Doo doo, doo doo doo doo, doo doo doo doo doo, doo doody doo doo, doo doo doody dee doody doo, doody dee doody doo...'

'The Magnificent Seven! Right? So, you're not a farmer, you don't kill coos and you're no' a landscape gardener. But it's something to do with coos, I'm sure.' Two-Gun Jake thought hard. After a minute or so, his eyes lit up.

'You're a milkman!'

'I'm a fuckin' singer,' said Wild Bill, putting his inquisitor out of his misery. 'I play guitar and sing around some of the pubs in Glasgow. You've obviously never caught my act.'

'You sure you're not a milkman?' asked a clearly deflated Two-Gun Jake.

'Fairly positive,' said Wild Bill.

'What do you do for a living, Andy?'

'Oh, me? I'm a joiner, mainly working in Glasgow and airts and pairts.'

'So you're a real cowboy?'

CHAPTER SEVEN

EARLY SUNDAY MORNING, SEPTEMBER 2

Chief News Reporter Griff Stewart, aka as R.I.P., quickly typed out an e-mail for his News Editor Martin Gilhooley, a pleasant, white-bearded, roly-poly sort of person who would never be out of work around Christmas time.

He also possessed a flytrap mind and had also been one of the finest news reporters in the business as he climbed the editorial ladder to pole position. R.I.P. often wondered why such excellent operators were taken out of the field where their expertise was of more use to the newspaper. Now Gilhooley was behind a desk and was sending out news reporters who couldn't lace his boots to cover jobs he could do in his sleep. It was the same with photographers. The best guy would invariably end up as Picture Editor and would never take another snap in his life.

R.I.P. was aware of the cast-in-stone habits of his News Editor. Gilhooley was always the first journalist on the vast editorial floor, sitting at his desk by 7am with just the cleaners and copy staff for company. The copy boys and girls always knew to get his newspapers sorted out on his desk by the time he arrived. A cup of strong, black coffee would be required at the same time. Gilhooley didn't read newspapers. He devoured them. Cover to cover, pausing every now and again to tear out a story or two of particular interest. He coined the phrase, 'Put a kilt on it.' He could find an obscure tale tucked away at the bottom of a column in a rival newspaper and instinctively know it could be developed into a better story for the News. It could be a murder in Mexico, but he had a sixth sense that somehow told him there could be a Scottish connection and, after a bit of good old-fashioned newspaper work, his reporter could then 'put a kilt on it.'

He always laughed at the story that continued to do the rounds that summed up the small town thinking of local papers. When the Titanic sank, a Dundee paper ran the headline, 'LOCAL MAN DIES IN SEA TRAGEDY!' Actually, Gilhooley, in his meticulous fashion and to satisfy his own curiosity, checked out the validity of the claim. It wasn't true. Good tale, though.

Every Friday evening, around eight o'clock, he would collect all the local newspapers from the copy staff who stored them for him as they arrived on each of the newspapers' preferred publication days, normally a Thursday. By the end of the week, they had assembled the lot, from the John O'Groats Journal to the Gretna Post, and Gilhooley would put them in an enormous hold-all and take them home. As a daily newspaperman he had every Saturday off while the Sunday News took over the editorial on the third floor of the five-storey custom-built offices on the Clydeside.

And every Saturday Gilhooley would place the local newspapers in a neat pile in his study at home and work his way through them. Again, he would tear out one or two items of particular interest and would later present them to a news reporter to work on. He never ceased to be amazed at the stories that were tucked away in the local newspapers. One of the best was about the priest up north who had been having an affair with his married house cleaner for about ten years. Eventually, the story broke and the local newspaper put it on a wing column on page ten. Apparently, the editor was a devout Catholic and tried to bury the story. He was under pressure from his bosses to expose the priest when it appeared the entire community was in on the cleric's dirty little secret.

Gilhooley, with his trained eye, spotted the tucked-away tale immediately. The following Monday, the News splashed it on the front page, had four more pages inside, talking to anyone who had come within touching distance of Father Filth, as the newspaper decided to headline him. Parishioners, neighbours, the neighbours' cat, the lot were interviewed. There was also a colour piece from one of the features writers, digging out past misdemeanors by men of the cloth who combined sermons with sex. No denomination was safe. By the end of the day, every national newspaper was heading north to follow up the story. TV camera crews, radio and every other media strand got in on the act. That was all down to the diligence of one man, Martin Gilhooley, workaholic News Editor of the biggest selling daily newspaper in Scotland, a man who never married and would often say, 'I came out the womb a journalist.' Many agreed.

Gilhooley switched on his computer. Another saying of his was, 'I'm yesterday's man in tomorrow's world.' He had been brought into newspapers in the hot metal era when typewriters were solid items that roughly weighed the same as a small car. Cast-iron Imperial typewriters were built to last. You could fire an Exocet missile at one of these things and the flying bomb would come off worse. Now it was all lightweight plastic stuff that seemed to have a life expectancy of about a year, if you were lucky. At the beginning of the advanced technology, the News Editor could never quite get his head round being told to 'reboot' his computer. Why not switch it off and switch it on again?

The News Editor checked his e-mails. First one up was from his Chief News reporter Griff Stewart, timed at 12.34am. 'Good murder story breaking in Millport. I'm off on the first ferry. Told they might be cancelled, so I might have to swim! Hope not. I'll phone at 10am. Okay?' Gilhooley nodded his head in agreement. He liked his top man, but wasn't overly fond of his nickname R.I.P. That bastard Brock had lumbered him with that moniker. Gilhooley rated Brock highly too and believed the sports section was the poorer without his contribution. 'My day will come, as well,' he sighed. For the moment, though, the News Editor was happy to have Griff Stewart on board. He was always impressed by his Chief News Reporter's willingness to work on his initiative. He didn't need to be led by the nose as so many other reporters did.

Gilhooley looked at the clock on the wall. It was just beyond eight o'clock. He still had plenty of time to put together his news schedule before the day's first conference at eleven o'clock sharp in the Editor's office. These could often be fairly dull, mundane, run-of-the-mill affairs. He, as News Editor, would read out his list of stories for the day and the Sports Editor, Features Editor, Picture Editor, Circulation Manager and a few of their deputies would read from their respective schedules. Everyone was invited to throw in their tuppence worth.

Decisions could be made fairly swiftly by professionals used to working with tight deadlines, but there could be the odd disagreement or two. Take Rangers going into liquidation and being dumped into Scotland's Third Division, for instance. Obviously, it was of news *and* sports interest. The Sports Editor would want the best story of the day for the back page, the News Editor would push for it to be on the front page. They would discuss the merits of the story before a decision was finally made.

Heads of departments were precious things. They always wanted their own way for their respective sections of the newspaper. Petted lips could go up like bouncy castles if they didn't get the nod from Vic Bernard, the managing editor. There had never been blood shed at these meetings, but they could get feisty. All that for fifty pence.

Saturday disappeared into oblivion as the clock ticked away to fifteen minutes past midnight. R.I.P. made one final telephone call before calling it a night in the newsroom which, by now, was mainly silent, the drone of the twenty-four hour news service on satellite TV gently humming over his head. He punched out the number of his good long-time friend, close confidant and boozing buddy Tommy Booth, Detective Inspector with the Strathclyde CID. 'Not too late, Tommy?' asked the newspaperman knowing only too well the cop was a night owl.

'Of course not. What's happening at this time of night, my old tart?' Booth was also known as El Cid. El Cid and R.I.P. An interesting double-act.

'Thought I'd give you a quick head's-up with this one, mate,' said R.I.P. 'It looks like we've got a murder in Millport. The first ever on the island.'

'Not being rude but, this should interest me ... why?'

'It's not just an ordinary old murder. We've got a guy dressed up as Wild Bill Hickok and it looks as though he's been shot between the eyes.'

'Fuck off.'

'No, honestly. It's the Country and Western Festival on the island. The place is heaving and Brock's just phoned to let me know there are 12,000 cowboys on the island and they're all carrying guns. The beat cop's on the verge of a nervous breakdown.'

'Is Brock pished?'

'No, he sounds good. I talked to the cop, anyway, just in case.'

'Christ. Aye, that sounds like good stuff, right enough.'

'Fancy coming over? It could be fun.'

'Don't you think there's enough happening in No Mean City to keep me busy?' The cop didn't wait for an answer. 'You going?'

'Try and hold me back. Tell your chief there'll be nothing happening in Glasgow over the next few days, everyone's decanted to Millport.'

'I'll see what I can do, but the place will probably be flooded with CID tomorrow, anyway. I can only ask.'

El Cid smiled. He liked nothing better than a good western.

CHAPTER EIGHT

EARLY FRIDAY AFTERNOON, AUGUST 31

'Howdy, purdner, what time's the bar brawl?' The cowboy with the abandoned hair and the chaotic moustache leaned forward to rest his elbow on the bar.

Hughie Edwards looked up from washing a couple of pint glasses. 'Oh, I'm not sure we're having one. We'll see how busy we are. Not a lot of space in here for a floor show. Maybe about six o'clock, if it's quiet. Not too mad at that time. Have it around eight or nine o'clock and it will turn into a real fist fight. I learned that lesson a wee while ago. What will it be, mate?'

The cowboy appeared to bristle. 'A pint of your best heavy. And don't call me "mate". I'm Wild Bill. Wild Bill Hickok.'

'I would never have guessed,' thought Hughie, looking at the shoulder-length hair, the large Stetson, the long black coat, the guns and the assortment of elaborate cowboy gear. He poured the pint. 'I'm Hughie, owner of this saloon. Pleased to meet you, Wild Bill. Tell me, when you get really, really angry do you become Livid Bill?' Hughie smiled, pleased with himself.

'I haven't heard that one before,' answered the cowboy, rolling his eyes skywards.

'If we're having a bar brawl later, do you want to take part, Bill?'

'It's WILD Bill,' corrected the cowboy. 'No, I was involved in one down at the Kentuckian earlier. One fight's enough in one day. I'll maybe watch this one, though. See if I can pick up some tips to help my act.' It was Hughie's turn to roll his eyes skywards. 'Improve his act? What the fuck's he talking about? Marlon Brando's got a lot to answer for with all this method acting shite,' he thought.

'Aye,' he said, 'we've got the iced candy bottles ready just in case.'

Last year Hughie had to let one of his staff go for failing to switch bottles. Some poor cowboy suffered severe concussion and was out for about half-an-hour. Wasn't in any condition to finish his pint of Guinness and whisky chaser. Apparently, it took his wife an entire weekend to convince him he wasn't Wyatt Earp.

Charlie Brock looked down from the Schloss Adler. The town was beginning to come alive. Cowboys and cowgirls were arriving by the busload. It was good to see the place busy. He knew only too well what a successful Country and Western Festival meant to the locals. He had already had a couple of beers in the Georgics, aka the Confederate HQ, and, sensibly for a change, put a lining in his stomach with a fish supper from the Hippy Chippy. Blotting paper, he realised, would be required. He would go over and see his pal Hughie in a minute before bedlam ensued.

'Did you know Wild Bill Hickok was born in Illinois?' asked the cowboy. 'Homer, Illinois. It's now called Troy Grove, Illinois.'

'Is that right?' said Hughie. 'You learn something new every day.' The pub was beginning to rapidly fill up and he was actively engaged in pouring six pints of lager for some incoming cowboys, eager to get involved in the fun and frolics of the weekend.

'Did you know he was appointed town marshal of Abilene in 1871?'

'Just what I need,' thought Hughie, 'a history lesson of the Wild West.' 'Really? Well, I never'.

'And do you know why he was appointed the town marshal of Abilene in 1871?'

'Wyatt Earp was otherwise engaged?' ventured Hughie, his back to Wild Bill as he frantically poured dark rums from the optics for a party of pink-hatted cowgirls who, if they kept necking the booze at this rate, wouldn't be awake in three hours' time. They might not be *alive* in four hours' time. Hughie had seen it all before. 'Hello, girls,' smiled Hughie. 'Having a good time?'

'Just keep the fuckin' drink coming,' answered one particularly fat and obnoxious cowgirl, who, in a certain light, resembled Pavarotti, beard and all.

'I'll keep the fuckin' drink coming as long as you can keep fuckin' paying for it.' Hughie thought to himself.

'Hey, barkeep, do you know the answer?' asked Wild Bill, who wasn't about to allow his prey to wriggle clear of his clutches.

'Eh? Sorry. What was the question again?'

'Do you know why Wild Bill was appointed town marshal of Abilene in 1871?'

'He was the only guy with a gun?'

'Nope.' Wild Bill was happy with himself and knew he was well ahead on points. 'The original marshal was a guy called Tom "Bear River" Smith. And he died because he refused to use his guns. Believe it or not, he was a pacifist. Imagine that. A marshal in charge of a Wild West town a pacifist. Anyway, he was beaten to death by an angry home-steader.'

'Why?' Hughie asked, getting sucked in.

'Don't know. Just some sort of argument, apparently, and the marshal refused to use his guns. The other guy chopped him up.'

'And in stepped Wild Bill Hickok?' queried Hughie.

'Yessssireeebob. The town council had a meeting after the death of Tom "Bear River" Smith and they voted unanimously to bring in a marshal who wasn't afraid to blow people away, waste them where they stood, blast them to fuck, fire them straight to hell.'

'And Wild Bill fitted the bill? Hughie laughed at his wit.

Stoney-faced, the cowboy continued. 'The town council had heard of Wild Bill's reputation. He was the most flamboyant, most feared of all gunmen who drifted from mining camps to cow towns and back again after the Civil War.'

Hughie, still furiously pulling pints, wondered if the cowboy had committed the entire history of Wild Bill Hickok to his memory banks. Grudgingly, he gave him some credit. 'You certainly know your stuff,' he said.

'Yessssireeebob. Here's another one for you, barkeep.'

'Hughie. You can call me Hughie.'

'Okay, Hughie. Do you know how many men he killed?'

'Oh, for fuck's sake, it's turning into a full-blown Mastermind,' muttered Hughie under his breath. The cowboys and cowgirls kept arriving and he kept pouring. The Jewish Piano would be going into meltdown at this rate.

'I said do you know how many men he killed?' repeated Wild Bill, fumbling in a pocket of his waistcoat.

'Five? Ten? Twenty?' Hughie's voice was flat. He didn't really want to be captured any more by this conversation. Unfortunately, all his beer fonts were right at the point where Wild Bill had parked his elbow. There was no escape. Another day, when the place was quiet, he would have been only too happy to find out more about his customer's specialist subject. 'Maggie, can you get the guys in the corner?' He pointed his wife in the direction of the table at the fruit machine where five guys were sitting with empty glasses.

Wild Bill spread out a well-thumbed newspaper clipping on the bar. 'This is a copy of an original interview with a journalist from one of those eastern newspapers. It says here that a guy called Henry Morton Stanley asked Wild Bill straight out how many men he had shot down. And it says here he answered, "I suppose I have killed more than a hundred...and not one without good cause." There you go. Straight from the horse's mouth.'

'The horse's arse, more like,' thought Hughie.

Wild Bill carefully folded the newspaper clipping and tucked it back in his waistcoat. He replaced it on the bar with another cutting. Hughie's heart plummeted towards the cellar beneath his feet. 'This is going to be a long day,' he thought. He had hoped to be home by three in the morning.

'It says here he left Illinois for Kansas in 1855. He was going to work as a farmer. Wild Bill Hickok? A farmer? Thank the Good Lord and praise the angels that didn't occur. Nope, he was appointed town constable before he was twenty-one-years-old. He must have been pretty handy with a gun even then. According to legend, he shot and killed his first man, a hombre by the name of David McCanles, in Nebraska in 1858. Imagine having the honour and privilege of being the first man to be gunned down by Wild Bill Hickok? That guy must have died a happy man.'

'Doubt it,' thought Hughie. He looked pointedly at Wild Bill's emptying pint glass. If his ears were going to get a bashing, the Jewish Piano might as well get in on the action. 'You for another?' he asked.

'Yessssireeebob,' smiled Wild Bill. 'A cowboy can't walk on one leg alone.'

Hughie wondered what the fuck he meant by that, but he poured the pint, anyway. He was intrigued, though. 'How did the first bloke die? Does it say in there?'

The cowboy smoothed the newspaper clipping on the bar again. 'Wild Bill was working in a Nebraska freight station and it says here that a persistent customer demanded money he claimed he was owed by Wild Bill. Imagine picking a fight with our hero? Wild Bill blasted him, using both guns.'

'Was it a good old-fashioned gunfight? Two guys out on the street ready to draw on each other?'

'Well, no, actually it wasn't,' Wild Bill answered, a little sheepishly. 'The other guy wasn't actually armed.'

'Not armed? Wild Bill shot and killed an unarmed man? Was that not a hanging offence back then?'

Wild Bill was suddenly indignant. 'It was self-defence! It says it right here in the newspaper, so it must be true.'

'So, the first-ever guy murdered by Wild Bill didn't even have a gun on him?'

'Killed, not murdered. He was killed by Wild Bill. In self-defence. It says it right here.'

'Doesn't sound like a fair fight to me. Was the guy shot in the back, by any chance?'

Wild Bill sniffed, 'I don't have that information.'

'Hey, you, geez another six dark rums,' interrupted one of a group of ladies Hughie had mentally christened the Spice Witches.

'Certainly,' beamed Hughie. 'Coming right up, ladies.'

Wild Bill neatly folded his newspaper clipping and placed it in his waistcoat pocket. From an inside pocket he produced a copy of a cutting from another journal. Meticulously, he wiped the bar with his hand just in case there had been any spillage of alcohol. He placed it in front of him.

Hughie, from the corner of his eye, saw the movement. 'Fuck me, he's got an entire library in that waistcoat,' he thought. 'What next?'

'How about this, Hughie?' said the cowboy.

'Be with you in a minute, Bill. Sorry, *Wild* Bill,' he corrected himself. 'The guy's a fuckin' nutter,' he thought.

'Right, this one is from a newspaper called the Springfield Missouri Weekly Patriot and it's dated 27 July 1865. It says that Wild Bill had served as a Union scout along the Missouri border during the Civil War and then became a professional gambler. This newspaper guy, Timothy J. Higginsworth, wrote that Wild Bill had earned the reputation as a man it was best not to cross.' The cowboy paused. Hughie was certain he could see his chest puffing up with pride. He continued, 'David Tutt, of Yellville, Arkansas, was shot in the Public Square at six o'clock on Friday last by an individual known in the southwest Missouri as Wild

Bill Hickok. And it says here, "The difficulty arose from a game of cards." How about that? Blew the cheatin' bastard away.'

'Did he have a gun?' asked Hughie.

'What do you mean? Of course, he had a gun. He shot him, didn't he?'

'No, not Wild Bill. The other guy. Did *he* have a gun?'

The cowboy sniffed again. 'It doesn't say,' he answered, carefully folding away the newspaper clipping.

Hughie Edwards' eyes, behind his dark-rimmed spectacles, lit up as he looked over Wild Bill's shoulder. The heavy wood-pannelled door had swung open. 'Charlie Brock! How the hell are you? When did you come down? You should have given me a wee warning.' He looked genuinely pleased to see his journalist pal.

Brock managed to squeeze between two burly, gun-totting cowboys. One had a plastic arrow sticking through his Stetson. He made it to the bar and stood beside Wild Bill. He extended his hand across the bar to Hughie. 'I'm fine, mucker. How you doing? Good to see you swamped. Hope you've got enough beer for an army of thirsty cowboys.'

'When did you ever see me run out? We've got enough down in that cellar to take us through to next year.' He repeated, 'When did you come down?'

'I got the 10.15 ferry. I'd have been in earlier, but I had a couple of pints over at the Georgics with my old neighbour, Tam Nellis. Christ, he's in good nick for a bloke closing in on ninety, isn't he? There must be some medicinal value in a steady diet of large whiskies.'

'Och, he probably died a couple of years ago and is too drunk to notice,' smiled Hughie, pouring a pint of lager as a reflex action. 'I take it you haven't taken up drinking Cinzano? You here for the duration? The full three or four days of insanity?' he asked his friend.

'Last man standing,' answered Brock, adding quickly, 'I hope.'

'I'm Wild Bill Hickok,' said the long-haired, mustachioed stranger to Brock's left. He offered his hand.

Brock shook it, 'I'm Charlie Brock.'

'What's your stage name?'

'Stage name?' queried Brock. 'I don't have one.'

'Oh,' sighed Wild Bill, looking sorry and almost embarrassed for the new arrival. 'No stage name, huh? Oh, well.'

'Wild Bill here has been regaling me with all sorts of stories about the Wild West,' said Hughie. 'All very educational. He's brought some interesting stuff with him. Old newspapers. So old maybe your name's in them.' Hughie was in fine fettle. Even the Spice Witches weren't going to rattle his cage today.

'Hey, you! Merr dark rum ower here. Pronto.'

Hughie smiled, 'Yes, my sweets, coming right up.'

Wild Bill eyed his latest drinking companion. He wasn't one bit impressed by his dress code. 'You ain't got a gun?' he asked with a semblance of pity in his voice.

'No, never owned one,' replied Brock. 'I'd probably blow my fuckin' toes off if I ever put on a holster. No, I don't want to be walking funny for the rest of my life.'

'Show him one of your newspaper cuttings, Wild Bill,' said Hughie. 'Honestly, Charlie, he's got everything in that waistcoat.'

Wild Bill fumbled about inside his waistcoat. 'Ah, here we are,' he said with a degree of satisfaction. 'This is what I've been looking for.' Again, he went through the ritual of cleaning the surface of the bar with his open hand. He carefully unfolded the piece of paper. 'Right, how about this? This is from the Topeka Daily Commonwealth and it's dated 22 July 1870. It says, "On Monday last, Wild Bill Hickok killed a soldier and seriously wounded another at Hays City. Five attacked Wild Bill and two got used up."'

'Two got used up?' interrupted Brock. 'Is that what it said? Used up?' It appeared newspapers back then were as well versed in succinct descriptions as they are today.

Wild Bill placed the cutting in front of Brock. He dragged his forefinger along the line of print. 'There you are. "Used up." That means shot to fuck, you know.'

'I guessed that.'

Wild Bill dragged on the end of his droopy moustache and beamed. 'I like this part. "The sentiment of the community is with Bill." It was claimed he acted in self-defence.'

'He seemed to do a lot of shooting in self-defence, didn't he?' offered Hughie. Then he asked Wild Bill, 'Can a man walk on two legs alone?'

Brock's brow furrowed. He had never heard that expression before.

'Eh?' queried Wild Bill. 'Oh, yup. Good one. I'll have another beer. You for one, Charlie?'

'Won't say no. Let's see what else you've got there.'

Once more Wild Bill, meticulous as ever, folded away the piece of paper and replaced it on the bar with another. 'This one is from the Leavenworth Kansas Times and it's dated 26 August 1869. What does it say now? Here we are. "Wild Bill Hickok shot one Mulrey at Hays on Tuesday. Mulrey died yesterday morning." Oh, look at this. "Bill has been elected sheriff of Ellis County."'

'Did he get the job because he shot this bloke Mulrey, the guy with no first name?'

'Doesn't say.'

'Did Mulrey have a gun?' asked Hughie, mischievously.

'Doesn't say.'

Once more Wild Bill went through the rigmarole of perfectly preserving his copy of the clipping. He stopped reading from a script. 'You know there were those in Hays who didn't always appreciate Wild Bill? Imagine that.' He removed his black Stetson and shook his head while running his hand through his long hair. 'Okay, we know he was a bit wild. Well, where do you think he got the nickname? Wild Bill. Not Mild Bill, but Wild Bill. And, okay, he roomed with a succession of prostitutes. Okay, he drank himself into a stupor every now and again. And, yes, he ran the town from the card tables in the Long Branch Saloon. He would kick the shit out of a passerby when he felt like it. And I'll give you he was a heavy and reckless gambler. Okay, he might have been too ready to pull out his guns and wave them under someone's nose when he was pissed. But, hey, no-one's perfect.'

'Clearly,' said Brock.

'There was a lot of jealousy back then.' The cowboy felt the need to jump to the defence of his hero. He climbed upon his high horse. 'Take a look at this clipping. It's from the St.Joseph Union newspaper. It's not dated, but it would have been around 1869, I reckon. It says, "If the enthusiastic admirers of this plainsman called Wild Bill Hickok could see him on one of his periodical drinking sprees they would have considerable romance knocked out of them." See what I mean? Jealousy. The town council unanimously voted him into office. They knew what they were doing. This was the Wild West, for fuck's sake. Everybody wanted to shoot each other, didn't they? Law of the gun. They made him sheriff and he cleaned up their town and that's the thanks he gets for it. Some mealy-mouthed little newspaper weasel reporter was probably envious.'

Brock could see Hughie was about to inform Wild Bill that his new beer-swilling companion was a journalist. Brock quickly put his forefinger to his lips. Hughie nodded and let his pal off the hook. Wild Bill's high horse was still rampaging towards a grande finale. 'Here, have a gander at this,' he said, producing yet another cutting from within the labyrinth that doubled as a garment of clothing as well as a mobile library.

'Have you got a printing press in there?' queried Brock. Wild Bill said nothing.

He continued. 'This is a cowboy talking. "When I came along the street, he was standing there with his back to the wall and his thumbs hooked into his gun-belt. He stood there and rolled his head from side to side, looking at everything and everybody from under his eyebrows - just like a mad bull. I decided there and then that I didn't want any part of him." How about that? Respect, man! And how about this piece from the Abilene Chronicle? This is brilliant. "Hickok has posted up printed notices, informing all persons that the ordinance against carrying firearms or other weapons in Abilene, will be enforced." And it's got Wild Bill talking, too. He says, "There's no bravery in carrying revolvers in a civilised community. Such a practice is well enough and perhaps necessary when among Indians or other barbarians, but among white people it ought to be discountenanced." Wise words from a wise man. What do you think?'

'But Wild Bill carried guns, didn't he, Bill?' ventured Brock.

'Wild Bill, Charlie. Don't forget the "Wild". Of course, he did - he was the law. Maybe he had to gun down someone every now and again. In self-defence.'

Brock was catching up with the thinking of his pal behind the bar. This guy's sanity was a tad suspect. 'Okay, *Wild* Bill. But if memory serves correctly, I believe he was kicked out of his job as marshal in Abilene. Is that not right? Am I getting him mixed up with some other cowboy?'

Wild Bill slugged back his pint, coming close to slamming the empty glass on the surface of the bar. He looked a mite flustered.

'You for another one?' asked Brock. Wild Bill looked mortally offended by his drinking partner's impeccable recollection. He was right, but he wasn't aware there was anyone else on this island who knew that fact about his hero. Piqued or not, he agreed to another beer. Before Hughie could get his hand to the pump there was the Valkyrie-like shrill from the other end of the bar.

'Hey, you! What's a good-looking bird got to do to get a drink around here?' It was one of the Spice Witches. Hughie looked at her.

'She's a double bagger,' he whispered to Brock.

'A double bagger? What the fuck's that?'

'You would have to wear a bag over your head just in case hers burst when you're shagging her.' He turned to the Spice Witches, 'Dark rums, my lovelies? Coming your way in an instant.'

Wild Bill fumbled inside his coat. Remarkably, he seemed to have a filing system all of his own. He appeared to know where everything was stowed away. This was one strange dude. With systematic precision, he once again swept the bar with his open hand. Before he folded open the clipping, he said, 'I've done a bit of research of my own on this. Here's what I found. Okay, what you have got to remember is that there were no incidents involving gun play in Abilene back then. No shots were fired for a full eight months in that town. That was down to one man and one man only - Wild Bill Hickok. His gun control was working. Then, unfortunately, Wild Bill shot dead two men. Sounds bad, gentlemen, I know, but let me continue. Wild Bill had had a few drinks while playing cards in the Long Branch Saloon. There was a quarrel with a lowlife called Phil Coe. It might have had something to do with the affections of a woman. Okay, a prostitute, I'll give you that. There may even have been something about Wild Bill owing the guy a gambling debt. Not sure about that. Anyway, Wild Bill, very politely I must stress, invited the man to leave the premises.'

'Probably booted the guy in the nuts, battered him over the back of his head with the butt of his gun and booted him through the swing doors,' mused Brock, finding difficulty in keeping a straight face.

'Wild Bill went back to playing cards when he heard a couple of shots outside the Alamo Saloon, which was close by. He ran through the swing doors and raced to the Alamo. He saw Coe and told him to drop his gun. Coe told him he had been shooting at a stray dog. Imagine expecting Wild Bill Hickok to swallow that? No chance! He drew both his guns and started shooting at Coe who returned fire. Now, please remember, this was late at night, so it would have been very dark. Anyway, there was a gunfight. Bullets were flying everywhere. Wild Bill had a special deputy named Mike Williams and he raced to the scene when he heard the firing. Unfortunately, he didn't identify himself and, in the dark, Wild Bill shot him twice. He was dead before he hit the ground. It was an accident. Then Wild Bill put one in Coe. Two guys were shot. It could have happened to anyone.'

'And that's why he was sacked?' asked Brock.

'He *wasn't* sacked. You don't sack a man like Wild Bill Hickok. Here's what the Abilene Chronicle said.' He smoothed the newspaper cutting on the bar. "Wild Bill Hickok rushed to the scene, saw Coe with his revolver in his hand and drew his own. Both men began firing. Mike Williams, the special deputy, hurried round the corner to help the marshal and ran into two of Hickok's bullets. The whole incident was the work of an instant. The marshal, surrounded by the crowd, did not recognise Williams whose death he deeply regrets. Coe was shot through the stomach, the ball coming out of his back. He lived in great agony until Sunday and he died that evening. He was a gambler, but a man of natural good impulses in his better moments." Wild Bill was absolved of all blame. It's there in black and white in a newspaper, so it must be true.'

Brock smiled and said nothing.

Hughie repeated the earlier question, 'Why was he sacked?'

'I told you he *wasn't* sacked. The city council simply decided not to renew his contract. But look at this item in the paper. Again, we're talking jealously here. It's from a citizen. It says, "Wild Bill Hickok acted only too readily to shoot down, to kill outright instead of avoiding assassination when possible, as is the higher duty of a marshal. Such a policy of taking justice into his own hands exemplified a form of lawlessness." Bastards. Unappreciative, ungrateful bastards.' Wild Bill stopped short of advocating his hero should have filled every citizen in Abilene with lead before leaving town.

'Hey, you! Fuckin' hell.' The piercing wail of a Spice Witch.

'Ah, the children of the night,' whispered Hughie in his best Bela Lagosi/Dracula impersonation. 'Yes, my petal, another round of dark rums, is it?'

'He catches on quick, this wan. Aye, and be quick about it.'

'Yes, dear heart, coming right up,' said Hughie, stifling, 'Right up your fat arse.'

'Anyway, gentlemen, I'll make my farewells,' said Wild Bill, as he swept back his coat to display his immaculate ivory-handled guns. Brock looked at them somewhat quizzically.

'Ah, I see you have noticed my two equalisers. Wild Bill used to have his revolvers reversed in their holsters to help speed up his draw. It was known as a reverse-twist and it was used quite a lot by the cavalry. If it was good enough for Wild Bill, it's sure as hell good enough for me. And with my final act I bring good news. I will make my return this evening. There is more, much more you need to know about Wild Bill Hickok. So long.' And with that, he turned, maneuvered a safe passage around an unsteady cowboy and made his way through the door.

'Is there *anything* else we really need to know about the man?' queried Brock. 'That bloke's a walking encyclopedia on Wild Bill Hickok.'

'Aye, it could be the death of him some day if he's not careful,' said Hughie.

CHAPTER NINE

FRIDAY EVENING, AUGUST 31

'BANG! BANG! You're dead!'

A startled Charlie Brock almost peed down his right leg. He looked over his shoulder and there was a grinning Wild Bill Hickok, holding two guns to his head. 'For fuck's sake, Bill, I'm having a pish.' Brock was not amused.

'It's not Bill,' chided the cowboy. 'It's *Wild* Bill. Shufty up, I need a pee, too. Even legends have lavatorial requirements. Time to syphon the python.' Both men stood in silence until their 'requirements' had been taken care of.

Brock finished first, stuck his hands under the tap, dried them quickly and said, 'See you later.' He fought his way past a posse of drunks to the bar. 'Hughie, he's back!' Hughie Edwards was still pouring pints at a rate that might have interested the people who compiled the Guinness Book of Records.

The bar owner looked up. 'Eh?' He cocked his hand to his left ear and stretched forward. 'Who's back?' Brock had to compete with screaming and screeching of the Spice Witches. They weren't handsome when they wobbled into the pub and, four hours and Christ only knows how many dark rums later, they were now suitable life models for Picasso.

'Wild Bill Hickok! Wild Bill's back!'

'Sure am, purdner,' said Wild Bill, still slinking up behind people, but, at least, his ivory-handled pistols were holstered now.

The Spice Witches were shrieking, squawking, whooping and hollering their way towards registering on the Richter Scale. 'Girls, can you give it a wee rest for a moment?' pleaded Hughie.

'Go fuck yourself,' he was told.

'Country and Western Festival, ye cannae whack it,' he thought and smiled.

Brock finally caught up with his pint at the bar. To his consternation, Wild Bill had followed him to his favourite spot. Polite to the end, Brock motioned to Wild Bill, 'Are you up for a pint? Heavy, wasn't it?'

'Well, that would be mighty neighbourly of you, fella,' said Wild Bill.

'Oh, fuck he gets worse as the beers go down,' detected Brock. 'Hughie,' he shouted, 'when you've got a minute. Two down here, please. A heavy for Wild Bill. One for yourself.' Hughie nodded. He looked at the clock on the wall. It was just past nine o'clock. Four hours to go and he gets the place back to himself. And the day's takings would go straight into the safe. He smiled again.

'Hey, bartender! Get yer arse ower here. Merr dark rum.' The banshee-like demand from a Spice Witch could be neither ignored nor disobeyed.

Hughie yelled back, 'Be with you in a second, my flower. Dark rums all round?' Swiftly, he poured the drinks and set them up on the bar.

'Hey, you, ya dirty bastard. Ur you looking at ma tits?' Hughie didn't want to inform Miss Blubber 1986 that he would rather have his eyes spooned out.

'Could you blame me if I was?' he said, smoothly, adding, 'Beauty is always something to behold and appreciate.' Privately, he believed she was so repulsive that the tide would refuse to take her out.

Miss Blubber 1986 informed Hughie, 'Ye can look, but ye can-nae touch. Sorry, but Ah'm spoken for. Ah've got a fella.'

'Poor bastard,' thought Hughie.

'He's been lookin' at ma tits, tae,' said another Spice Witch. 'Ah've been watchin' him. Bet ye he fancies ma rose tattoo. Hey, you, do ye want to know where the stem ends up?'

'Ah, my little sugar cube, that's for you to know and for me to find out. If I'm ever lucky enough.'

'Whit does that mean? You watch yersel. Ah've got a man, tae.'

'Poor bastard,' thought Hughie, again.

'Right, Charlie, where did we leave off?' Wild Bill asked his new best mate. Brock winced. He had been looking forward to the pandemonium of the Country and Western Festival, but to have a crazy bastard who thinks he is the reincarnation of Wild Bill Hickcok stick to him like a limpet mine was overpowering.

He failed in his effort to feign interest. 'Oh, I can't remember.'

'I do, though,' said Wild Bill triumphantly.

'Great,' said Brock. A voice inside his head screamed, 'HELP!'

'We left off with Wild Bill moving from Abilene. Remember? Not sacked, they just didn't renew his contract as town marshal. Bastards! Well, I know you'll find this hard to believe, but it gets even *more* interesting from now on. Amazing, eh?'

Brock nodded wearily. 'Can't wait,' he lied.

'Bet you can't,' enthused Wild Bill. 'Okay, he was hurt by the people of Abilene's attitude towards him when he shot and killed his deputy. Remember, he wasn't charged with anything. But Wild Bill was obviously made of good stuff. Okay, he was jobless for awhile and maybe he took to the drink. Who wouldn't after being treated like that in Abilene? Bastards! Thankfully, he was in great demand by the easterners. People say a lot of what was written was exaggerated, but not me. I read some newspaper that insisted Wild Bill killed fewer than ten people. I remember the same reporter also wrote, "Some of his motives for killing them didn't always bear close scrutiny." Now, that's slander.'

'No, actually, it's libel,' corrected Brock. 'It's slander if you *say* something and it's libel if it's in print.'

Wild Bill's eyes narrowed. 'How do you know? Are you a lawyer?'

Brock wasn't about to get caught up in a whole new debate about the merits and demerits of newspapers and journalists, even ones from another century. 'Oh, it's just something I picked up at school. Some things just stick in your head.'

'Right, okay, buddy. Listen, you'll love this. I can see you're enjoying yourself. There's more. Lots more.'

Brock was wondering if there was the possibility of a stagecoach leaving any time soon for Arkansas.

'The easterners took to Wild Bill's colourful ways and he actually became a tour guide for awhile. The people from out east wanted to see something of the old Wild West and who better to show them than Wild Bill? Man, could you ever imagine being given a tour of the old towns, the saloons, the plains by a real-life legend?'

All Brock could imagine at that moment was jumping on a stagecoach and heading for Arkansas.

'And, then in 1873, another remarkable thing happened. A lot of folk thought Wild Bill and Buffalo Bill were enemies. Nothing could be further from the truth. They were best of pals, in fact. So, after he had finished with the tour guide stuff, Buffalo Bill invited him to go east and tour with him. He had put together some sort of melodrama and called it 'The Scouts of the Plains'. Hell, was there nothing this guy couldn't do? Now he was a fuckin' actor.'

Brock awoke from his revelry. 'Really, Wild Bill was an actor?'

'Ah, you see, there's a lot about Wild Bill Hickok the world doesn't know. He was an extraordinary character, right enough. Sadly, things didn't go too well with the play. Well, he wasn't a trained actor, was he? And some even said he had a high-pitched sort of girlish voice. And, okay, there were stories about him getting drunk and forgetting his lines. There was also talk of him having some trouble with the stagehands. They were slow sometimes to keep him in the spotlight. Apparently, Wild Bill threatened to shoot them. The story goes Buffalo Bill asked Wild Bill to sign a pledge promising to give up alcohol. He didn't sign anything, but he gave Buffalo Bill his word he would do his best to stay away from the bevvy. So, at rehearsals, he would get a little bored, a wee bit restless.

'Wild Bill believed it would be a hoot to fire blank cartridges at the actors playing the Indians in the play. Hilarious, eh? Buffalo Bill asked him to refrain, but Wild Bill told him he was just having some fun. Harmless, eh? The fuckin' actors playing the Indians threatened to walk out. No sense of humour, those guys. Well, Buffalo Bill wanted Wild Bill in the show, but the show was doomed without the fuckin' Indians. That bastard Buffalo Bill sacked him.'

'Hollywood's loss was the Wild West's gain, I suppose.' Brock thought he might as well throw in a word or two every now and again.

'You betcha! Yesssirreeeebob. That's exactly what happened. Wild Bill was no pansy easterner. He was a Wild West frontier-type of bloke. He told Buffalo Bill to shove his play - and his Indians - up his arse and he came home to the west where he belonged. Unfortunately, he couldn't find work, what with the drinking and all. And he had another problem. His eyesight was worsening. A bit of a hindrance to a guy with a fierce reputation as a gunfighter. Wild Bill knew he had to stay off the streets, especially at night, because too many people would want to make their name gunning down a guy with his sort of celebrity. Do you know what happened next?'

Brock stared blankly, close to defeat.

'He took up gold mining. Brilliant, eh? All those wide open spaces and people only working during daylight hours. Another problem, though.'

'He didn't find any gold?'

'How did you know? Yup, God made life tough for this guy. He was forced to return to his old haunts. The eyesight, by this time, was deteriorating at an alarming rate. He got back into his normal routine, drinking and playing poker. And then he broke a golden rule.' Brock detected a sniffle from Wild Bill.

'Jeezus Christ Almighty! Ah've no' had a swally for at least two minutes. Whit kind of pub is this?' The Spice Witches were still gracing Hugh's Bar with their presence. The pink cowboy hats had long since been lost during the six's many sojourns to the Ladies' Powder Room. Or, as they preferred to call it, 'The Dumping Ground'. Hughie had discovered they were from Paisley and he wondered how the town could live without these good-time, fun-loving gals even for a few hours. 'Geez a drink, specky.' Hughie was already heading for the dark rum optics.

'Ah, the lavender-scented phrases form so easily upon your lips,' he said.

'Whit ur ye talkin' aboot? The only thing Ah want near ma lips is another fuckin' dark rum – and wan a' they Chippendale guy's giant walloper.' Her friends positively screeched.

Brock, interrupting Wild Bill's lecture, asked, 'Do you take those newspaper cuttings everywhere you go?'

Wild Bill looked him square in the eye and answered, 'Do you think I'm daft? Of course, I don't. Why would I?'

'To bore some poor bastard into oblivion,' thought Brock.

Wild Bill cleared the slops off the bar. He removed his necker-chief to wipe down the surface. Happy that it was safe to proceed, he tossed the neckerchief back round his neck. He spread the clip-ping on the bar.

'Right, this is from the Cheyenne Leader. It says, "Uncharacteristically, Wild Bill Hickcok didn't face the door as he played poker with friends. A demented little man named Jack McCall slipped up behind him. McCall had evidently persuaded himself that Hickok was responsible for the death of his brother in Hays City, Kansas. No evidence of such a crime was ever found.

He stood watching the game for a moment, then drew his revolver and fired into the back of Wild Bill's head. Hickok died instantly, scattering the cards as he fell.'

Tears were now evident in Wild Bill's eyes. He made no effort to disguise his emotions. Brock wondered how many times he put himself through all this story-telling just to end up a gibbering, sobbing wreck. Wild Bill sniffed and swallowed and shook a bit. 'They called it a Dead Man's Hand in cards forever after that. Jack McCall. Bastard!'

Wild Bill neatly folded away the newspaper clipping and secreted it somewhere upon his person.

'This McCall guy was charged with murder and knew he was heading for the rope, but he still wanted to sell his story to the newspapers. A reporter by the name of Leander Richardson, who wrote for something called Scribner's Monthly, got in touch. The newspaper agreed to cover his burial costs and suchlike. The little arsehole didn't have a bean to his name. He fuckin' murdered a true legend of the Wild West and he was skint. He was acquitted at first, but there was a retrial and he was charged with willful murder. They hanged the little bastard on 1 March 1877, seven months after they buried Wild Bill Hickok. Justice served in the end.'

'Amen to that,' said Brock, throwing a mouthful of lager down his throat.

CHAPTER TEN

LATE FRIDAY EVENING, AUGUST 31

'Hughie! We've got a technicolour yawn over here!'

'Oh, Christ,' thought Hughie, 'there's always fuckin' one.' He looked over to the table beside the fruit machine. Who was the heaving culprit this time? It could have been any one of the five who had been drinking steadily since opening time. 'I'll be over in a minute,' shouted Hughie to Tip-Toe Thompson, one of the locals. 'Make sure nobody stands in it, will you?'

'Aye, aye, captain,' said Tip-Toe.

The bleary-eyed cowboy, an accountant from Tarbolton, gazed down at the regurgitated mess at his feet. He had spewed up all over his chaps and his boots. He tried to make sense of it all as he peered into the hotchpotch that had just been deposited on the floor. Pints of heavy, Bacardi and Coke and five or six packets of pickled onion crisps mixed together presented a strange-looking concoction when they made their splattering comeback. 'Why are there always carrots?' he thought, blinking and eyeing the brightly-coloured vomit. 'I don't even eat carrots.'

Involuntarily and violently, he jerked forward again, his head thumping off the edge of the table. There were some more dregs apparently eager to catch up with the contents that had already escaped his stomach with such a vibrant flourish moments earlier. The cowboy looked up, dazed after his brow had had a sudden and painful collision with a solid oak table. He squinted around and slowly and unsteadily managed to get to his feet. 'Who are you fuckin' punching?' he said, before promptly sticking the head on the fruit machine.

'Whit a smell!' observed a Spice Witch, only yards from the action. 'Ya dirty wee bastard. That's bawfin'.' One of her drinking companions, her neck struggling to keep her head upright, looked as confused as the retching cowboy.

'Christ, that might have been me,' she said. 'Ah think Ah've just had a wattery wan.' Her pal looked at her,

'Aw, no' again, Senga. Can ye no' just fart like the rest of us?'

Wild Bill Hickok had just about exhausted his tales of his hero. He turned to Charlie Brock. 'You know he was only thirty-nine when he was murdered? What sort of age is that for a genuine Wild West legend to die? He didn't even see forty. That's just not fair. Jack McCall. Bastard!'

'Maybe that's the way he would have wanted to go,' nodded Brock, who, by this time, clearly didn't give a monkey's how Wild Bill had met his untimely demise. They could have strung him up by his balls in the town square and invited people to throw rocks at him for all he cared.

'No, I don't think so,' said Wild Bill, a serious tone in his voice. 'No, I don't think he would have wanted the back of his head blown clean away by some sniveling little coward who sneaked up behind him while he was playing cards. Fuck, he was actually winning the poker game, too. Now that's bad timing.'

'Aye,' nodded Brock, closing in on a state of comatose. Wild Bill was appearing to have more effect on him than the alcohol.

'Look, I've got a cutting from the Black Hills Pioneer of the actual death notice for Wild Bill.'

Brock didn't reel back in surprise. 'Really?' he asked, trying not to roll his eyes too obviously. 'That must be interesting.'

'You bet, look at this. "Died in Deadwood, Black Hills, August 2, 1876, from the effects of a pistol shot, J.B. Hickock (Wild Bill), formerly of Cheyenne, Wyoming. Funeral service will be held in Charlie Utter's Camp on Thursday afternoon, August 3, 1876, at 3 o'clock P.M. All respectively invited to attend."'

Brock peered at the copy. 'Can I have a look at this, Wild Bill?' He lifted the newspaper clipping closer to his eyes. 'Have you noticed that Wild Bill's name is misspelled in this death notice?'

'You're fuckin' joking,' said the cowboy. 'Can't be. That's the official death notice written out by Charlie Utter.'

'Charlie Utter might have been a friend, but he couldn't spell. He's spelled Hickok with an extra 'c' before the final 'k'. Here, have a look.'

Wild Bill took the clipping back. He stared at it for a moment. 'For fuck's sake,' he muttered. 'You're right. I've never noticed that before. Nice words, pity the arsehole couldn't fuckin' spell.' He folded it carefully and put it away, saying nothing at all. Brock cheered his little victory silently.

Hughie nudged his way through the little gap in the bar. 'There's always some bampot who can't hold his bevvy.' He came back with a mop and bucket. 'Okay, which one was it?' he asked the five cowboys. One was still sitting with his head between his spread-eagled legs. 'I guess you're favourite,' said Hughie. 'I should make you clean up this fuckin' mess.' The cowboy wearily looked up at the bar owner. His forehead was covered in blood.

'Shorry, bosh. Ah had a wee accshident. Shorry.'

Hughie put the mop to work, thinking, 'Just as well Maggie took up the carpets this morning.' The perpetrator fumbled to find a pocket in his jeans.

'Look, Ah've got money. Ah'll pay for it. Okay? Nae worries.' He produced a pile of smash and scattered it on the table. 'Is that enough dosh, bosh?'

Hughie laughed. It was Country and Western Festival. These things happened. 'Keep your money, you'll need it for a fish supper.'

'Fuck the fish shupper. Ah want merr bevvy.' Suddenly the cow-boy let out a rasping 'Yahoo!' If he had possessed guns, Hughie could envisage him pointing them at the ceiling and blasting away great chunks of plaster.

'If you want more drink, you'll have to go elsewhere, I'm afraid. Go round the corner to McIntosh's, the Varmint Inn. He'll serve you, no problem.' Hughie didn't particularly care for the owner of that establishment. The five cowboys prepared to leave.

'Just roon the corner? Thanksh, bosh. Any burdsh in there? Maybe I'll get lucky,' said the drunkest, still covered in puke and now the possessor of a crimson forehead. He dragged himself to his feet. The cowboy tried to focus on Hughie. 'See that bastard there? He punched me.' He pointed to the fruit machine.

'Me want firewater!' Hughie looked round. Sitting Bull had arrived, the front of his garish headdress settling on his nose, his legs a little unsteady. 'Sitting Bull demand more firewater.'

'Fuck off, ya eejit,' said the cowboy with the burst forehead stumbling past on his way to the pub round the corner.

'I knew this was going to be a long day,' sighed Hughie.

'Me come in peace, white man. Me friend of the yellow legs. Me friend of the pony soldiers. Me no take scalp. Me like white faces. Me want firewater.' Hughie returned the mop and bucket to the closet at the corner of the bar. 'Me want whisky,' said Sitting Bull. 'Me dry of mouth. Many travels today. Me journey many places. Me very tired.' Not wanting to spoil his image, he whispered, 'Make it a large Bell's, please, Hughie. A couple of chunks of ice.'

'When yer finished with Big Chief Bastard Face, geez six merr dark rums. As fast as ye like, four eyes.'

Hughie was wondering what was holding up the Spice Witches, apart from the bar. He looked for invisible strings. Give them their due, they could take their drink. 'Yes, my little piece of sweetness and light, I'll be right with you.'

'Sooner the better, ya wee turd.' The Spice Witches cackled together.

Hughie thought momentarily about wringing the contents of the mop into their drinks.

Maggie returned with a pile of empties from the snooker room. Hughie motioned conspiratorially. 'Do me a favour, Maggie,' Hughie said to his wife, who was putting in a shift above and beyond. The thought of the cruise keeping her focused. 'Discreetly, can you find out when these "ladies" are going home? Are they here all weekend? If they are, I'll take any amount of shite they want to throw at me. Their money's as good as anyone's.'

The pub was calming down to a storm. 'Have you had a good night, mate?' asked Brock.

'Christ, aye, you better believe it.' Hughie looked at the clock. It was just coming up for 11.30. 'Not long to go now,' he said. 'You want to come over to my place for a wee bite to eat?'

Brock didn't have to think too hard. 'I'd much prefer to stay here and have a few with my old mucker once Wild Bill shoots the crow.' Hughie laughed,

'Christ, really? You want more drink? You'll be getting journalists a bad name.'

Wild Bill was playing the fruit machine, wondering why there was a large crack in the glass. 'Wild Bill? Pint of heavy over here with your name on it,' shouted Hughie above the racket that engulfed his bar. Wild Bill turned and gave the thumbs up. 'Ach, he isn't too bad, is he?' asked Hughie.

'No, he's harmless enough,' answered Brock. 'Told me he's a singer in a few pubs back at the ranch. Fuck me, he's got me as bad as himself. Glasgow. He's going to give me a list of his gigs. And

I've to pop in some night. Maybe I will. I'll make sure my earplugs are fitted securely, though.

'What's his real name?' asked Hughie.

'Don't know. I'm frightened to ask,' answered Brock. 'He just likes to be called Wild Bill. Maybe he's a bit squirrely. Cheers for the drink. Are you having one?'

Hughie hesitated for a nano-second. 'Aye, why the hell not?' He poured a large brandy and port. He wouldn't be driving tonight.

'Me want more firewater. Me still dry of mouth. Me still heap thirsty. Me need whisky.'

'Same again, chief?' asked Hughie, already heading for the Bell's optic. Sitting Bull whispered,

'And a packet of Salt'n'Vinegar, too, Hughie, please.'

Tip-Toe Thompson put away his snooker cue and returned to the bar. 'Pint of lager, please, Hughie, when you've got a minute,' he said. Tip-Toe Thompson actually started life as Matthew Thompson, but picked up his moniker after moving from the mainland to Millport a couple of years ago. Apparently, he was very light on his feet. Not gay, just dainty on his toes. He was the chef next door at The Pier and had finished his shift at six before making a bolt of all of four yards to join the maddening throng in Hugh's. Or Nashville, as it had been renamed.

'Busy next door?' asked Hughie.

'Stowed all day,' replied Tip-Toe. 'Must have made about two hundred breakfasts. Those cowboys can put it away. One bloke had three sittings, Hughie. Three full Scottishes. Four rashers of bacon, two fried eggs, black pudding, white pudding, two tattie scones, mushrooms, tomatoes, square sausage, beans, bread and butter and chips. Chips are compulsory, by the way. Hey, Hughie, do you know what a Scot calls cold chips? No? A salad!'

'Three full Scottishes? I wouldn't like the task of cleaning out his cage in the morning.' muttered Brock.

'Hey, shit-face! It might have escaped your attention, but ye've got six thirsty wummen parched ower here.' Once more the clarion call of a Spice Witch reverberated around the bar.

'Let me guess, six dark rums, my wonderfulness?'

'Never mind that shite, just get pouring.'

'Your wish is my command, madam,' smiled Hughie.

'Just get yer skinny arse in gear,' came the response. As long as they kept drinking and kept paying, they could verbally abuse him until the cows came home.

Wild Bill returned to the bar to join Brock, Hughie and Tip-Toe. 'Do you know you've got a crack in the glass in your fruit machine?' he said.

'They're going home tomorrow,' said Maggie, her sleuthing done for the night. 'They work in the cosmetic department at Fosters in Paisley. In the beauty salon.'

'Fuck me,' blurted Hughie. 'That lot work in a beauty salon? Christ almighty. Imagine one of that lot trying to give you beauty tips? The mind boggles. I'm more likely to look for beauty advice from Sitting Bull here. Tomorrow, eh?'

'Aye, one of the early ferries,' said Maggie. 'They start work at nine.'

'Interesting,' smiled Hughie to his wife. 'Great work, Mrs Columbo. Very interesting. I must remember to wish them a fond farewell when they leave. Oh, no, can't have them leaving without the appropriate send-off. Oh, no.'

'Me ride prairie all day. Me swallow much dust. Me still thirsty. Me want more firewater.' Sitting Bull put in his usual request. 'Remember the ice, please, Hughie,' he whispered.

Wild Bill checked his pocket watch attached to his waistcoat by a chain. It was just past the midnight hour. 'Time this hombre was heading for some shut-eye,' he said.

'Thank fuck,' Brock and Hughie indulged in some synchronized thinking.

'Big day ahead tomorrow. People to see, things to do.' He stretched his arms wide and arched his back. 'Might get in some shooting practice. I'm going in for the Gary Cooper Cup on Sunday. I've got my name down for the High Noon shoot-out.'

The cowboys took the midday Sunday showdown on the Newton Beach across from the Mitre, aka the Kentuckian, very seriously. Down the years Hughie had witnessed a few spectacular disagreements over some of the judges' calls. 'Maybe just as well they don't use real bullets,' he mused. 'Having said that, if they did use real bullets it would settle all the arguments, wouldn't it? Maybe I should put that forward as a motion at the meeting of the Country and Western Committee for next year's festival.' Then he frowned and thought maybe he better not. The donkey rides were close by and he could envisage all sorts of carnage that might be brought to the attention of the RSPCA.

'You tried to win it before?' asked Hughie.

'No, this is my first time,' said Wild Bill. 'First time I've been here, as a matter of fact. I've been meaning to come for years, but, until now, I kept getting gigs on the same weekend and a man's got to eat. Clear this weekend, though, and I aim to make the most of it.'

'You any good with those guns?' asked Brock. 'They look impressive enough.'

'Clean them every day,' said Wild Bill, pulling both from their holsters and looking at them proudly. 'Genuine replicas, these. Look real, don't they? They're just like the ones Wild Bill carried. I've even got the guns holstered with the ivory handles pointing out the way, just like Wild Bill.' He got a little misty-eyed at this stage. 'I hope to make him proud of me on Sunday. That Gary Cooper Cup's got my name on it. I'm sure of it. I reckon I've got a secret weapon.'

He moved closer to Brock, Hughie and Tip-Toe. He spoke gently and, although the din in the pub was actually dying down, they could barely hear him. 'I'm going to stop drinking tomorrow before eight. A lot of these guys will still be getting pissed out of their skulls way after midnight. By the time they turn up at High Noon, a lot of them won't be able to hold a boulder straight. They'll be shaking all over the place. I'll let them see how fast I am with the equalisers.' Suddenly Wild Bill Hickcok had become Wild Bill Hickok. He had a strange glint in his eye. The pub singer from Glasgow repeated, 'I'm going to make my hero proud of me.'

'In the name of holy fuck! Dry up here! Nae chance of a wee scatter, Ah suppose? Wid that be oot of the question?'
Hughie grinned and took a quick look at the clock on the wall. Ten minutes past midnight. 'Yes, my little personification of charm,' he responded. 'Six dark rums, by any chance?'

'Ye should know by now, ya wee pervert. Get the bevvy on the bar the noo. And keep yer eyes aff Pinky and Perky.'

'Thank you for your hospitality, gentlemen,' said Wild Bill. 'I hope you have enjoyed yourselves as much as have I, but my bunk is beckoning. I must say farewell before I outstay my welcome.'

'Not at all, good to spend some time in your company,' lied Hughie. 'Are you in tomorrow?'

'Oh, we shall have to wait and see. Couple of things I need to take care of, so no promises.'

'What a shame,' lied Brock. 'We'll keep our fingers crossed. Very educational. I learned more today than I did in school.'

'My pleasure, sir. Until the next time, may the spirits be with you.' He turned his back and paused. 'And I'm not talking about the ones on the wall behind the bar.'

Brock, Hughie and Tip-Toe saw his shoulders jiggling under his jet-black ankle-length coat as he jostled his way to the door.

'Fuck me, he had a sense of humour all along,' said Brock. 'I have to say his disguise was perfect.'

'Me have throat as dry as cactus leaves. Me feel baked tongue in mouth. Me victim of much prairie dust. Me yearn for firewater.'

'Same again, Sitting Bull?' said Hughie, realising only too well it was a daft question. He poured the drink and placed it in on the bar. The Indian chief motioned for Hughie to come closer. 'And a packet of dry roasted as well, please, Hughie,' he whispered.

Hughie responded in equally hushed tones, 'Just for future reference, a cactus does not have leaves. It has spines. Just thought you might want to update your material.'

'Me heap impressed,' said Sitting Bull.

Hughie looked once again at the clock on the wall. Bang on thirty minutes after midnight. He sighed and looked at his pal Brock. 'What a day I've had. Mental. Absolutely mental. Run off my feet. Same with Maggie. She'll sleep well tonight. Thank Christ.'

'Why don't you get someone else in to help out?' asked Brock. 'You know it's going to be crazy. Another pair of hands would surely help.'

'Aye, I know, Charlie, but it's been a bugger of a year, to tell the truth. Unfortunately, the recession hasn't missed Millport. Calamity Jane's in tomorrow, but do you remember Mondays when we used to have about twenty to thirty punters in doing the giant crossword in the Express? Now I'm lucky if we've got five. Honestly. The folk just don't have the money. Take this lot that come down for the Country and Western Festival. I know a lot of them save up for a year. A whole year. Seriously. Then they just go nuts for a few days and nights and blow the lot. Then they go home and start saving again. Thank goodness.'

'Is there a fuckin' ban on booze in this pub? Hey, you, geeky. Are ye still breathing? Or ur ye sleeping with yer eyes open? Ah've seen merr life in a lump of wid.'

Hughie walked once more to the dark rum optics. 'I take it you wish to avail yourselves of the delights of the liquor this proud establishment provides for your enjoyment, my fine young maiden?'

'Just pour the drink. You talk a lot of shite.'

'Put a pin in her,' thought Hughie, 'and she would whizz around the bar for at least an hour'. He laughed out loud. He put the drink on the bar and took the money. He counted it and, sure enough, it was there to the penny, as it had been all night. 'What, girls, no tip for your hard-working bartender?'

'Aye, here's wan. When ye jump in the Clyde make sure yer wearing heavy boots.' The Spice Witch named Sharon positively squawked. 'Did ye hear that, Senga?' Her rotund chum was getting close to waving farewell to anything remotely approaching consciousness.

'Aye. Clyde. Boots. Where's ma drink?'

'I've got to take my bunnet off to you, Hughie,' said Brock, in admiration as his pal returned. 'Despite the crap you've taken off the Shelley Winters Fan Club up there you've not thrown them out. Commendable.'

'Commendable?' said Hughie. 'Fuck commendable.' He pointed over his shoulder at the cash register. 'Old Sammy Davis Jnr there has been close to bursting into flames several times tonight. The harem from hell have been buying dark rums all day. Christ knows how many. I reckon they've put the thick end of about three hundred quid in the kitty. They don't know it, but they have helped subsidise me and Maggie's cruise around the Med in November. I'll hoist a large one to absent friends while the sun beats down on my grateful little body.

The cowboys, in various states of drunkeness and distress, were calling it a day as they trekked groggily towards the door. 'See you tomorrow, lads,' beamed Hughie. 'Remember to bring money.' The smile disappeared very quickly. 'Oops,' said Hughie, as he raced round the bar. 'One puke is enough for one day, mate.' A bewildered cowboy looked as though he was about to decorate the entire bar with the swilling contents of his gut as he aimlessly lurched around. Hughie grabbed him by the shoulders, pushed him in the back and propelled him towards the door. 'Dead soldier coming through, make way, please. Thanks, lads.' Hughie's timing was perfect. He just managed to shove the cowboy through the door when there was a distinct rumbling from the guy's insides, quickly followed by a gurgling bellow. Whoosh! The eruption scattered all over the pavement. 'The road sweepers certainly have their work cut out on Country and Western Festival,' thought the bar owner as he returned to his post.

Hughie checked the clock. Fifteen minutes to one o'clock. 'Last orders, PULLEEEZE, cowboys and cowgirls,' he shouted. He rattled the bell on the wall behind the bar. No psychic powers were required.

'Hey, Harry Potter's da. Six dark rums afore Ah collapse wi' thirst. Right noo, okay?'

Hughie smiled. 'Of course, my little cherub, six of my most excellent dark rums are on their way for your edification and approval.'

'Fuck aff wi' the speeches and jist dae yer joab.'

Hughie eyed the obese shrew and pondered for a moment. Was there ever a time when some granny or auntie juggled this vile creature on their knees and said, 'Oh, who's a pretty baby? Oh, who's a beautiful girl?' What on earth happened on the journey in between?

He placed the drinks on the bar and said, 'No tip necessary, ladies.'

'Get fucked,' was the curt reply.

'Me feel as I have wood scrapings in throat. Me feel barren of liquid. Me feel...'

'Oh, give it a rest, John. Do you want a large Bell's?'

'That would be very kind of you,' said Sitting Bull. 'And a packet of scampi fries, please, Hughie.'

'Right, lads, what's yours?' enquired Hughie. 'Charlie? Pint or do you want a short? Tip-Toe? Pint or a short?'

Brock was first in, 'I'll stick to lager, thanks.'

Tip-Toe Thompson looked at his watch. He was due at The Pier at seven to begin preparing the breakfasts. He had done around two hundred today and he knew there would be more tomorrow with another deluge of cowboys on the island. The wise thing would have been to have gone home, a two minutes' walk up Cardiff Street to the top floor flat he shared with his wife Liz and their cat Claude. He was just about out on his feet. Jiggered. Knackered. Exhausted. 'I'll have another lager, please, Hughie,' he said.

A couple of stragglers made it to the bar for last orders. Hughie shook his head and smiled. 'Two large whiskies, gentlemen?' he asked.

One blinked drowsily. 'Aye, how dae ye know?'

'Just a lucky guess,' replied Hughie. 'That and the fact you and your mate have been drinking in here for the past five hours. Have these on me. Cheers, lads.'

The Man in Black also made his way to the door. 'Cheers, mate,' offered the bar owner. Johnny Cash said nothing.

Hughie shrugged. 'Well, Charlie, this is where the fun begins. Watch this. Time PULLEEEZE, cowboys and cowgirls. Time to go home. If you want more you can come earlier. Thank you.'

'Hey, Joe 90, let's have six dark rums up here. Pronto. Zoom! Zoom! Get yer arse shifting.' The Spice Witches had spoken.

'Sorry, my little tub of lard,' smiled Hughie. 'No can do. Time for you and your obnoxious pals to depart the premises. Hit the road. Bite the dust. Drag your carcasses elsewhere.'

'Whit ur ye talkin' aboot? Six dark rums. Here. Right noo. Get shifting.' The Spice Witch named Kylie wasn't overly happy about the change in demeanor of the serf behind the bar.

'I'm afraid the only thing that will be shifting will be your rear ends. Right out that door. Vamoose! Adios! Skedaddle! Skoot! Allez! Allez! Areeba! Areeba! Whichever way you want it, but just vacate the building.'

The six members of the Shelley Winters Fan club were dumbfounded. Pissed, befuddled and insulted. 'He's no' serving us,' wailed Kylie.

'Why no'?' asked Sharon. 'Whit's the fuckin' problem?'

Senga observed, 'Cos he's a fuckpig. That's why. A fuckin' wee fuckpig.'

They went into a huddle, putting their heads together to come up with some sort of brilliant strategy that would see them getting more much-needed alcohol.

'Do you want me to wheel a cauldron up there?' asked Hughie, helpfully. 'You know? Hubble, bubble, toil and trouble? No? I didn't think Macbeth was your thing.'

'Whit's he talkin' about? Ah think he's had merr tae drink than us put thigither,' said one of the Spice Witches. Through the haze of booze, she believed she had concocted what she thought was a certain winner. 'Chantelle, show him yer tits.'

Chantelle wasn't entirely convinced that her showing Hughie her tits would persuade the barman to give them drink. 'Ma Justin widnae like it,' she said. 'He went fuckin' ga-ga when Ah showed them to the rugby team the other night. Didnae help, either, when they a' copped a squeeze. They're still fuckin' sore.'

'Go on,' urged a Spice Witch named Tiffany. 'Ye've got the best diddies oot o' the lot of us. Ye used to get them oot a' the time. Couldnae keep the puppies in. Remember?'

'Aye, but that was afore Justin. He disnae like me flashin' ma tits.'

'Time to go home,' said Hughie. 'Mind how you go. Don't go near anything sharp. We don't want you lot getting punctured and circumnavigating the globe for the next one hundred years. There's enough useless crap up there already.'

'How about if Chantelle AND Tiffany both show him their tits?' said Sharon. 'He's bound to give us drink then.

'Naw, Justin wid beat the shit oot o' me if he ever found oot,' said Chantelle.

Tiffany wasn't sold on the idea, either. 'Ma nipple piercings ur still murder,' she explained. 'Senga, why don't ye show him where the stem ends on your tattoo? That would dae it.'

Senga, coming back to the planet earth, sniffed rather haughtily which was quite amazing when all things were considered. 'That's for Lionel. Naebody else has ever seen it doon there. Apart from the tattooist. Took him half-an-hour to do the rose and the stem and then about two hours a day for two weeks to finish it aff doon there. Said he wanted to get it just right. Took pictures, tae. Very professional. Nice man. Cold hands.'

Slowly they appeared to admit collective defeat in their quest for six dark rums. They started to pick up the debris round about them, handbags, jackets, cardigans, shoes. 'Where's oor fuckin' hats?' said Senga. 'Some bastard's had it away with oor hats. They cost a quid each.' She turned and looked accusingly at Hughie. 'You fuckin' stole oor hats, didn't yae? Ah thought ye looked dodgy when we came in. We were nice to ye and ye stole oor hats. Dirty thievin' bastard.'

'Aye, that's right. Got them on e-bay straight away. Now I've got enough for an ocean-going liner. Now beat it. I'll see you lot to the door.'

'We'll no' be back,' threatened Chantelle.

'Christ, that's like being told I'll never die,' said Hughie.

'Ye huvnae treated us like ladies,' said Sharon. 'Ye should be ashamed of yersel.' The Spice Witches struggled towards the door. 'Whit ur ye lookin' at, Chief Fuckheid? Away and get a proper job, ya wanker,' Kylie felt she had to comment on something, anything. Sitting Bull was in direct line of her venom.

They gathered at the doorway. 'We ur definitely no' comin' back here and we'll tell a' oor friends,' they hissed. 'And we're very popular.'

'Aye,' said Hughie. 'I can tell by the way you walk.'

'Whit dis he mean by that?' Tiffany asked.

'Never mind that wee shite,' said Chantelle. 'He's just trying to be cheeky. Don't let him see he's getting tae ye. Remember, dignity at a' times,' she said, scratching her particularly bulbous right buttock, doing its best to break free from a straining blue denim mini-skirt.

Hughie saw them to the door. 'Safe journey home, girls. Don't any of you stumble and demolish a building, for fuck's sake. If you're looking for company, the bouncy castle is just across the road. The crazy golf is over there, too. You'll feel quite at home. Mind you don't block out the moon or people will think we're having an eclipse. You'll startle the cows.'

'Whit's he sayin' aboot moon?' asked Kylie. 'Ah didnae moon anywan. Did Ah?'

Hughie grinned and waved and prepared to return to the bar. 'Goodbye girls. Make sure you give my best to Beelzebub, eh?'

'Ah've never been so insulted.'

'You should get out more,' grinned Hughie. 'There they go, The Elephant Walk.' He started to sing, 'Nellie the elephant packed her trunk and said goodbye to the circus.'

'Your years at Charm School didn't go to waste, then, Hughie?' smiled Brock.

'I've been bottling that up all night, Charlie. You get the grief and then you take the gravy. Right, eh?'

'You never spake a truer word, my friend,' said Brock. 'Cheers. Fancy another? Or do you want me to fuck off, too?'

The Spice Witches staggered, wiggled and quivered in three rows of two back to their guest house beside the Garrison. Chantelle and Senga were at the front. Senga was doing her best to stagger in a straight line. Her eyes were closing, her head was nodding. She farted loudly and seemed to alarm even herself. She hiccupped and said, 'Ye know somethin', Chantelle? Ah think that bastard was wattering doon oor drink.'

And with that she veered off violently sideways towards the road, picking up speed as she tried to arrest the sudden, unexpected surge of acceleration. Not unlike an angry, charging rhino, she rammed the driver's side of a black Land Rover Discovery parked at the kerb. As she frantically tried to restore her balance, she threw out her hand and ripped a wing mirror off the side of the car. She spun backwards and was sent careering towards a lamp post. She crashed against it awkwardly, spun again and finally came thudding to a halt on the pavement, her head bouncing off the concrete before her face settled in a discarded carton of cold chips and curry sauce.

There was a caricature of a happy, smiling fish on the carton. There was a bubble coming out of its mouth. 'Mr Fishy says - Have A Nice Day.'

Chantelle carried on. 'I hope that fart wisnae a follow-through like the last wan, Senga.' Unfortunately, she had totally missed the impromptu display of stunning sideways sprinting and spectacular acrobatics by her friend.

Kylie and Sharon stumbled past their stricken bar buddy. 'Look at Senga, she's made an arse of hersel' again,' said Kylie. 'Whit that lassie does to attract attention.'

A couple of minutes later Shelley and Tiffany, clinging to each other, passed the fallen body. 'Oh, fuck Senga's done it again. At least, she's no lyin' in the dug shit this time.'

As they turned the corner, Tiffany took one last drunken look back. A golden labrador was sniffing Senga's crotch.

CHAPTER ELEVEN

SATURDAY MORNING, SEPTEMBER 1

'What are those Elvis Presley guys all about?' thought Wild Bill Hickok. 'Do they know how daft they look?'

Wild Bill fingered the ivory-handled revolvers in the holsters of his gun-belt, adorned with the enormous brass Bald Eagle buckle. He then pushed his black Stetson high on his head, swept his black ankle-length waxed coat to both sides, displaying his scarlet-coloured garishly embroidered waistcoat enveloping a green and black plaid shirt. He checked if his tan knee-high boots needed a polish. 'Perfect,' he decided before summoning over the bartender at the Confederate HQ. 'A pint of your best heavy, purdner,' he said. The bartender, a pump attendant at the island's only garage, was earning a few extra quid during the festival.

'Coming right up, mate,' he said.

'It's not 'mate'. It's Wild Bill. Wild Bill Hickok.'

'Aye, whatever, chief,' said the bartender/pump attendant and started pouring.

The main doors to the hotel bar were pinned back to maximise the effect of the radiant sunshine as it flowed down majestically upon the island, bouncing light into the darkest of corners, the Firth of Clyde positively shimmering and gleaming in its glow. 'Any chance o' getting Jailhouse Rock on the jukey, pal?' An Elvis lookalike had spoken. A serene moment of sheer tranquility was about to pass. 'Went to a party at the County jail...'

Wild Bill sipped at his beer and wondered what Elvis Presley had to do with the Country and Western Festival. It was for cowboys, real-life cowboys like himself. 'This is a lot more like it,' he mused as five guys walked towards the inviting open door of the hotel bar. They were dressed in long, brown coats - 'dustcoats', he thought they were called - and the quintet looked as though they had just arrived from a particularly long and grueling cattle drive; the dust still in their faces. He liked their look. Long hair, unshaven, a couple of rambling, shambolic moustaches, not unlike his own proud creation. A mishmash of clothing, a clutter of colour. A steady stroll towards the door, the five all spread out in a line. A mean look in their faces and a purposeful stride. A look that said, 'Don't fuck with us.' 'Hey, you guys, look the real deal,' thought Wild Bill, again involuntarily touching the ivory-handled revolvers.

In his mind, all five were about to draw their weapons on him. In his mind, he would remain calm. In his mind, he would show no fear. In his mind, he would blow the shit out of all of them the first moment one of them went for his gun. The two guys on either flank would be the first to go, a single bullet through the heart for each. The guy in the middle was just unlucky, he was getting both barrels. There would be bloody carnage at the Confederate HQ. And one man would walk away, blowing smoke from the barrels of his ivory-handled revolvers. Wild Bill Hickok.

'We're the Culpepper Cattle Company,' said one, breaking Wild Bill's reverie. 'We've come all the way from Troon.' The guy sounded a bit like Julian Clary. 'Oh, what are we going to have? Five half-pints of lager with a suspicion of lime in one, please, if it's not too much trouble, thank you very much. Oh, that ferry was so busy. Wasn't it, boys? I didn't know where to put my six-shooter.'

Another said, 'I was having trouble with my chaps, if you know what I mean.'

Another piped up, 'Did you see the cute bandoleer on the one in front of me? It took me all my time to keep my hands to myself.' They all giggled.

They never showed you that side of the Wild West in Rawhide, thought Wild Bill. Trail boss Gil Favour and lead cattle hand Rowdy Yeats were close, he knew, but he assumed they slept in different bunks. He never gave it a second thought that the cook was called Wishbone.

'What next?' thought Wild Bill. 'Sid James coming through the doors, shouting "Yippee" and telling us the Rumpo Kid was in town? Were they filming Carry On Cumbrae this weekend? Just my luck.'

'Ooh, I'm woozy already,' said one of the Culpepper Cattle Company, 'and I've only had the tiniest sip. I say, barperson, what do you put in your lime?'

'Lime,' was the reply.

Unbeknownst to the cowboys, the barman had the Alabama

Lie-Detector behind the bar. And his boss had told him to use it any time he saw fit. Any hint of trouble and the Alabama Lie-Detector was to come straight into action. The Alabama Lie-Detector was a large baseball bat.

There was the sudden growl and snarl of reverberating engines and Wild Bill looked out to see a dozen or so bikers pulling up on their hogs outside the hotel.

'Oh, great,' he thought, 'here come the fuckin' Village People.'

CHAPTER TWELVE

SATURDAY MORNING, SEPTEMBER 1

'Captain America can get right on your tits, can't he?' stated Boring Brian, sitting at the front window of the Nashville.

'Not your shrewdest observation, I have to admit,' landlord Hughie Edwards said.

'Och, you know what I mean. He thinks the whole fuckin' Country and Western Festival exists just for him. He's a fuckin' nuisance. What time is the parade today? Midday? He'll want to be right at the front, as usual. The wee lassie who's won the Queen of the Parade title - Willie Mack's daughter this year, isn't it? Wee Jennie? - she'll have to get him in a Boston Crab and throw him into the fuckin' Firth to have any chance of getting her picture in the Largs and Millport News. That halfwit always wants to be in pole position. Anybody got a gun? Let's shoot the bastard.'

Boring Brian went through the same ritual every year. And he wondered why people called him Boring Brian.

Captain America was the owner of Millport Transport, a portly, pint-sized bloke called Tommy Cunningham, and this day was built for him. Star-spangled banners, confederate flags, cowboys, cowgirls. Even a Red Indian. He could look out his white Stetson and his tan suede knee-length coat with all the fringes down the sleeves. Yahoo! Could there be anything better? There was one flaw in Captain America; he had never actually been to America. He had spent six months in Vancouver in Canada once, so that might allow him to creep under the radar. But the way he talked he had done the whole New York, Boston, Chicago, Washington, California, Texas and New Orleans bit. However, what really amazed the Cumbrae residents was the fact that Tommy, who had been born in the local Lady Margaret Hospital fifty years ago, had undergone some sort of voice box transplant during his six-month excursion to Vancouver.

Hughie noticed the change immediately. He opened the doors to the pub at 11am one day and in stepped the Cumbrae King of Transport. Before Hughie had a chance to welcome him home, he was greeted by a, 'Hot diggety, what a day. I say, hot diggety, what a day.' Hughie removed his spectacles and rubbed them with a dishtowel. It looked like Tommy Cunningham. But it didn't sound like Tommy Cunningham. 'How ya doin', ya old mother-fucker?' Hughie put the spectacles back on.

'Tommy? Tommy Cunningham?'

'Sure'n hell is, Hubert. In the flesh.'

'You okay? You haven't fallen on your head, have you?' asked the bar owner.

'No way, no how, no sir. I'll just scramble atop a stool here, good fellow, and try some of that goshdarn Jack Daniels.'

Hughie squinted. 'Goshdarn Jack Daniels?' He said. 'I thought you were a wee Bailey's man, Tommy?'

'Times, my friend, they are a'changin'.

'You haven't changed your name since we last saw you? An eagle hasn't dropped a rock on your head?' queried Hughie. The name Tommy Cunningham seemed positively mundane now.

'Nope, my moniker is as it always was and always will be, Hubert. Tommy Cunningham, a good ol' boy from these here parts. Hey, man, give me five, let's clash some skin. Jumpin' Jehosophat and gee willikers, where's my goshdarn Jack Daniels, ya motherfucker? My, my it's good to be home and see nothing's doggone changed. Yahoo! Hot diggety-doooooo.'

Hughie smiled at the memory. The bloke was relatively sane when he left the island, his first holiday in years, and came back a raving lunatic. Wish to fuck he would go back to Vancouver and annoy the hell out of them. Did a Dr Frankenstein get a hold of him during his travels in Canada? Did he force in a new brain? Wonder what he did with the old one? It had hardly been used.

Hughie skipped round the bar, made for the door and looked along Stuart Street onto Guildford Street and beyond. Sunshine covered the island and he thanked God. There had been a couple of times in recent years when the heavens had opened and, try as you might, it's not easy to go through a line-dancing routine on top of a moving lorry in gale-force winds that threaten to remove lampposts from their stanchions. 'At least, Mustang Mags will be a happy gal today,' said Boring Brian. 'She'll be able to get the line-dancers doing their thing down at the harbour without the risk of being swept off to Rothesay. I've got to say old Mustang puts her back into this weekend. How she gets all those daft old farts to go through those fuckin' crazy routines is beyond me.'

'Most things are beyond you, especially looking down and locating your feet.' Mustang Mags had sidled in unnoticed through the side-door.

'You want to get out there and do a bit of exercise yourself, Brian. Wouldn't do you any harm.'

'It would probably bring on a heart attack,' complained Boring Brian.

'Okay, it wouldn't do US any harm,' returned Mustang Mags.

'Ready for the big day, Hughie?' she asked.

'The parade is ready to go. Everyone's got their slot and they're all happy. Makes a change. The motorbike guys are coming up the rear. They've been warned not to ride through the procession. Remember that idiot last year? Straight through the middle and startled the lead horse on the stagecoach? Didn't know that old nag could move so fast. Found it galloping towards Fintry Bay at the speed of light. Took about a week for it to settle back down. Farmer Jack wasn't best pleased. Thought he might have to get Henrietta destroyed. Our main problem will probably be Captain America again, no doubt. We've tried to work out a little surprise for him. We'll have to wait and see. He might make the front page of the Largs and Millport News again.'

'That'll keep him happy,' said Boring Brian.

'No it won't,' corrected Mustang Mags.

'Have you guys prepared yourself with the Cowboy's Prayer, Hughie? Can you remember it from last year? You know you've got to clear the bar, get everybody out and recite it as the procession goes by. Don't forget now.'

'Aye, I know,' said Hughie. 'And, I know it's tradition. It's been going on since 1994. And the pox and plague will be visited upon my establishment if I don't keep up with tradition. Ready, Brian? Let's keep Mustang Mags happy and prove we should get a gold star in our jotter for doing our homework.

The two men stood bolt upright at the door, placed a hand on their heart and solemnly proclaimed,

'Lord, please help me, Lend me thine ear,
The prayer of a troubled cowman to hear,
No doubt my prayer to you may seem strange,

But I want you to bless my cattle range,
As you, Oh Lord, my fine herds behold,
They represent a pure sack of gold,
I think that at least five cents on the pound,
Would be a good price for beef the year round.'
Hughie and Boring Brian waited for applause.
'Once more with feeling,' said Mustang Mags.
'Fuck off,' dueted Hughie and Boring Brian, no rehearsal required.

CHAPTER THIRTEEN

SATURDAY AFTERNOON, SEPTEMBER 1

A seagull, swooping urgently and dramatically, let out a tortured scream and fired its messy cargo towards the ground below. Wild Bill Hickok, just stepping out of the front door at the Confederate HQ on Quayhead Street, appeared to be in direct line for an unexpected gift. He paused though for a vital moment to remove his Stetson and run his fingers through the long locks he favoured in homage to his great Western hero. Splosh! The white deposit splattered onto the pavement at his right foot. The pointed toe of his tan knee-high boot was merely brushed by the offending offering from above. 'That was lucky,' he said to himself, hoping the same fortune would favour him for the rest of the day.

He hitched up his gun-belt, with the pistols, as ever, reversed in their holsters. He had a couple of things he wanted to take care of during the early evening. He also had every intention of being in his bunk at a reasonable time in preparation for the High Noon shoot-out the following day. 'They might as well just give me the Gary Cooper Cup right now,' he thought confidently. It was a sunny day, brightness bathing the town, fondly stroking the mild ripples of the passive waters of the Firth of Clyde. The Eilean rocks, normally a dull grey, sparkled as silver. Wild Bill was pretty pleased with himself, a man on a mission.

Wild Bill checked the pocket watch on the chain attached to his waistcoat. 'Only two o'clock,' he mused. 'Plenty of time.' He strode off in the direction of Kames Bay. He attracted some strange looks from many of the other cowboy visitors.

One surprised onlooker said to his wife, 'Look at him. You can fry eggs on the pavement today and he's wearing a big ankle-length coat. Must be fuckin' bananas.'

Wild Bill overhead the observation and shrugged. 'If it was okay for Wild Bill Hickok, it's okay for me.' The heavy, waxed coat remained where it was. However, he had to admit he was sweltering under the garment, which was unbuttoned and flapping merrily at the Cuban heels of his boots.

He crossed over to Stuart Street and walked straight-backed towards the Nashville where he had enjoyed the company of somebody called Brock the previous afternoon and evening. And the barman, Hughie, was very friendly, too. There was another guy, as well. What was his name? Flat Feet? Something like that. Very pleasant, he thought, as he glided past the massive window that doubled as a mirror at the front of Hugh's Bar, one of those trick glass concoctions that allow insiders to see out, but outsiders can't see in. Hughie loved sticking his tongue out at people who stopped to check their looks, comb their hair and make all sorts of adjustments to their apparel while gazing unwittingly into the mirror.

Hughie saw Wild Bill striding towards the pub. He nudged Charlie Brock. 'Oh, fuck, he's not coming in, is he?' he hissed. 'God what have I done to deserve this? I'll give more to charity. Honest, Lord. Please don't let him come in.' Brock was wondering if there was anywhere he could hide behind the bar. Wild Bill continued his saunter. The main door didn't swing open. Hughie and Brock breathed a joint sigh of relief.

Wild Bill walked past the Nixe Cafe, now Katy's Cantena, and inwardly growled at other cowboys who had capitulated and bowed to the blistering unseasonal temperatures and had swapped their plaid shirts for colourful open vests. Christ almighty, some had shorts on. Could anyone imagine John Wayne in The Searchers wandering around in shorts? How about Ernest Borgnine in The Wild Bunch traipsing around in sneekers? Call yourself a cowboy? Wild Bill was not impressed. He knew how the real Wild Bill Hickok would have coped with such desecration of cowboy gear. He knew his hero would have blazed away with both barrels, slaughtering the lily-livered, fake fuckers on the spot. They wouldn't have stood a chance as hell beckoned.

'Nice day, son,' said old Mrs Johnston, the kindly diminutive spinster who ran the scone shop.

'Yup, mighty fine,' said Wild Bill. He wondered if his hero might have taken her out, too? May have hesitated a moment. Then Wild Bill noticed the tartan slippers. They would have offended his hero, no doubt about it. With her choice of casual footwear, old Mrs Johnston had signed her own death warrant. She would have to be blown all the way to Kingdom Come.

Wild Bill was lost in thought as he continued on his way. He passed the Garrison and turned left at College Street. The sweat was running off him, but he wasn't going to wave any white flag. Nossirreeejack. He passed the Cathedral of the Isles on his right as he continued up the hill. He stopped at a bench seat beside a farm gate. He was impressed by the panoramic views of the lush green golf course, the sparkling Little Cumbrae, the stunning Sleeping Warrior range of hills on Arran and Bute. Ailsa Craig, isolated and proud, where blue hone granite was once quarried to make curling stones, was just visible on the horizon. The glistening Firth of Clyde was simply breathtaking. The highest part on the island was Glaidstane Point, exactly 417 feet above sea level. Wild Bill drank in the awesome views for another fifteen minutes or so. Another check at the pocket watch. Just twenty-five minutes past three. Still plenty of time. He turned to walk down the way he had just travelled.

The smile melted and was replaced by a grim expression on his face, the eyes looking meaner. Something he had to take care of. 'A man's gotta do what a man's gotta do.' Then he stepped into a large mound of horse manure.

Maybe it wasn't going to be his lucky day, after all.

CHAPTER FOURTEEN

EARLY SATURDAY AFTERNOON, SEPTEMBER 1

'Christ, that was close!' Hughie Edwards and Charlie Brock looked relieved as Wild Bill Hickok meandered past the front window and, more importantly, the front door of the Nashvile. Right behind him, though, shuffled the unmistakeable figure of Vodka Joe. There was no chance he wasn't coming through the front door.

Vodka Joe reckoned Hugh's Bar was his home from home. 'It's time you began paying your Council Tax here, Vodka,' Hughie said often to his little world-weary chum who lived alone in a small apartment in Cardiff Street just around the corner from the pub. Vodka Joe, with tired eyes that had seen it all during his sixty-five years, had his own personal space at Hughie's front window where he told everyone he liked to sit and watch the world go by. He wasn't going to wear out his eyeballs on an island of twelve hundred inhabitants, many of whom never seemed to leave their front rooms. Vodka's space in the corner had been invaded by a party of six unruly bank workers from Auchinleck, each one more absurdly dressed than the other.

'Fuckin' cowboys,' said Vodka Joe as he found a place at the bar.

'Vodka, Joe?' asked Hughie, as he started pouring from the optic without waiting for a reply. In fact, it had been noted by Hughie's regulars that Vodka Joe rarely used the word 'vodka'. He would put his money on the bar, nod and, as if by magic, some brand of clear Polish alcohol would materialise in front of him.

He threw Hughie, and the entire island, into a flat spin when he changed his tipple to whisky. The Isle of Great Cumbrae had been thrust into turmoil. No-one was more perplexed than Hughie. 'What do I call you now, Vodka? Whisky Joe doesn't sound right. For fuck's sake go back on the vodka.'

The jubilant islanders thought about throwing a street party when Vodka Joe announced, after seven eventful days, 'Whisky's shite.' He pointed to the upturned vodka bottle behind Hughie. The bar owner was so overcome by emotion he poured him a large one on the house.

Vodka Joe, about five foot four inches tall, was obviously a creature of habit who was rarely seen without his black leather jacket. The garment remained stubbornly in place even on afternoons like this one when the island was blessed and engulfed in glorious sunshine. He had just overheard some bloke say, 'You can fry eggs on the pavement today.' Then there was a reference to someone being "fuckin" bananas.' Vodka Joe didn't know if he was referring to him or the big hairy eejit with the daft coat down to his ankles walking just in front of him. He didn't really care. Four minutes had just drifted beyond 2pm and it was time for his first vodka of the day. His normal kick-off time at Hugh's Bar was dead on eleven in the morning which, by happy coincidence, was precisely the time Hughie Edwards opened the doors of his establishment for business. But Vodka Joe liked to pace himself during the Country and Western Festival.

He would be in bed by about 4pm.

Vodka Joe was a man of few words, which betrayed a certain intelligence, a streetwise knowledge. No-one really had too much of an idea about his background. He had arrived on the island twenty years ago, seemed happy with the one-bedroom abode the North Ayrshire council had allocated him, and was even more delighted to discover there was a smashing wee boozer practically on his doorstep. 'This will do for me,' he said, his tired brown eyes twinkling. And he knew the only way he would be leaving the island was in a wooden box.

Until then, shares in an obscure make of Polish vodka would continue to rocket. He had become what was known as a local worthy. Undoubtedly, he was a character. And when locals tried to push him and get him to open up about his past, he would merely smile. End of conversation. Like Clint Eastwood's Man With No Name, Vodka Joe was a man with no history. He started life at forty-five and appeared to be more than content with his lot. No-one ever queried where his money came from, but he always had a few quid to spend on vodka. 'Maybe he's wan of them Great Train Robbers,' mused a local on one occasion. No one discounted the theory. Apart from his physical structure, Vodka Joe was never short.

Two locals, Tommy and Mary Gilmour, never tired of telling their favourite story about Vodka Joe. Their two dogs, Ziggy and Rosie were agitating for their usual daily walk along the beach.

The dogs, normally so placid, were barking wildly and loudly. The persistent canines got their wish when Tommy stumbled out of bed, followed by his wife. 'What time's it, Tommy?' she asked, still in mid-slumber. He looked at the electric bedside clock.

'Fuckin' far too early. What's the matter with these dogs?'

The Gilmours had had a few the previous night. 'What time did we leave Hughie's?' asked Mary.

'Pass,' answered Tommy.

'Did you take the dogs down to the harbour for their last round-up?'

'Pass,' was Tommy's reply again.

'Christ, Tommy, they've been locked in the kitchen for about thirteen hours. They'll be burstin'. Shift your arse. Come on, let's get them down the stairs before I'll need a rowin' boat to get to the cooker.'

It was in moments like this that the Gilmours wished they had a bottom floor flat where they could open the back door and kick the dogs out to do their business. They lived in a top floor flat in Crichton Street, so any question of their dogs being booted out of back windows might just seriously cost them some of their popularity among the neighbours. Ziggy and Rosie raced threw the front door of the tenement close and didn't wait to get to their respective favoured spots on the beach where Tommy and Mary always cleaned up their mess. This morning, though, Ziggy and Rosie changed a routine of six years. The large black public dust-bin outside the front door got a doing.

Tommy and Mary then ventured into their own routine. The couple detected a slight mist. The lazy old town was wiping the sleep from its eyes. They continued their walk along the white-walled promenade, both still half-asleep, both more than just a tad hungover. 'Once they've had their shites, I'm going back to bed for a couple of hours,' Mary informed her husband.

'You'll have company,' he nodded. They were both awakened by the sound of clattering bottles. They both peered ahead and there was the slight figure of Vodka Joe, sixty yards away, walking in their direction. He was carrying four plastic bags.

Clink! Clank! Clink! Clank! 'Morning, people,' said Vodka Joe, with his usual happy wee face and heading back along the prom-enade on his way to his flat in Cardiff Street.

'Fuck's sake, Vodka,' said Tommy, asking needlessly, 'What have you got in there?'

Vodka Joe didn't hesitate. 'Vodka. What do you think I would be carrying at this time in the morning?'

Tommy looked at his wristwatch. 'Christ, Vodka, it's not even 6.20. Where are you going?'

'Home. I'm having a wee party,' answered Vodka Joe with almost childlike innocence. 'My pal's over from Kilbirnie, so we're going to have a wee party. You and Mary are welcome. The more the merrier.'

Momentarily, the Gilmours were tempted. 'Christ, Vodka,' said Tommy, 'your mate's only over from Kilbirnie not Krakow. He's five minutes away. And you're celebrating at this time in the morning?'

'Aye, we don't see that much of each other.' It seemed a perfectly reasonable response to Vodka Joe.

'Hey, wait a minute, Vodka, where did you get a carry-out at this time in the morning?'

Vodka Joe smiled his knowing smile and continued on his way.

'You fancy popping in for a snifter, Mary?' asked Tommy.

'Don't be insane,' was the curt answer.

'Did you know cowboys were smelly bastards?' Vodka Joe asked Hughie. 'Hardly ever washed.'

'Personal hygiene wasn't a strong point, then?'

'Stank the place out.'

'That must have been bad news for Big Nose Kate.'

Vodka Joe was serious. 'No, Hughie, I mean it. Look at the way they are portrayed in films. Paul Newman and Robert Redford in Butch Cassidy and the Sundance Kid. Hardly a hair out of place between them. All their gear looked freshly laundered. Fuck me, they had smiles that would have blinded you. Where did they get teeth like that back then? They never even had Colgate. Yet there was those two doing their thing and attracting a bird like Katherine Ross.'

Vodka smiled and continued, 'I blame Paul Newman. He milked the west for all he could get. Remember he played Billy The Kid in The Left-Handed Gun? I saw a picture of Billy The Kid, the real Billy The Kid. He was an ugly, spotty, rat-faced, rotten-toothed, humphy-backed wee individual and I'll bet no-one dared to walk downwind of him.'

'Didn't realise you felt so strongly about it, Joe,' said Hughie, noting that there was a freshly-drained vodka glass in front of his wee mate and automatically turned to the optic of his customer's choice. Not for the first time Hughie wondered about Vodka Joe's past.

'And don't get me started on Yul Brynner, either,' said Vodka Joe, putting cash on the bar with his left hand and raising the alcohol to his lips with his right. A move he had perfected over the years.

'Did you see him in The Magnificent Seven?'

'You're not going to say he never had a hair out of place, are you?' said Hughie, trying his stand-up routine once again.

'He could have had a fuckin' Afro under his hat for all we knew, Hughie,' replied Vodka Joe. 'Do you know how many times he took his hat off in that movie? Go on, answer that one. Get it right and I'll buy you a brandy and port. Wrong and I'll have...' he pointed to the vodka.

'Jeezus Christ, Vodka, how am I supposed to know that? How many times did Yul Brynner take his hat off in The Magnificent Seven? Who was counting?'

'Me,' smirked Vodka Joe.

'Ten? Twenty? Thirty? One hundred and eleven?'

'Once,' said Vodka Joe, happy in the knowledge he was one hundred cent accurate. 'Just the once. He was digging a ditch outside the Mexican village they were protecting from Eli Wallach and his bandits. That's when he removed his hat, wiped his brow and immediately put his hat back on his head. I'll have that drink now, thanks.'

'Just the once? You're joking. I'll have to watch the movie again.'

Vodka Joe was on a roll. 'Now Eli Wallach, he looked real. He looked like a Mexican bandit. He looked manky, could've done with a right good hose down with a flame-thrower. Filthy, he was. Fuckin' honkin'. Didn't look like he had come into contact with soap for about a year. Mind you, if you are a murdering scum bastard, I don't expect you bother too much about toilet requisites. In any case, who was going to tell Eli Wallach he had a bad case of body odour?'

'Fair point,' mused Hughie. Sometimes Vodka Joe could be worth the admission money. The bar owner shouted over to

Charlie Brock, talking football, for a change, with complete strangers who always wanted the inside track on what was happening at Celtic, Rangers and anyone else close to their hearts. 'Charlie, fight your way over here, if you can.'

'Be right with you, Hughie. Stick up a pint, will you? Whatever Vodka Joe's drinking and one for yourself.'

Hughie pondered for a moment. 'What the fuck else would Vodka Joe be drinking?'

'Hey, Brock, what did you think of The Magnificent Seven?' asked Vodka Joe, refusing to let go of the theme. 'Yul Brynner dressed in black all the way through the film. Was that the same outfit? Did he only have black in his wardrobe? Did you even see him carrying a change of clothes? Or did he wear the same gear for the entire duration? Can you imagine how he ponged after all his exertions under the Mexican sun for weeks? Christ, it's a wonder his horse didn't faint from the fumes when he rode off at the end. The horse's arse probably smelled fuckin' positively fragrant compared to his oxters.'

Vodka Joe stopped for breath, then added, 'Yet did you spot a wrinkle out of place in his shirt?'

'I hadn't really viewed the film from that angle to be honest,' answered Brock. 'No, I suppose he might have been a bit whiffy at the end.'

'Whiffy? He would have smelled like a New York subway,' said Vodka Joe.

'What about Charles Bronson? He was believable, wasn't he? Had a face like it had had a fight with a combine harvester. I liked him. Steve McQueen? Far too handsome. He didn't look like a cowboy.'

Brock saw an opening. 'Actually, that's how he first came to the attention of the Hollywood people. He played a town marshal in a TV series called Wanted Dead Or Alive. Big hit back in the fifties.'

'Aye, I remember it. Thought he was a tad suspect. Got that wrong. Now Richard Boone, I liked him. He was in a TV series called Paladin.'

'Want to bet?' asked Hughie, still smarting after losing the earlier wager. 'I'll bet you a vodka to a brandy and port that it wasn't called Paladin.'

Vodka Joe was on the ropes. 'Aye, it was. I'm sure of it.'

'The clock's ticking,' said Hughie, smelling blood. Or, at least, a brandy and port. 'Tick, tick, tick, tick..'

'Fuck off, I'm trying to think. Richard Boone. Remember him well. Shaved with a chisel. Had a face that looked as though it had been hit by a freight train. A nose that resembled an exploding giant red pepper.'

'Tick, tick, tick, tick...'

'Ah, fuck it. I don't know.'

'Have Gun Will Travel,' said Hughie triumphantly, already moving to the gantry to collect his prize.

'You sure?' asked Vodka Joe. 'It wasn't Paladin?'

'I'm afraid he's right,' chimed Brock. 'His name was Paladin and the series was called Have Gun Will Travel.'

'Why should I take your word for it?' Vodka Joe looked at the sportswriter shiftily. 'You and him are bum chums. You could be covering up for him.' 'Right,' said Hughie, placing his untouched brandy and port on the bar. 'Before I take a sip of this I'll give you a chance for double or quits. Okay? Right. What was Slim Pickens' name in Blazing Saddles?'

Vodka Joe smiled his little smile. 'Taggart,' he answered unhesitatingly.

Hughie had the good grace to look dumbfounded, thunderstruck, the dream of a large brandy and port being demolished before his incredulous stare. 'Fuck me, how did you know that Joe?'

'It's my favourite movie,' grinned the winner, mimicking 'There's been a murrrrderrrr. I'll have a large one of them, thank you very much.' He pointed to the vodka bottle on the gantry.

The bar was beginning to throb with thirsty cowboys. Maggie had just arrived to begin her shift. Hughie thought she could take care of business for a while. He was having too much fun. 'Hello, my dear, thank you for joining the working classes. There's a pile of guys down at the window been gasping for a drink for the last five minutes. Can you take care of it, please?'

Maggie muttered something under her breath that sounded like 'Ruck moo'.

'Right, my turn now,' said Brock.

'You only know about football,' said Vodka Joe. 'What do you know about Westerns?'

'I knew Have Gun Will Travel was the name of the TV series, didn't I? And you didn't,' said Brock.

'Never liked you,' said Vodka Joe. Hughie glinted at his diminutive mate. 'Is the vodka taking hold already?' he mused. 'He's got at least another hour-and-a-half to go.' Hughie knew this because he had been serving Vodka Joe with vodka - apart from that mad week when he took up whisky - for thirteen years and had a better idea of what his wee chum could take before falling over than Vodka Joe himself. Hughie had misread the signs only a few times over the years and found himself giving Vodka Joe a Fireman's Lift home.

And then Vodka Joe smiled. 'Go on then, Brock, give it your best shot.' All was well with the world again.

'I take it we've got the same bet as you and Hughie? A drink for a drink? Okay? Here goes. Charles Bronson starred in a movie from 1954 called Apache. What was his name in the film?'

'Shit!' said Vodka Joe, now giving the sportswriter more respect than he had done only seconds beforehand. 'Charles Bronson in Apache? I can see him sitting on a horse with a head band, braided long hair, beads round the neck and the war paint. Bronson, not the horse. What was his name? Good question, I'll give you that. Right, let's see. There were several different types of Apache. The son of Cochise was called Nachez and he was a leader of the Chiricahau Apache. But, then, you had the Kiowa Apache and I'm not sure who their chief was. Let me think.'

'Very impressive,' said Brock, 'but I'll have to hurry you along. And, remember, I can only take the first answer.'

'Will I start the clock?' asked Hughie.

'Fuck you,' said Vodka Joe. 'I can see Bronson on the horse. I thought he made a good Indian. Had good muscles. Mind you, a lot of them were on his face. Ach, I give up.'

'Hondo,' said Brock. 'I'll have that pint now and, coming from you, it will taste like an angel's tears.'

Vodka Joe squinted at Brock. 'Wait a fuckin' minute, Charles Bronson wasn't even in Hondo. Don't bother pouring that pint, Hughie.'

Brock smiled. 'That might have been my next question. Hondo was made in the same year and it starred John Wayne and, you're perfectly correct, Charles Bronson wasn't in it. But he was in

Apache and his name in that movie was Hondo. I can taste that lager coasting past my Adam's Apple already.'

Vodka Joe remained silent. Hughie piped up, 'I think he's right. John Wayne was in Hondo with Ward Bond. Charles Bronson was in Apache with Burt Lancaster.'

'Does your wife know you're a poof?' queried Vodka Joe.

'Okay, I'll give you a chance to win a vodka,' said Hughie, ignoring the question.

'They made a movie, Apache Rifles, in the mid-sixties. Who was the lead?'

'No problem with this one,' smirked Vodka Joe. 'That was the Twenty-Four-Hour Irishman. Audie Murphy.'

Vodka Joe slurped the remains of his glass and put it in front of Hughie. 'One of those, please, barman, quick as you like.' He wondered if sarcasm had gone out of style. 'And I suppose I better get this bastard a beer.' He nudged his elbow in the direction of Brock, who was standing about six inches away.

Brock acknowledged his gift. 'Right, Joe, for a bonus point...'

'I don't want a bonus point. I want one of those.' He pointed to the vodka bottle on the gantry.

'Okay. What was Charles Bronson's name?'

'Do you only know questions about Charles Bronson?'

'I'm sorry I've started, so I'll finish. What was Charles Bronson's name in the movie Once Upon A Time In The West? Start the clock ticking, please.'

'Tick, tick, tick, tick,' Hughie was enjoying this. Maggie was going off her head.

'You sure you two aren't turd burglars?' Vodka Joe scratched his chin.

'I'm sorry you can't answer a question with a question. I'll have to hurry you along.'

'Tick, tick, tick, tick...'

'Ach, put a tock in it,' snapped Vodka Joe. 'Right. Let's think. I don't believe he had a name. It's a trick question, isn't it?'

'Is that your final question?'

'Tick, tick, tick, tick,' from behind the bar.

'I'm going to have to ask you for an answer, please.' Brock real-ised he was turning into Dale Winton.

'Ach, aye. He didn't have a name.'

'Wrong! In the list of credits for the movie entitled Once Upon A Time In The West, starring Henry Fonda, Claudia Cardinale and Jason Robards, Charles Bronson's character's name was, in fact, "The Man Harmonica". That one would have beaten most people. A very good answer, though.'

'Right, my turn,' said Hughie. 'High Noon was an all-time classic, I think we'll all agree? Gary Cooper saved a town from the bad guys. What was the name of the town and, as a bonus point, can you tell what was controversial about the film?'

'What the fuck's a bonus point? I don't want a bonus point. I want one of those,' said Vodka Joe. He pointed to the bottle of vodka on the gantry.

'The wee man's right, Hughie. What's a bonus point?' asked Brock.

'I'll make them doubles, okay?'

Vodka Joe thought hard. 'Abeline? No. Nashville? No. Boot Hill? No. Laramie? No...'

'Give in, Vodka. I've already had to shave twice since the start of the question,' said Brock.

'Ach, okay. I don't know.'

'The answer to the first question was Hadleyville...'

'No such place. That Hollywood again,' said Vodka Joe.

'And the big controversy among the public was that Gary Cooper was fifty when he made the movie, almost thirty years older than his co-star Grace Kelly. That was a big no-no back then, some decrepit old bastard getting his leg over a bird just out of High School. Good question, eh, lads?'

Bungalow Bob elbowed his way to the bar beside Brock and Vodka Joe. Bungalow Bob was the island's window cleaner. He had a fear of heights, so only took care of the downstairs windows. 'Looks like you're having fun over here. Can I join in?'

'Have you got money?' asked Vodka Joe, cutting to the chase.

'What are you having? Pint, Charlie? Vodka, Vodka Joe?'

His new drinking partners nodded in unison. 'Maggie, when you've got a minute, dear. Vodka, lager and a wee gin and tonic, please.'

Bungalow Bob was sweating. 'Warm day, eh?' said Brock.

'The sweat? Naw it's fuck all to do with the weather. Someone's just asked to me to do their windows on the second floor. I had to tell them I don't even like being this tall.' Bungalow Bob was roughly five foot eight inches. 'Thanks, Maggie,' he said passing over the money as the drinks arrived. 'One for yourself.'

'I'll have a pint of Creme de Menthe, thanks,' said Maggie, who didn't do busy.

'Okay, what's all the fun and laughter about in this corner? You pissed? Been here all day? Your secret's safe with me, I'm a window cleaner.'

'How good are you on westerns? On the TV and at the cinema?' asked Brock.

'I'd prefer Great Window Cleaners of the Nineteenth Century, but I'll give it a stab,' said Bungalow Bob, wondering what he had got himself into. Maybe he should go out and attempt to wash those second floor windows, after all.

'I'll go next,' volunteered Vodka Joe. 'Is there a drink on this? You both get it wrong, you both buy me a drink?'

'Aye,' said Brock, 'just as well as you buy me and Bungalow one each if we get it right. Deal or no deal?'

'That's not a western,' laughed Vodka Joe. 'Just my wee joke. Can't see Noel Edmunds taking on Lee Van Cleef in a gunfight, can you? Right, let's go. In the movie El Dorado, James Caan starred alongside John Wayne and Robert Mitchum. What was James Caan's character's name? And I can only take your first answer.' Vodka Joe was confident.

Hughie joined the company again. 'I think I've got a couple of minutes to myself. What a day I've had. What's the question?'

Vodka Joe repeated it.

'You've got me stumped there, Vodka Joe,' conceded Brock. 'I've seen the movie, too. John Wayne played John Wayne, didn't he? Do you know John Wayne probably accepted that Donald Duck had a superior acting technique? The only thing he knew about horses were all four legs touched the ground. No, it's not there. I give in.'

There was a triumphal look in Vodka Joe's eyes. 'James Caan's character's name was Alain "Mississippi" Bouroillon Traherne...'

'Wait! I was going to say that,' protested Bungalow Bob. 'I haven't given in yet.'

'Haven't you got any fuckin' windows to fall through?' snapped Vodka Joe. 'Get the vodka on the bar.'

'Well, it was worth a try, Bungalow,' said Brock. 'Right, Vodka Joe, two can play at that game. Kirk Douglas starred alongside Burt Lancaster in Gunfight At The OK Corral...'

Brock could see the immediate twinkle in Vodka Joe's eyes. He continued, 'What was...Kirk Douglas' real name? You didn't really think I was going to ask you his name in the film, did you? Doc Holliday? After your fuckin' James Caan question?'

'Bastard!' said Vodka Joe, realising a vodka had been prised from his very grasp. 'Bastard! Fuck you! Haven't the foggiest.'

'I can throw this one open to the floor,' said Brock,

'Last chance, Vodka Joe,' offered Brock.

'Fuck you!' was the response.

'It's Issur Danielovich Demsky. He was the son of an illiterate immigrant Russian-Jewish ragman in Amsterdam, New York, twenty-eight miles northwest of Albany. His father, Hershal Danielovich, was born in Moscow around 1884 and fled Russia in 1908 to escape being drafted into the Russian army to fight in the Russo-Japanese War. His mother was Bryna Sanglel, from a family of Ukrainian farmers, and she remained behind to work in a bakery for two years before joining her husband in America. Kirk's original choice of new name was Norman Dens because he wanted a surname that started with the letter "D". A friend suggested Douglas and he liked it right away. Later on another pal suggested Kirk. It was only later he realised Kirk Douglas sounded very Scottish.'

'You sure?' asked Vodka Bob.

'You making that up?' queried Bungalow Bob.

Brock wasn't disappointed when he didn't get a round of applause. 'I believe you gentlemen owe me a small drink after that, don't you think?'

'Why did he change his name?' asked Vodka Joe

'That one's got me stumped. Why did a bloke, who wanted to see his name in lights, called Issur Danielovich Demsky change his name to Kirk Douglas? That's a toughie.'

'Aye, it's a puzzler, right enough,' said Bungalow Bob, stroking his chin.

At that instant Brock wondered if Bungalow Bob got his nickname because possibly he didn't have too much up top.

'Fuck's sake,' said Vodka Joe. 'Was Champion the Wonder

Horse the only one in Hollywood who didn't change his name?'

'Or Trigger?' offered Bungalow Bob.

'Or Silver?' chucked in Brock.

'I wonder if Rin Tin Tin was born Rin Tin Tin?' pondered Vodka Joe.

Another round of drinks gave the great minds time for a welcome rest.

'Okay, to start again, lads?' said Brock. 'Bungalow Bob, I still think you owe me a pint?'

'And me a vodka,' said Vodka Joe, not sure at all of his facts.

'Whoa! Hold your horses,' said the island's window cleaner. 'Just a cotton-pickin' minute.' He wondered briefly why he had used that expression. 'Just give us a second here. Remember, I've come in cold. Let me pick up speed. Okay, let's try this one. Who played Matt Dillon in Gunsmoke?'

'James Arness,' answered Vodka Joe and Brock in a dead heat.

'...on the radio?' concluded Bungalow Bob. 'Everyone knows who played him on the television.'

'Get lost,' said Vodka Joe, another vodka disappearing back into the bottle on the gantry. 'Didn't even know they did Gunsmoke on the radio.'

'I'm not even going to try with that one,' said Brock. 'No idea whatsoever. Absolutely none.'

Bungalow Bob flashed a smile Vodka Joe would have been proud of. 'It was William Conrad.'

'William Conrad?' spluttered Vodka Joe. 'That fat bastard who played the private eye on the telly? Cannon? He could never get on a horse. He would break the poor creature's back.'

The Man in Black at the corner of the bar almost smiled.

CHAPTER FIFTEEN

EARLY SATURDAY EVENING, SEPTEMBER 1

'Me heap no pleased. Paleface pony soldiers are scum who speak with forked tongue. Me believe all white men are breath from Satan's rectum.'

'Aw, Christ, Sitting Bull's kicked off early tonight,' observed Hughie Edwards, owner of the Nashville. He checked the time. Bang on twenty minutes past six. Tip-Toe Thompson had finished his shift as the chef next door at The Pier twenty minutes earlier. 'Who's been winding him up again? Tip-Toe? You got anything to do with this?'

'White man deserve to die while lying in own pish...'

Tip-Toe grinned. 'Ach, Hughie, it's been a long day. I've been serving full Scottish breakfasts next door for the last ten hours. I got bored. I fancied a wee laugh. Sorry.'

'You mentioned that Sitting Bull did fuck all at the Battle of the Little Bighorn again, didn't you? You've always got to mention that. You know it sets him off. Now there's no stopping him.'

'Well, it's almost the truth, Hughie,' said Tip-Toe. 'Sitting Bull might have been there in the movies, cutting off Custer's head and everything, but he wasn't actually riding on a white charger into the thick of the action, using his hatchet, preferring not to use a firearm and wiping out the Seventh Cavalry. Nonsense. He preferred to watch from the safety of a faraway ridge, ready to scarper if everything went tits up.'

'But do you have to mention it when he's been drinking firewater all day? He's not even got a lining in his stomach. He's only had a couple of packets of mini cheddars.'

'Paleface deserve to die the death of a thousand cuts and entrails fed to rabid prairie dogs...'

'Oh, that's a new one,' said Hughie almost admiringly. 'He's been working on new material. Okay, give it to me again, Tip-Toe. What is it exactly that you say to him that causes him to go on the warpath?

'The history books I read don't exactly square up with Hollywood.

But, as your journalist pal Brock would say, "Never let facts get in the way of a good story." Sitting Bull? A Great warrior? My dick. I've told you this before. There was a battle just before the Little Bighorn and he was stuck in his bed, letting all his warriors do his dirty work. The night before the confrontation, Sitting Bull did a war dance, or sun dance as they preferred to call it, in front of his braves, preparing them for battle the following day. Well, the war dance entailed a lot of cutting of his own flesh with extremely sharp knives. The chief would show how brave he was by slashing at his arms and legs. If you could do that to yourself, imagine what you could do to your enemy. Sitting Bull, the daft, old cunt, got a bit carried away. By the end of it all, he was practically carried to his teepee by a couple of his warriors. The following day, he had lost so much blood overnight that he could barely get out of his bed.'

'Black Hills is my land and I love it. And whoever interferes will hear my gun...'

'I think he's preparing for war now,' warned Hughie. 'Just as well Vodka Joe's not here because he's in his space. Then, there really would be trouble. Gave him a Fireman's Lift home at 4.15pm. That extra fifteen minutes did in the wee man.'

'Anyway, Sitting Bull, this great warrior, remained in his scratcher while he sent his men went off to join up with Crazy Horse...'

'Aw, Tip-Toe, you didn't mention Crazy Horse, did you?' said Hughie. 'You know that drives him mental. He doesn't like Crazy Horse.'

'Crazy Horse and Low Dog combined their forces as Custer, who thought he was invincible, led his soldiers to their death.'

'Any chance of a couple of Guinnesses over here, chief?' The shout came from a cowboy at the bar.

Hughie presumed the bloke didn't actually want served by Sitting Bull. 'Give us a minute, Tip-Toe, I'll get this guy.'

Maggie, wife and barmaid, and Calamity Jane were working behind the bar. Calamity Jane was actually a piper in the Cumbrae Pipe Band and was Kathryn Casey in real life. 'She smashes more glasses than she cleans,' wailed Hughie, who, stuck for staff, checked his insurance policies for the pub before letting her back behind the bar. All day there had been a steady tinkle of pint tumblers going to their final resting place.

'Me believe all paleface are waste matter from my bowels...'

'Oh, another new one,' said Hughie, almost impressed.

'...the dirt on the soil at my feet.'

Hughie returned to sit down alongside The Pier's chef. 'Tell me, Tip-Toe, how come you know so much about all this?'

'I was brought up with the Cisco Kid. Did you know it was the first all-colour western series on American TV? It ran from 1951 to 1955. Duncan Renaldo was the Cisco Kid. Brilliant, fancy gear and a huge sombrero. Two big silver guns. White horse. A lot better than Tales From The Riverbank.'

'Oh, that explains it, then,' said Hughie, trying not to look mystified.

'Right, where was I? Custer's Crow scouts spotted an encampment at Rosebud Creek on 24 June...'

'Custer had Indians working for him? How did that happen? Cash? Firewater?'

'No, not at all. The Crow hated the Lakota, Sitting Bull's tribe, who had taken some of their land in the north. The Cheyenne moved in, too. So the Crow were happy to work for the white man.'

'Me scalp-lifter and have many brave companions in arms...'

'About two or three weeks before the massacre, something like 3,000 Lakota and Cheyenne warriors were camped in readiness. Custer hadn't been informed of an attack on a column of soldiers led by General George Cook around that time. Someone hadn't done their homework, that's for sure. The General and his soldiers stopped at the banks of the Rosebud to brew coffee and possibly have a game of whist. The Indians were camped just over the ridge. Cook's troops were attacked by around five hundred Sioux and Cheyenne warriors, around twice the size of the American soldiers' column. Cook survived, thanks to the help of his Indian allies, the Crow and the Shoshone.'

'And you learned all this from watching the Cisco Kid on the telly?' asked Hughie, slightly incredulously.

'White man deserve to die with balls in mouth...'

'Do you know, the Indians never named the battleground the Little Bighorn?'

Hughie felt as though he was back in school.

'No, they named it Greasy Grass because it was set up beside a winding stream. The soil was never dry. Anyway, that pillock, Custer, marched ever onwards to his death and met up with another American column led, if memory serves correctly, by Brigadier General Alfred Terry at Yellowstone River. Custer then took the Seventh Cavalry towards Rosebud. It was then his Crow scouts warned Custer that there were enough Indians to fight for many days. Do you know what that arsehole said? "I guess we'll get through them in one day." Arrogant buffoon.'

Hughie had never heard Custer being called an arrogant buffoon before.

'All paleface are bags of shit...'

'Anyway, Custer, and, remember, his men and the horses were knackered after riding under a merciless sun for three days; twelve miles the first day, thirty-three the second, twenty-eight the third. When he was told where the Indians had set up camp he wanted to attack right away. Total tosspot.'

Hughie had never heard Custer being called a total tosspot before.

'And where was Sitting Bull, the real Sitting Bull, not the one making an arse of himself over in Vodka Joe's spot?' asked Hughie.

'Oh, he was lording it up with the other chiefs. Their encampment had by now stretched to three miles along the river and another 3,000 Indians, angered by what was going on with the white man's invasion of the Black Hills, had joined up with them. The tribes of Oglala, really fierce fighters, Hunkpapa, Miniconjou, Sans Arc, Blackfoot Sioux and Northern Cheyenne were all there. While Custer's men were out on their feet and the horses were out on their hooves, the Indians had been dining on freshly-killed antelope. They were ready for battle.'

'White man stench of cowshit...'

'Custer decided to try to take them by surprise. He didn't bother to send his Crow scouts out again to get an update. He refused to send for reinforcements. When he saw forty warriors on top of the ridge, and without knowing anything of the terrain beyond, he ordered his troops to attack. He must have shat himself when he saw 6,000 Indians waiting for him.'

The image of Custer shitting himself swiftly formed in Hughie's mind. It wasn't a pleasant one. Robert Shaw soiling his breeks?

Not nice. He had cut such a heroic figure in The Buccaneers. Was very good in Jaws, as well.

'Low Dog told his men, "This is a good day to die. Follow me."'

'So, he said that? Not Sitting Bull?'

'Sitting Bull did what he did best. He sat on his duff. Why do you think he was called Sitting Bull? He let all the others do all the fighting and he took all the glory. Fuckin' old charlatan.'

Hughie had never heard Sitting Bull called a fuckin' old charlatan before. He also wished he had watched more of the Cisco Kid on the telly.

'White man only good for kissing my arse...'

'Very good, Tip-Toe. I enjoyed that. Fancy a pint?'

'Okay, Hughie, and I'll throw in my favourite Indian joke, too, if you want.'

'I'll get the beers. Give me a minute.' Hughie dodged his way to the bar, wondering for a moment if there were a lot of drunken cowboys around when they named Dodge City. 'Everything okay, girls? Maggie? Calamity?' Both of the bar staff had lost more weight in a day than they would in a month of aerobics classes.

'Don't call me Calamity,' said Kathryn Casey, precisely two seconds before smashing a pint glass. 'Oops.'

'I hate the sound of breaking glass, oh, oh, breaking glass,' sang the bar owner, before joining Tip-Toe at a table which was awash with beer slops. He thought briefly about cleaning it up. 'I'll leave it for Maggie,' the decision was instantaneous. 'Let her think she's important.'

Hughie clinked glasses with Tip-Toe and said, 'Right, let's have your favourite Indian joke.'

'Well, there's an Indian chief called Red Wolf and his wee boy wants to know how his parents came to give him his name. His dad says, "When Rain-In-The-Face was born, there was a cloudburst moments later. The parents took it as a sign from the gods and called him Rain-In-The-Face. Okay, son?'

'I don't understand, father,' said the boy.

'When Crazy Horse was born, his parents looked out of their teepee and saw a horse without a rider running around wild and going up on its hind legs. They took it as a sign from the gods and they named their son Crazy Horse. Okay, son?'

'I don't understand, father,' said the boy.

'When Running Deer was born her parents saw a beautiful deer running in the woods. They took it as a sign from the gods and they called their daughter Running Deer. Okay, son?'

'I still don't understand, father,' said the boy.

'When you were born, my son, your mother and I looked out of our teepee and saw two animals. We took it as a sign from the gods. Does that answer your question, Two Dogs Fucking?'

'Aye, very good, that's another pint on me. Two Dogs Fucking? I'll try to remember that.'

'I hate all pony soldier yellow-bellied scum bastards who must die at my feet.' Sitting Bull was preparing for war. Drunkenly, he pushed his way through some cowboys to the front of the bar. He tried to focus, peering left and right. His headdress slipped to his chin as he fumbled for his rubber tomahawk. He tried to lean on the bar, missed by at least a foot and slithered to the floor, banging his head on a bar stool on the way down. His last barely audible words were, 'Me resolute to end and fight any pony soldier...' And then he fell asleep in a crumpled mess.

Tip-Toe asked for a piece of paper and a black marker pen. He scribbled on it and placed the A4 piece of paper on the stricken Sitting Bull. It read,

CUSTER WAS HERE!

CHAPTER SIXTEEN

SATURDAY EVENING, SEPTEMBER 1

'Aye, the nightsssssss are fairrrrrrr drawinnnnn' innnnn, Cap'nnn Mainwarrrring,' observed Hughie Edwards, in his best John Laurie impersonation.

'Christ, I thought I was in an episode of Dad's Army then,' said Charlie Brock. 'Don't wish your life away, my boy. Plenty of time for you to sit with your feet up, Hughie, when the dark nights arrive. Until then, you've got a few pints to pull. This lot look like they're in for the duration.' He pointed to the mingling, heavily-drinking cowboys who had annexed the bar.

'That's the way Sammy Davis Junior and myself prefer it,' smiled the bar owner of the Nashville. 'There will be plenty of cold, lonely nights coming up to give me time to count my money. It's been a good day so far. Captain America got booted off the stagecoach. Nice one, Wee Jennie. Who saw that one coming? Certainly not Captain America. Who knew Wee Jennie was such a devotee of Bruce Lee? I've given Vodka Joe a Fireman's Lift home after he got blotto and Sitting Bull has also declared war on all palefaces. And we've managed to body swerve Wild Bill Hickok. Wonder where he was off to this afternoon with his mobile library? So, all things considered, we've not had a bad day. Better than sitting here doing the crossword on my own.'

Brock ordered another drink for himself and his mate. 'Might as well get one in while there's a window of opportunity,' he thought. 'Hey, whatever happened to that old cop who lived on the island? What was his name? Old Bill? I haven't seen him for a while.'

'I'm afraid we lost him,' answered Hughie.

'What do you mean "lost him"? You make it sound as though he was a British fighter pilot who hasn't returned from a mission behind enemy lines.'

'No, he had some problems. He was losing it a bit.'

'Aye, I could detect that. He was slowing down, but I didn't think he was that bad. I liked him. Smashing old guy. Used to give me sweets.'

'Aye, the ones he nicked from next door at the newsagents. He didn't think anyone knew. He would help himself to a handful every time he went in to buy a newspaper. Same when he was over at McIntosh's when they left all the bowls lying around with the little sachets of sauce, mustard and vinegar and the like. Old Bill would go in, order a half-pint of cider and then swoop round the tables and stuff his pockets with bundles of sachets. I think it was around then that we all realised not all was well with Old Bill. Pity. As you say, a nice man. Missed by everyone over here. Mind you, Bert at McIntosh's doesn't have to replenish his sauces stock every five minutes these days.'

Lennie, the island's only painter and decorator who also answered to Leonardo, joined Brock at the bar. 'Hughie, pint, please. Brock, you for one? Whatever Brock's having and one for yourself, Hughie,' he said. 'Whit a fuckin' day. Ah've been working my balls off...'

'You mean you've had them stitched back on since Sandra last cut them off?' smiled Hughie.

'Hilarious. Naw, Ah've been trying to get a flat ready for some punters coming over next week. Ah've been putting it aff for ages. They've already settled their bill. Banked and spent. Ah told them it was ready months ago. Noo they're coming ower in a couple of days' time and Ah huvnae done a thing. They'll smell a rat...'

'They'll smell five coats of Crown Silk,' smiled Brock.

'Aye, Ah know that. Ah'm goin' to hae tae leave the windaes open fur the next couple of days. Thank Christ it's sunny. Pray to God it disnae rain. Five coats of Crown Silk? Ur ye fuckin' kiddin'? Two coats of the economy stuff and it'll be well wattered doon, tae. But Ah should be suing them for compensation when Ah think aboot it.'

'How come?' asked Hughie, pushing a pint across the bar.

'Ah was painting up above the door when a fuckin' mounted fish came alive and started signing, "Don't worry, be happy..." Ah fell aff ma ladder. They might warn you aboot these fuckin' things. Who invented these daft bastards? Almost brought on a heart attack. You know these things? Rubber fuckin' fish that burst into song when you activate them? Whit the fuck's that all aboot?'

'One wee thing before you bring in Sue, Grabbit and Run, Lennie,' said Brock. 'I'm no painter and decorator, but don't you take everything off the walls before you start painting and all that stuff?'

'Oh, suddenly it's Micky Angelo at the Cistern Chapel...'

'It's Michelangelo and it's the Sistine Chapel, Lennie.'

'Ach, how would Ah know? Ah'm a Rangers supporter.'

Brock and Hughie both looked at each other and shrugged.

'Ah suppose ye've got somethin' there, Brock. Fuck it, man, Ah'm in such a hurry to get this job done. Ah've got tae cut corners, you know.'

'So, try to remember to paint round the telly, will you?' laughed Hughie.

'Hilarious. You should take your act on the road. The sooner the fuckin' better. They'll no' know the difference. Ah might even get a bonus. Cheers, guys.' He lifted the pint to his lips and swallowed. 'Ah hope you're no' puttin' watter in your beer, Hughie. That wid be right dishonest.'

Maggie, sweating profusely, sidled down to the bottom of the bar. 'Hughie, my darling, would you like to extract your finger, please? Just a request, you understand? Not a requirement. Thank you, dear.' She moved back up the bar. Hughie thought he heard her mutter something like, 'Muck do.'

Calamity Jane stared into space while it looked as though most of the population of Cincinnati were screaming for a drink. The Man in Black seemed fairly content at the corner of the bar.

'Hey, chief,' said a cowboy the worse for wear. 'Can ye play "Ah Done It Ma Wey?"' He began singing without the use of the karaoke. 'And noo the end is hereah, and so Ah face the final fuckin' curtain...'

'That's no' the way Sintra wrote it,' said Lennie the Painter.

'Actually, he didn't write it all,' said Brock. 'I think you'll find it was Paul Anka.'

'Whit the fuck dae ye mean? Paul Wanker? It was fuckin' Ole' Blue Eyes. Course it was.'

'...and merr, much merr than this, I done it ma fuckin' weyaah.'

'Maggie, dearest, turn up the karaoke will you? Shove on Bruce Springsteen or someone loud. Drown out this guy, please,' requested Hughie. Did he hear his wife say 'Luck who?'

'Actually, Sinatra bought the rights for the song of Anka for a zillion dollars,' corrected Brock. 'Sinatra heard it, went bonkers over it and immediately wanted it as his signature song. He wrote the cheque there and then and that was that. I assure you, though, it was Paul Anka who wrote it.'

'Paul Wanker,' said a deflated Lennie, muttering to himself, 'Ah'm sure Sinatra wrote it. Course he did. What does Brock know? He's a sportswriter.'

'Where's Boring Brian, Hughie?' asked Brock. 'I've hardly seen him since I've been down. Have the natives got restless, fitted him with a concrete overcoat and tipped him into the Firth? He wasn't *that* boring.'

'Oh, he's around somewhere,' said the bar owner. 'I think he's at the Millerston tonight. He's got some relatives visiting from Glasgow and they've got a room over there. He'll be in later, I'm sure. You missing his patter?'

'No, not really,' smiled Brock. 'You never did tell me how he got the moniker in the first place. How did he earn the valued esteem of an entire island? That couldn't have been easy.'

'In Boring Brian's case, it was a shoo in. He took pole position within minutes of arriving on the island. How long has he been here now? About three years? Four? Too fuckin' long, that's for sure. He's alright in small doses, but if you're not in the mood for him he can really do your box in. I'm a captured entity in here. Millport is like Alcatraz. There's nowhere to run. He'll come through the door, settle down on a seat at the bar, order up a gin and tonic and say, "Did I ever tell you about the time I got a trial for St. Mirren?" And then you know this story will stretch on for about an hour or so.'

'Did he ever get a trial for St. Mirren?' asked Brock, showing some interest. 'What was his second name? I might have heard of him.'

'I think Brian is his second name,' laughed Hughie, frantically pouring four pints of heavy in an effort to attempt to get back into Maggie's good books. 'I think his parents took one look at him and christened him Boring.'

'Seriously, what's his second name?' persisted the sports reporter.

'Genuinely, I don't know. He's so boring no-one has ever thought to ask him. St. Mirren? Maybe he did play for them. I'm a Morton man myself as you well know, so I don't take much interest in what is happening over at Paisley. What I do know is that he'll tell you about scoring on his first team debut. Another couple and he's scoring goals all over the place; Ibrox, Parkhead, Hampden. The man's a fuckin' goal machine. Another couple of gins and he's joined Barcelona for a hundred million quid and he's playing in Champions League Final against Real Madrid. Barcelona are losing 2-0 with five minutes to go when the manager turns to him. He's on the substitutes' bench because he's got a broken leg. The manager pleads, "Brian, you must score three goals. Only you can achieve this." He sends him on as a substitute, plaster and all, and Boring Brian rattles in a hat-trick in five minutes and the Spaniards are the best team in Europe. By the end of the night, and another couple of gins, he leaves believing he is the White Pele.'

'Aye, I think I might have heard of him if he had scored three goals in a Champions League Final,' nodded Brock. 'Wish me luck, I'm off for a pee. Should take me about half-and-hour to get to the toilet by the time I've battled my way through this lot.'

Hughie looked through the window at the front of the pub. 'Talk of the devil,' he said. 'Here comes Boring Brian now. Wonder what he's going to come up with tonight?'

CHAPTER SEVENTEEN

'Yippie yi ohhhh, yippie yi yaaay, Ghost Riders in the Sky...'

'Shut the fuck up!'

Clearly, the Alka Seltzer had failed to make its soothing impact on the individual with the thumping sore head sitting beside the open window at the top floor flat in Miller Street. He was gasping for the fresh air very kindly provided by the motion of the Firth of Clyde, gulping it down greedily before his eardrums were so rudely and savagely invaded by the throaty tones of a stumbling, singing cowboy, wending his way home after a hard night's boozing session down at Newton Beach. 'Whit's the matter wi' you? Ah'm only singin',' he said, looking upwards trying to locate where Foghorn Leghorn was situated. 'Ah, there ye ur.' He waved up. 'Mornin'.'

'Fuck off!'

'Well, huv it yer oan way. Yippie yi ohhhh, yippie yi yaaay, Ghost Riders in the Sky...'

'Shut the fuck up!'

Possessing the hangover from hell, the sorry character felt as though he had come off second best following an argument with a wrecking ball. Even his eyebrows pulsated. His nose hair hurt. He realised he was going around the room walking in much the same manner as Groucho Marx, with his hair too heavy for his head.

He almost laughed. He almost threw up. What on earth happened last night? He tried to piece it all together. It had all started so sensibly. Millport didn't normally encourage 'sensibly'. Certainly not during the Country and Western Festival. He flicked on the switch of the electric kettle and sat at the table. He held his head in his hands, groaned and looked at the clock on the wall three feet above the ancient electric two-bar fire. The tasteful wall-mounted plastic geese looked as though they were already flying out of the window in formation to their freedom. 'Remember that wee man at the start of the Rank movies?' he said to the boiling kettle. 'You now the guy in the tight trunks and muscles on his muscles? The guy with that bloody big gong? And that big hammer-type thing? He's in my fuckin' head just now and he's giving it fuckin' laldy. Why do I do this to myself? Year after year? I can't drink with these guys. They're all professional drunks.'

Carefully, he poured the hot water on top of a teabag in a mug emblazoned 'I'd Rather Be In Millport'. 'You are in fuckin' Millport. Where else would you be?' He realised he was talking to a piece of pottery. 'Oh, dear, not good,' he moaned and slumped into a chair beside the table. He poured in a dollop of milk or 'cow juice' as he had been told to call it this weekend. He wondered for a moment. Did all cowboys say cow juice when they were talking about milk? That didn't make sense. If they looked at a particularly well-endowed female with a rack that would take your eye out at twenty paces, did they not say, 'Look at the milkers on that?' Didn't seem right to say, 'Look at the cow juicers on that.' He thought a bit more. 'Did cowboys even drink tea?' He couldn't remember Clint Eastwood riding into town, all mysterious, The Man With No Name, and asking for a nice cup of Twinings with a smidgeon of milk.

'What happened last night?' he thought again. He took a slurp of tea. 'Ah, thank you, nectar from the gods.' He realised he was talking to a cup of tea. Making sure his frail, pain-wracked body didn't snap in two, he made his way back to his chair. 'Let's see. I started off at the Kentuckian. What time did I leave here? About threeish? Aye, about threeish. Met a nice bloke in the bar. What was his name? Ah! Two-Gun Jake. Yes, I remember him. We had to move along to the door to allow the bar brawl to take place. That went on for about five minutes and some bloke said, "Right, that's in the can" as though he was a big-time Hollywood director. Had a couple of drinks with Two-Gun Jake, can't remember his real name. Then I went along to Cactus Jack's. That was only about five minutes along the road. Felt perfectly fine, no problem. Good wee pub.'

He stopped the thought process to have a sip of tea; both physical and mental activities impossible on a simultaneous level at this stage in the healing process. This time he refrained from having a conversation with the piece of pottery. 'Ah, lovely,' he thought as he gulped. 'Now where we? Cactus Jack's. Everyone was having a good time. Robbie was behind the bar, pouring the drinks. There were a couple of busty females who had picked up a couple of stray seagulls' feathers and fitted them into their hair. Pocahontas One and Pocahontas Two. Both looked as though they were about to fall out of their tops. Neither would ever land on their face if they toppled over. They would just lurch forward and stop, held upright at an angle, unable to move for an eternity. What a way to go.' He almost laughed. He almost threw up. 'Oh, Christ, Man From Rank, fuck off, will you? Go and batter your gong elsewhere.'

'Yippie yi ohhhh, yippie yi yaaay, Ghost Riders in the Sky...'

Groucho scrambled to the open window. The singing cowboy was on the way back. 'Yippie yi ohhhh, yippie yi yaaay, Ghost Riders in the Sky...'

'Shut the fuck up!'

'Oh, hi,' said the singing cowboy, gazing up again, shielding his eyes from the glare of the wall-mounted light. 'Christ, am Ah lost or are there two o' you? Oh, fuck, please tell me Ah'm lost.'

'You're lost.'

'Thank fuck for that. Yippie yi ohhhh,yippie yi yaaay, Ghost Riders in the Sky...' He stumbled back in the direction he had just come.

Groucho couldn't summon up the energy for another bellow. He sat down again. He was determined to put the jigsaw together. 'Right, where are we?' he asked himself in the belief he might get a better answer from a living being rather than a kettle or a piece of pottery or the contents of a piece of pottery. He also admitted it might be a close-run thing. 'No problem in Cactus Jack's. A couple of drinks with a couple of locals. Just shooting the breeze, everyone happy at the parade. Went well. Apparently, there was some bloke called Captain America making a bit of an arse of himself, wanting to be in every photograph. Does it every year, I'm told. The committee are thinking of banning him next year. Or, at least, locking him in a cellar until the parade is over. Probably the latter was the better option, he remembered. That was the consensus of opinion.

Things were coming back to Groucho. He remembered being told that Wee Jennie Mack had obviously been taking karate lessons. Captain America did not see that straight-foot approach coming when he jostled to get on the stagecoach with her.

'Wow! Could that wee girl kick. One flash, right in the orchestra stalls,' said Mrs Muggins, the seventy-five-year-old retired head-mistress, complimenting the ten-year-old on her deadly accuracy and devastating power with her flying kick. 'Sweetest thing I ever saw,' she said. 'What reflexes. Quality. Sheer quality.'

Apparently, Captain America screamed something like, 'Jump in'fuckin'Jehosafuckin'phat.' And then collapsed off the rig and onto the street, the wheel of the coach narrowly missing his head. Then there was sustained applause from an appreciative audience. Queen for a Day Jennie Mack was urged to take a bow and the cheering lasted something like another ten minutes. Captain America didn't join in from his prone position. The procession continued without him.

The Line Dancing on the lorries went well, too, Groucho seemed to recall through the fog. Great innovation that from Mustang Mags, everyone agreed. Apart from the old librarian bird who fell off when the lorry had to make a sudden stop after a kid cut across the truck on his bike. The OAP will probably be in traction for awhile, they said, but she's not going to sue. What a way to spend your seventieth birthday. Okay, so far, so good. Came out of Cactus Jack's and then where did I go? Left or right? Right, definitely right, back along towards the Kentuckian. What happened then?'

He drained his cup and moved gingerly towards the kettle for a refill. He waited for the water to boil again when he caught sight of his image in the mirror. 'Aw, for fuck's sake. Who would do that?' Someone had drawn a cock on his forehead in lipstick. 'How long has that been there? Aw, for Christ's sake, have I been walking around all night with a big cock on my forehead?' He picked up a dishtowel, wet it through and started to scrub furiously at his forehead. 'Animals! Fuckin' animals! You come out for a good day, a couple of swallies, make a bit of small talk and then some bastard draws a big cock on your forehead. What's this country coming to? I blame the Lib-Dems.'

He looked again in the mirror. Apart from a couple of smears, the offending body art was as good as removed. He thought, 'I suppose I should be thankful. It's only a matter of time before some arsehole will do a tattoo for "a wee laugh". Christ, imagine going through life with a cock tattooed across your forehead?

Wouldn't go down well in job interviews, I wouldn't have thought. No point in applying for a post where you have to deal with Joe Public on a face-to-face level. Wee Mrs McEwan going into some electrical goods store looking for a new microwave and you go up to her, a cock emblazoned across your forehead, and ask if you can do anything for her.

'Who would draw a cock on your forehead? How many people are on the island at the moment? About 12,000, I heard someone say. Aye. It could have been any one of 12,000. Christ, I must have been in a bad way. Was I with a bird last night? Did I get lucky? Think I might remember that. Mind you, there were some mincing cowboys on the island, too, so it could have been any one of them with their lipstick. Where did I go after Cactus Jack's? When did I get home? HOW did I get home? Let's go back to Cactus Jack's. I turned right and walked back towards the Kentuckian. Let's think. Did I go in again? Yes! Yes, I went back in. The door was open and that guy, Two-Gun Jake, was having a cigarette outside. He offered to buy me a drink. Yes, I remember it now. Did he spike my drink? Surely not. One of those date-rape drugs?'

Cautiously, he touched the cheeks of his backside. 'No, feels okay down there,' he thought. 'He bought me a drink and I bought him one back. A couple of other guys joined us at the bar. It's all coming back now. Oh, Christ, the drink was flying about, wasn't it? My God, I looked down and I had about four or five drinks on the bar in front of me. Someone said, 'That's known as a "Heathrow", mate. All that stacking. Get them down you. Do you good.' Now they wanted to come back up again. Do him good. 'Right,' he thought, 'what happened after the Kentuckian?' He shook his head as though the action would jog his memory bank. 'I started to walk towards the harbour. Aye, I remember that. I got some strange looks. Did I have a cock on my forehead at the time? No, I don't think so. Surely, someone would have come up to me and told me I had a cock on my forehead? No, it must have happened later. But where?'

'Yippie yi ohhhh, yippie yi yaay, Ghost Riders in the Sky...'

'Aw, fuck me, it's Gene Autrey again.' He struggled back to his feet and stumbled towards the open window.

'Shut the fuck up!'

The singing cowboy looked up. He shielded his eyes again and squinted. 'Whit happened to yer cock?,' he asked. 'The cock ye had oan yer heid?'

'None of your fuckin' business. Now fuck off!'

'Nae problem, mate. Ah've just remembered where Ah parked ma car. Ah'll be aff yer island in a jiffy.' He added, 'And ye can go back to drawin' cocks oan yer heid. Nice one, mate. Whitever floats yer boat. Yippie yi ohhh...'

Groucho gathered as much power as he could, pushed his head as far outside the window as possible and positively roared, 'I don't draw fuckin' cocks on my forehead.' Two elderly ladies, taking their dogs for their early-morning constitution, stopped in their tracks before upping the pace as they hurried towards Quayhead Street.

'The strangest things happen down here during the Country and Western Festival, Agnes,' said one. Agnes asked,

'What did he say about cocks on his forehead, Babs? I'm a wee bit hard of hearing. He doesn't draw fuckin' cocks on his forehead? Oh, well, that's nice.'

Groucho looked at his wristwatch. 'It's not even 6.15am,' he noticed. 'Those old dears should still be in their bloody beds.'

All this didn't help him piece together the missing hours from the previous evening. 'Yes, I walked towards the harbour. I remember that. Was I going to buy a bag of chips from the Hippy Chippy? Aye, I think so. Queue was all the way round the Confederate HQ. Fuck that, I'll wait and get something later on.' Suddenly, he smiled, the quick-fire expression bringing immediate pain to his aching head. 'I went in to the Nashville. Yes, I went into Hughie's. It's all coming back now.' Then it faded again, just as swiftly as it had come. 'What happened after that?'

He wondered where on earth he had parted company with his headdress, his bow and arrow and his rubber tomahawk.

CHAPTER EIGHTEEN

6am SUNDAY

Newspaperman Griff Stewart, who Brock had christened R.I.P., met his good friend Tommy Booth, Detective Inspector of Strathclyde CID, known as El Cid, at the Largs slip at the pre-arranged time of 6am for the 6.45 ferry crossing, the first of the day, to the Isle of Cumbrae. Cal-Mac's service would not be disrupted, after all, and the ferry owners could get on with making their millions. Apparently, everything was under control on the island. There was just the little matter of finding a murderer.

'You swung it then?' asked R.I.P.

'The old man wasn't best pleased to get a call after midnight, but he owes me a few favours, so here I am,' said El Cid. 'He got his revenge by phoning me back about 2am to tell me the Saltcoats lads were already on the case. They had taken the call from the cop on the island. They whistled up a helicopter and got four of CID's finest to Millport along with a guy from forensics. Largs ferried over four cops last night, too.'

'They've got a helipad in Millport?' R.I.P. genuinely sounded surprised.

'Aye, they've had one over at the rear of the West Bay playing fields for years. They've needed it for emergencies since the cutbacks at the hospital.'

'Not quite a cast of thousands, but, at least, the cop on the island has company.'

'Aye, and there's more on the way, too, from Glasgow. A coach with ten, I believe, six CID with four constables to do the dirty work. They're taking over a couple of dogs, so they'll probably eat any evidence that's around. My mates might even catch this crossing if they get their backsides in gear. Old Man Briggs likes to staff up on murders. Maverick's in charge of this one, Chief DI Bert Martin. Good lad. I've worked with him a few times. I've to report to him this morning. Fair enough. A cowboy murder mystery? Right up my street.' Booth stopped short at yelling 'Yahoo!' But, as an aficionado of the Wild West, it was obvious he was eagerly anticipating getting involved.

'They've identified the body,' added the cop.

'Christ, that was quick,' said R.I.P., genuinely impressed.

'It's a James Hitchcock. Apparently he is, sorry, was, a Country and Western singer in Glasgow. And do you know what's quite intriguing about that, my old friend?' asked the cop.

'What? That he was a Country and Western singer in Glasgow?'

'No, no. His name. James Hitchcock.'

'Oh, yeah. Hickok and Hitchcock. Very good.'

'No. Wild Bill's real Christian name was James.'

'It's a bit early for your jokes, my old mate.'

'Seriously, his full name was James B Hickok. He even went by the name Haycock at one stage before reverting back to the original.'

'Why on earth did he bother to change it from James to Bill?' asked the newspaperman. 'Did he think Wild James didn't sound quite as menacing as Wild Bill?'

'No, there's a wonderful story behind that one that not a lot of people know. Wild Bill had quite a big hooter and he also had a protruding lip. A bloke called David McCanles, the first guy he shot, by the way, used to taunt him and call him "Duck Bill". So, instead, of being saddled with that nickname all his life he changed it first to "Shanghai Bill". Then he grew that extraordinary moustache that made him look a bit unkempt and someone renamed him "Wild Bill" and that name stuck for the rest of his life.'

R.I.P. looked at his cop friend. 'You know, El Cid, you might be the only guy around who would know that fact. Makes a reasonable line for the paper. You wouldn't know what the "B" stood for, by any chance?'

'Butler. James Butler Hickok was the name on his birth certificate. Handy having me around to do your research, eh? Anything else you want to know?'

'That'll do for going on with. Thanks.' The Daily News's Chief News Reporter looked at his wristwatch. Both the newspaperman and the cop, not sure of their precise schedules, had journeyed in their own cars on the hour-long trip from Glasgow to Largs. R.I.P. said, 'Okay, heads or tails to see who takes their car over. Have you seen the price to get a car on the ferry? Fuckin' astronomical!'

'Shouldn't worry you, you'll get it back on expenses.'

'So will you. At least mine might even be reasonably accurate.'

Booth smiled. 'I better take mine just in case I've got to do a Steve McQueen job. You saw Bullitt, didn't you? What a car chase. Brilliant. Tyres screeching and cars getting banged about all over the place. Aah, they don't make movies like that any more. Give me a good western or cop movie any time.'

'I don't know much about Millport,' confessed R.I.P. 'I was down last year for a couple of days with Brock and never left the pub. I was told if you do five-miles-per-hour, you'll be round the island in about ten minutes.'

'Walking or driving?' smiled the cop. 'Aye, I've been over a few hundred times, day trips and the like. The odd weekend. Lynda loves it. Quiet wee place. Even the seagulls fly in slow motion. It's just over ten miles all the way round, did you know that? So I don't think we'll be witnessing too many McQueen jobs. Maybe I should ditch the car and just run around the place. Save petrol. Old Man Briggs would like that.'

'You could probably do with the exercise, anyway.'

'Cheeky bastard! You're not likely to be ever mistaken for an athlete, are you? What about that big skinny footballer plays for one of the London clubs? You'll never be mistaken for him. Mind you, he's about a foot taller than you and probably weighs the same.'

'Let's get the ferry paid and get across,' said R.I.P..

'What's first on your agenda?' asked the cop. 'Go to the pub?'

'Seven in the morning is a wee bit too early even for me. No, I'll have to find a local photographer. In the good, old days they would have sent a snapper down with me, but that's all changed. Christ only knows when they'll stop the cutbacks. The body will be back in Glasgow by now. So, it will be the usual picture of a tent and a cordoned off crime scene and some totally pissed-off beat cop standing around trying to stifle yawns. Poor souls crawling around on all fours searching through mud and glaur for anything that might help solve the case.

'I'll be lucky if I'm able to pick up a "collect". The local newspaper guy will have taken thousands of shots because even I know the Country and Western Festival is the biggest event in Millport these days. Only problem is I have never come across a snapper who likes to actually caption his own pictures. Did you know that? Have I told you that before?'

'Only about three trillion times, mate,' answered the cop.

'Photo journalists, my arse. So, they'll have spread after spread of pictures, but no captions. What's-his-name? James Hitchcock could be in every snap and we would never know. Unless we get lucky and find someone on the island who can identify him. Wait a minute! Brock might come in handy here. He saw the body last night. We'll see. Anyway, pictures? Great for eating up space. Who needs reporters when they can just plaster pictures all over the place? Have you noticed that, Tommy? Massive photographs everywhere of showbiz nonentities that I've never heard of. Apparently, that's news these days. I'm sixty-two on my next birthday. Do you think it's too late to have a change of profession?'

'You coming up for sixty-two? That all? I thought you were older.' El Cid smiled, adding, 'I'm so much younger. I've got my whole life to lead.'

'Aye, very good, mate. I take it you guys are having a press conference? The usual guff?'

'Old Man Briggs loves his press conferences, too, as you know. One of the first things he did this morning was commandeer the Cumbrae Tourist Information Centre. We'll be working out of there. Could be a bit cramped if Old Man Briggs keeps sending in the troops.'

'I'll get the local guy to cover that. The Largs and Millport News should be on the case. I think we can afford a fiver these days for a freelance. The bloke will probably be covering it for the Press Association and they'll fire it out to the nationals. Brock's call last night gave us a head start, so I better give him an early buzz. I suppose I better buy him a drink, too. What time do the pubs open in Millport? Same as the rest of the country? Honestly, I don't remember from last year. Must have really enjoyed myself.'

'Afraid it's 11am.'

'Four hours without alcohol abuse won't do my liver any harm, I suppose.'

El Cid steered his Audi down the jetty and up onto the ramp towards the open mouth of the ferry. He was motioned forward by a Cal-Mac worker telling him to drive down the centre of the three lanes as the ferryman arranged the vehicles in the order he believed would be best served in preventing the vessel from capsizing into the Firth of Clyde. All very reassuring. The Cal-Mac employee looked about ten-years-old.

'Next stop Cumbrae,' said the cop.

'THE MILLPORT MURDER MYSTERY,' said the newspaperman, looking ahead to tomorrow's headlines.

But he couldn't help wondering. What if the bosses had come up with another fabulous competition? "WIN THE QUEEN AND RULE THE COMMONWEALTH." His story would be lucky to get a place on page fifteen.

CHAPTER NINETEEN

6. 27am SUNDAY

'CUSTER WAS HERE! Where the fuck did that come from? What the fuck does it mean? What happened to me last night?'

Sitting Bull, aka John Harris, stockbroker from plush Morningside, in Edinburgh, padded around his Millport flat, recollections of the previous evening gingerly feeding into consciousness. He made his way to the open window and sucked in what he hoped would be a lungful of fresh air, that lovely salty tang wafting up from the Firth of Clyde. He gazed across at Largs, the sun already breaking through the disappearing grey clouds, picking out the many shades of green on the fields over on the mainland. 'Beautiful,' he thought. Then he threw up all over the kitchen sink.

He refilled the kettle and pressed the 'on' button. 'Maybe a fifth cup of tea might do the trick,' he said to himself. 'Right, let's try again.' He was desperate to put last night's jigsaw together. There were many areas that remained unexplored. 'Who drew the cock on my forehead with lipstick? Who pinned that notice "CUSTER WAS HERE!" on my chest? Where's my fuckin' headdress? Where's my bow and arrow? Where's my rubber tomahawk? How the fuck did I get home? What's that strange odour coming from my buckskins?' Questions bombarded a brain ill-equipped, at that moment, to deal with such an avalanche of queries. 'What happened in Hughie's?' He remembered being in Cactus Jack's. No problem there. At the procession, some bloke called Captain America had got a boot in the Kelvin Halls, according to some elderly lady. No, it was the orchestra stalls, wasn't it? Some wee girl apparently had taken up Tae Kwon Do for the day. Right, that's all perfectly okay.

'Two outings in the Kentuckian. Far too many whiskies.' Some things were beginning to filter through. 'I walked into the Kentuckian and someone behind the bar - Hamish, was it? - asked me if I had a reservation. And I said, "Yes, quite a few, but I came, anyway." That got a wee laugh. That was first time around. A bloke called Two-Gun Jake was at the bar. He asked me if I wanted a drink.

'I was told I was doing "a Heathrow" with all my whiskies stacking up in front of me. Did I drink them all? Christ, I can't drink like that. Back at McLay and McAlister, of Thistle Street, Edinburgh, we always go out for a quick one at Jermaine's Wine Bar on a Friday. Just the three of us. Norman would have three half-pints of shandy. Same line all the time. Buys one and then twenty minutes later asks barmaid Liz for the other half. And, after he has taken about half-an-hour to drain that, he says, "Oh, hell, it's the weekend and I'm feeling adventurous. Let's have another half, Liz." Every fuckin' Friday. He must have had the same script-writer as Reg Varney. About as funny as an ingrowing toenail. And Lawrence's not much better. "I'll have a wee rum, just for my chest, you understand?" What was the matter with his chest? Was it a fuckin' alcoholic? He gets bladdered, goes home, falls over the dog, shits in the lasagne and blames it on his chest? He has three rums and starts to tell us he saw secretary Joan's knickers the other day. Fuck, I almost saw them once, but I managed to look away just in time. That was scary.

'I've always enjoyed my three whiskies with ice. No complica-tions. No daft remarks. No silly chat-up lines to Liz. I had never bothered to tell Norman and Lawrence that Liz was a raging les-bian and I had once seen her practically sucking the face off a prostitute in Rose Street one Christmas Eve after the office party.'

None of this though helped put Saturday evening back together. 'Another cup of tea will help,' he said, making his way back to the kettle. He realised he was still walking like Groucho Marx, his chin just a couple of feet off the floor. 'A woman is an occasional pleas-ure, but a cigar is always a smoke.' He put an imaginary cigar to his lips. 'I would never join a club who would have me as a member.'

He poured the hot water over the teabag for his sixth cup of the morning. He took a sip. 'Ach, this isn't helping, at all,' he rea-soned with himself. 'I need a wee half.' One snag, though. Sitting Bull hadn't bothered to bring over alcohol among his headdress, buckskins, rubber tomahawk, bow and arrow and moccasins in his cramped hold-all. 'And have you seen the price of a bottle of whisky down here?' he asked the cup of tea. 'They charge with the Light Brigade.'

He wondered if Hughie's was open. He couldn't see the pub from his flat in Miller Street, but he thought he would risk it.

Hughie was known to open that wee bit earlier during Country and Western Festival. A certain knock at the sidedoor and you were in. 'Boy's got to make his money when he can,' thought the stockbroker. He was still wearing his green and red silk dressing gown, festooned with fire-breathing dragons. He wondered what Sitting Bull, the REAL Sitting Bull, had worn as his night-time attire before going to war with the Yellow Legs the following day? 'It wouldn't have been a green and red silk dressing gown, festooned with fire-breathing dragons, that's for sure,' he told himself.

He motioned to pick up his buckskins, but thought the better of it. 'I'll leave them over at the window,' he mused, 'help get rid of that smell. Wonder what it is?'

He struggled into his jeans and pulled on a T Shirt emblazoned with the words 'Minnie-Ha-Ha Likes It Large'. There was a big arrow pointing down towards his crotch. 'If only Norman and Lawrence could see me now,' he smiled. Then he threw up.

'Me need firewater,' he said as he closed the door behind him.

CHAPTER TWENTY

7am SUNDAY

'R.I.P. Where are you? You on Fantasy Island yet?' Brock, enjoying his first pint along with bar owner Hughie Edwards in the Nashville at the ridiculous time of 7am, had just answered his mobile phone, his pal's name on the screen immediately identifying the caller.

'Charlie, we're just waiting to get off the ferry. I'm with El Cid. Listen, mate, quick question. You saw this Wild Bill Hickok bloke last night. Could you identify him in a picture?'

'That face is indelibly printed in my memory. He talked the ears off me for a huge chunk of Friday and then left me with a mental image of him lying dead last night. I could identify him wearing a blindfold. You looking for a "collect"? Christ, did I give you the right nickname or what, R.I.P?'

'Just doing my job, Charlie. You know the newspapers just love happy, gleeful portraits of someone who has just been decapitated or crushed to death. Sells newspapers.'

'Aye, now I know why I stuck to sport.'

'Where are you, Charlie?' The Daily News's Chief News Reporter swore he could detect some rattling in the background. 'Do I hear clinking glasses?'

'Sure do. Just popped over for a wee heart-starter with Hughie. You were in here last year with me, remember?'

'Aye, another lost weekend. Remember it? Just about. Right, I'll try to pick up a snap of this bloke from somewhere.'

'You won't have to look too far,' interrupted Brock. 'Hughie took some photographs on his mobile phone last night when he was left in charge of the body. And Wild Bill very conveniently was smiling at the camera with his eyes wide open. He looks alive, so the paper won't upset the faint of heart if they use the picture of a dead bloke.'

'Fuckin' brilliant,' said R.I.P. 'Well done to Hughie. Is he there? Can you put him on, please?'

Brock handed his mobile phone to Hughie. 'Hi, R.I.P. how you doing, my man?'

'A lot better for speaking to you, Hughie,' said the newspaperman. 'Good thinking with the mobile.'

'Aye, Wild Bill was most helpful, he stayed perfectly still while I took the pictures. Kept his eyes open and even smiled. How much you willing to pay for the snaps?'

'How about several brandies and port?'

'Done,' said Hughie. 'You can e-mail these pictures to your paper. They're good to go by the looks of them. Got lucky with the light, I suppose. I took about twenty snaps from just about every angle. Close-up and full length. You're welcome to them, but for fuck's sake don't tell Fiona.'

'Your secret's safe with me. I'd better tell my editor to leave off a picture credit. PHOTOGRAPH: HUGHIE EDWARDS. Fiona might spot that in the News tomorrow, eh?'

'Aye and then she might do unmentionable things with her truncheon to my backside.'

'Listen, we're only about five minutes or so from your establishment. Okay to pop in? My News Editor will already be in the office. I'll give him a quick call to give him the good news about the pictures. Well done. Wild Bill in all his cowboy gear. With his eyes open. I think this is going to be a good day.'

'I'm sure Wild Bill Hickok would give you a right good argument about that.'

'That doesn't make sense,' said R.I.P. 'He's dead.'

'Do you want to see these snaps or not? Bring your wallet. Drink isn't cheap in this bar.' Hughie laughed and handed the mobile back to Brock.

'I'll stick a couple up for you and Tommy with Hughie's money. Is El Cid allowed to drink on duty? At this Godforsaken time of the day?'

'Oh, I'm sure he'll relent with some arm twisting. The sun is over the yardarm somewhere in the world. Listen, we'll come in the side door. Too many cops down here just now with a platoon still to arrive. Can't wait to get a look at those snaps.'

'Lucky bastard,' said El Cid. 'So, you don't have to go banging on doors looking for snaps of Wild Bill? They've just landed on your lap? Manna from heaven. Is someone going to write your report, too? Or are you up to a couple of paragraphs of squiggles that some poor bastard back in Glasgow has to decipher and translate into understandable English and then put in the paper? Remember, I've met a few of those guys, the sub-editors. They've told me your stories are shite.'

'Ach, those guys are always complaining. My stuff's okay. And, remember, I've never been sued. I've handled a lot of volatile stuff and never given the paper or the lawyers a problem. How many can say that in my profession? Okay, I may have gotten lucky on this occasion, but good things happen to good people.'

'James Hitchcock might have been a good person. Nothing good happened to him. Who knows? He might have been the type to help old ladies across the road...'

'And mug them when he gets them safely to the other side out of sight and help himself to their pension. Aye, it takes all sorts, right enough.'

CHAPTER TWENTY-ONE

7.25 am SUNDAY

'Well, if it's not old Sitting Bullshit. Welcome back to the land of the living.' Hughie greeted the Edinburgh stockbroker's return to the bosom of the Nashville. 'What kept you?'

The hands on the clock on the pub wall were just nudging beyond 7.25am.

'What's good for a hangover, Hughie?' he wailed.

'You could try lots and lots of alcohol. That's great for a hangover. Works for me all the time.'

'You know what I mean,' moaned Sitting Bull.

'Or you could adopt the Dean Martin approach. Apparently, his ideal way of dealing with a hangover was to stay drunk.'

'Aye, I might try that. Stay drunk. Aye, that could be the answer. I'll try a wee Bell's, Hughie. See if that helps.' He turned to face sports reporter Charlie Brock. 'Fuck me, Charlie, you've started early, haven't you?' He didn't know the other two early-morning imbibers. Hughie didn't introduce him to Detective Inspector Harry Booth or Chief News Reporter Griff Stewart. Not through any bad manners. He just assumed that everyone on Millport knew everyone else. He wasn't often wrong.

'You guys want a drink?' offered Sitting Bull. Brock, El Cid and R.I.P. declined his kind offer. It was going to be a busy day for at least two of them. Brock smiled, ignorant of what lay ahead for him.

'Okay, Hughie, who do I need to apologise to?' It was a question Sitting Bull asked regularly during Country and Western Festivals. It was a rarity that he could ever remember leaving the Nashville on any of the three evenings during his annual stay. 'I'm going to have to learn how to drink,' he said.

'Hard to know where to start, Sitting Bull,' said Hughie.

'I'm just plain John Harris at the moment, Hughie. I'll get my Sitting Bull gear on later once I find where the hell I left it. Okay, hit me with it. Who's first for an apology?'

'Like I say, Sitting Bull, it's hard to know exactly what to start. Well, there's every cowboy on the island, that would be a reasonable place to kick off. You wanted to go to war with the palefaces last night.'

'Oh, Christ, not again.'

'Aye, we were all waste matter from the bowels, according to you. The breath from Satan's arse, as well. We were something you would scrape off the sole of your moccasin. We were all products of the devil's loins. We weren't even good enough for buzzard bait. All white squaws were hatchet-faced bitches from hell who all deserved your war lance up their rectums. All our wives were foul-smelling, syphilitic, blasphemous whores only to be reviled and defecated on. We were all the putrid stench from a longhorn's droppings. Pony soldiers were good only for worm meat. We all reeked of dead wart hog. No, you weren't exactly complimentary to the Yellow Legs.'

'Oh, fuck,' said Sitting Bull. 'Did I use some of my new material? I was keeping that for another night.'

'You were doing fine until you collapsed in a heap at the bar. Remember?'

'No, not really,' he said weakly. 'My party piece, eh? What happened next?'

'Tip-Toe eventually helped you back to your feet after you lay there for about half an hour. Everyone was stepping over you, spilling drink all over the place.'

'That would explain the smell from my buckskins this morning. I thought I had pished myself.'

'Tip-Toe sat you down in Vodka Joe's corner and you had another wee nap. When you came to, you looked over at Calamity Jane and ordered her to be scrubbed and taken to your teepee where you were going to give her a stiff, hard shag. You might owe her an apology. You tried to climb over the bar to get at her. She took you away to the Ladies' loo for a minute. We wondered if you were going to get lucky.'

'And I came back with a giant cock on my forehead etched in lipstick?'

'Ah, so you do remember some things?'

'Not really. I was having a cup of tea about an hour ago and just about collapsed when I saw myself in the mirror and there was a giant cock drawn on my forehead looking back at me. Remind me to say thanks to Calamity, will you?'

'You got off lightly, mate. The mood she was in you could have come back with the real thing nailed to your forehead.'

'Oh, dear. Not good. I'll buy her a box of chocolates, see if that placates her. My crown jewels stuck to my forehead? Not good, at all.'

Hughie suddenly had a thought. 'Presumably, you don't know about the excitement on the island last night?'

'What excitement? Me getting pished and making an arse of myself?'

'No a wee bit more exciting than that,' said Hughie, setting up another round drinks for his four early-morning drinking companions. And a small brandy and port for himself. 'That guy who was going around calling himself Wild Bill Hickok? He was found dead last night. Only a couple of hours after you left the pub, in fact. He was found with a bullet hole between the eyes.'

'Get lost,' said Sitting Bull.

'I'm afraid he's telling the truth,' said El Cid. 'That's why I'm here.' He put out his hand. 'The name's Harry Booth, Detective Inspector Strathclyde CID.'

Sitting Bull hesitated for a moment before accepting the handshake. 'Honest, I was only kidding when I said I wanted to kill every white man. I'm a stockbroker. From Morningside. In Edinburgh.'

'Not last night you weren't,' pointed out Hughie. 'You were Sitting Bull and you were on the warpath. All palefaces deserved to die. You said you would even put the pennies on their dead eyes yourself.'

'Not guilty,' shrieked Sitting Bull. 'Shove another Bell's in there, will you, Hughie? Make it large.' He handed over his glass. He could feel the eyes of the cop burning into the back of his head.

'And you don't remember a thing after you left here last night?' asked El Cid.

CHAPTER TWENTY-TWO

12.42pm SUNDAY

'Brock? That name rings a bell. Brock?' Detective Inspector Tommy Booth, aka El Cid, was pulling at his jaw and looking contemplative as he stood at the packed bar of the Nashville, a pint of heavy in his right hand. It was closing in on one o'clock and the thief-taker, as he was known to his two newspaper pals, was enjoying a half-hour break. Detective Chief Inspector Bert Martin, Maverick to his friends and enemies, told him to get some local knowledge. Where better way to get local knowledge than a local? El Cid headed straight for the Nashville. As Maverick knew he would. He owed him a couple.

'Of course, you know me, El Cid, are you going senile? Don't drag me and R.I.P. down with you,' said Charlie Brock. 'We've known each other for centuries. Or, maybe, it just feels like that.'

'I know. But, for whatever reason, I've never really thought about your name. Brock. It's unusual, isn't it? I've always thought of you as Charlie. Plain and simple Charlie. Don't take that the wrong way. But something has now just popped into my head. Brock? Where do I know that name from? You got millions of relatives?'

'Just a sister and she's now called Perrers. There's some French blood in her husband's family. If there are another million Brocks out there, then I don't know of them. I'm not even sure of the origins of the name. I've tried to look it up, but the net widens instead of narrowing, so I've chucked it. It's either Scottish, Irish, English, French, Dutch or German. Take your pick. I think I'm a bit of a mongrel. Not sure I want to know any more Brocks. I'm happy with my circle of friends.'

Hughie Edwards, bar owner and frustrated stand-up comedian, delved in, 'Christ, you're easily pleased, Big Man.' He looked at R.I.P. and El Cid and laughed. 'No offence, gentlemen.'

'Have you not got a job to do?' smiled R.I.P. 'You know, somewhere behind the bar?'

'Charming. I give you the scoop news picture of the year and that's how you treat me. I'll just fuck off and pour some pints, then.'

R.I.P. had already written his news story and would file in a couple of hours' time, although he realised only too well it might need a total rewrite at any time of the day if events changed dramatically. The dead man had been identified as James Hitchcock, a forty-two-year-old full-time entertainer from Glasgow. A helpful driving licence and credit cards in his jeans' pocket led the police straight to identification which had been verified by an aunt who had looked at the body at Glasgow mortuary in the early hours of the morning. 'Always knew dressing up like Wild Bill Hickok would get him into trouble,' she'd said, with a shrug of her shoulders.

It transpired he wasn't married, didn't have a partner, didn't have children and lived on his own in a top-floor flat in Maryhill, Glasgow, overlooking Partick Thistle's ground at Firhill. After the initial meeting with the aunt, who lived in a nearby tower block, several other relatives had been notified and given the information required before the police would release any details, however minor, to the media.

As ever, the police were asking the public if they had seen anything suspicious on Millport between eight and ten o'clock on Saturday evening, the two-hour period pathologists and forensics believed was around the time the incident had taken place. Had anyone had any contact with the victim? An emergency phone number had been set up and the police were continuing to work out of the Cumbrae Tourist Information Centre on Stuart Street. The police had also set up a caravan on the promenade appealing for any witnesses. Anyone who saw anything remotely suspicious was asked to telephone the two-foot high red-lettered number that had been put on posters and plastered all over the town.

The CID had also brought in the gun marshals for their assistance. There were twenty such professionals on the island during Country and Western Festival. And they took their jobs extremely seriously. Any gung-ho cowboy waving a toy gun around was running the risk of having it immediately confiscated. There were many cowboys who came onto the island who were in gun clubs, but, in the main, these enthusiasts knew how to behave and were also well aware of the gun laws. They realised it was strictly forbidden to even point a plastic gun at anyone. In fact, everyone carrying a gun had to keep it holstered. Even if someone took out a revolver to clean the barrel or some such chore ran the threat of having the 'weapon' taken off them. The organisers knew, though, that there were a few renegades willing to run the risk.

R.I.P. was intrigued. 'I've got to ask this question. How can you have High Noon when you are looking for the fastest draw? How does that work if you can't take the gun out of the holster?'

Hughie, that fount of all knowledge Cumbrae, was hovering nearby, cleaning some pint glasses when he provided the answer. 'You can take it out of the holster, but you must keep it pointed towards the ground. Seriously. Some of the shootists have caps in their guns and they make a realistic sound, but they are only allowed to fire them at the ground beside them. Anyone failing to do so is immediately disqualified.'

'Right, that's fine, I get that,' said the newspaperman. 'But how the hell do you determine who is the fastest gun on the island when you are not even allowed to fire blanks at each other?'

'Easy,' said Hughie. 'It's the fastest gun out of the holster and pointed downwards all in one movement. That's the rules, my friend.'

'The rules weren't even that strict in Dodge City. I take it there have been a few arguments over decisions, then?'

'You better believe it. There are no good losers in the High Noon shoot-out when everyone's got their eye on the Gary Cooper Cup. Aye, there's been a scuffle or two.'

'Are they allowed to actually hit each with their fists?' smiled R.I.P. He was joining in the general and infectious madness of Millport that his good friend Brock had warned him about. 'They don't have to punch the ground?'

Hughie was pensive for a moment. 'No, they batter the living fuck out of each other.'

A team of extra gun marshals had been brought onto the island to inspect the guns and rifles of the potential 12,000 suspects. Thankfully, there had been fewer than half that number of fire-arms and just about all of them were obvious fakes. Fifty beat cops got the job of knocking on doors at houses, apartments, guest houses, hotels, tents and caravans. Some cowboys were known to sleep rough, many on Newton Beach. They, too, were interviewed. Wild Bill Hickok had rented a caravan for the weekend in the grounds of the Westbourne Hotel not far from his final resting place at West Bay Park. No-one saw him come. No-one saw him go. Apart from a change of underwear, it looked as though he died wearing his complete wardrobe.

Pathologists had actually determined that Wild Bill Hickok, James Hitchcock, had been shot by a firearm. At the moment, they could not ascertain which sort of firearm until they finalised ballistic tests on the bullet they found between the victim's eyes. So, a team of highly-qualified scientists and forensic experts had taken hours to determine what PC Fiona Anderson, lowly beat cop of Millport, had deduced all on her own in a matter of seconds.

Holidaymaking cowboys queued to have their guns examined at the two centres set up on the promenade and also at the Police Station at the corner of Millburn Street and Crawford Street. Remarkably, it all went fairly smoothly. Those who needed to get off the island for a variety of reasons on Sunday were quick to hand in their weapon and all addresses were noted with contact phone numbers. Most of the guns and rifles were obvious plastic toys. Some were realistic-looking. And some were real. The Gun Club members were allowed to take their pistols, but the bullets stayed at home. It had been a perfectly-workable situation. Until now.

Every gun was checked and passed. That left the cops with a real problem. Could the assailant simply have dropped a firearm into the Firth of Clyde after shooting Wild Bill? Little rowing boats were dotted all around the island. Someone could have paddled out and ditched it and returned the rowing boat. The gun could be nestling anywhere out at sea. It could even have been dumped in the fields on the way to Fintry Bay. Or anywhere on an island where there was a fair percentage unoccupied and the fields can grow thick and wild. 'You could hide a tank in there,' El Cid confided to R.I.P. and Brock . El Cid reckoned his police colleagues had two chances of recovering any weapon. 'Slim and none. With the emphasis on the latter. Believe me, that's not defeatist talk. We might just get lucky and someone will let something slip and we'll get the killer. The gun, though, could be anywhere between here and Outer Mongolia.'

'No, that doesn't sound like defeatist talk, Tommy,' laughed the Chief News reporter. 'Slim and none? Not zilch and zero?'

'You've got to hope that someone saw something,' said El Cid. 'Then we've got a chance. Maybe someone confided in another. Shared the guilt. Even Jesus had his Judas.'

The cop straightened up at the bar and launched his drink down his throat. Suddenly he was serious. 'Ach, I'm fed up with all these American TV shows with all the new-fangled technology all the cops are supposed to have at their fingertips these days. Utter nonsense. I saw a show the other night, one of those CSI jobs. They were trying to piece together an updated photograph of someone who would now have been in their sixties. The only other picture they had was of the guy in a fuckin' pram. He was about six months' old, fuck's sake. So, they put that photograph into some machine, some bird with big tits hits a button, it whirrs along for a couple of seconds and up comes an image of what the bloke now looks like today. Jeezus Christ. The bloke's even got a wee goatee beard. How the fuck do they know that a wean in a pram might want to grow a wee goatee beard in sixty years' time? And what happens if the guy decides to have a sex change when he's twenty-two? He's fed up being a bloke, so he goes and gets his todger whipped off, develops boobs, gets those hair extension things and flounces around as Wilhemina when he used to be Willie? Oh, give us a break.'

He stopped, took a sip of his freshly-replenished pint glass and said, 'You know, a lot of these shows actually provoke nut-cases into trying to beat the system? They watch all this stuff on the box, take notes and then think they will go out and commit the perfect crime. There was a guy up north a few years ago who watched the make-believe nonsense and all the real stuff, too. He went through everything on some satellite channel and then set himself the task of going out to commit a double homicide and not leave a single trace of evidence behind. Honest, this is a true story. You'll remember it, surely, R.I.P? He waited until Christmas Day - did this guy have a sense of timing or what? - and then he went out and shot down and slaughtered a seventy-year-old grandmother and her daughter in their home. He burned the bodies that destroyed and degraded the bullets. He was very thorough and very premeditated. He had learned it all from watching these fuckin' TV shows.'

'Aye, I remember that case. The Aberdeen office - when we had an Aberdeen office - covered the story. He was caught, though, wasn't he?' said R.I.P.

'As a matter of fact he was. The best-laid plans etc. He disposed of his blood-stained boots by tossing them over a bridge into the river below. He didn't take into account the ice flows in the water, what with it being around Christmas. Anyway, the boots landed on the ice and didn't sink to the bottom. He strolled off, hands in his pockets, whistling merrily and didn't think to look over his shoulder. A walker spotted the boots a couple of days later, completely preserved. The criminal was already known to the local police. A quick check of the DNA and they were knocking on his door. He had never met either of his victims before. He said he picked their names randomly out of the phone book because they "sounded foreign". Just like that.'

El Cid was aware he now had two intrigued drinking companions. 'Any more like that?' asked Brock.

The cop took another sip. 'Och, there's a load like that, more's the pity. There are a lot of strange people out there...'

'There are a lot of strange people in here,' said Brock, pointing to the cowboys drinking as though they had just heard tomorrow had been cancelled.

'Aye, right,' smiled El Cid. 'Present company excepted, of course. There was another bloke who set up what he thought the cops would believe was a simple suicide of his missus. He decided to do away with his wife and planned it meticulously. She was found dead in bed and the husband raised the alarm himself. The cops arrived and what struck them immediately was how tidy the place was. It raised their suspicions right away. Why would anyone bother to do the hoovering, change the bedding, wear fresh pyjamas, wash and polish everything in sight and then quietly go to bed and commit suicide? Didn't ring true right from the off.

'The husband drugged her and then suffocated her and changed and destroyed her clothing. Put her into fresh jimjams and stuck her into bed. He even produced something that looked like a genuine suicide note in his wife's handwriting which she had signed. It was checked for forgery, but it was the real deal. It could have been a note she had left on another occasion. Something as simple as 'I've had enough of this,' written and signed by a fed-up wife after another domestic. The bloke kept the note for a rainy day.

Then he murdered her and left the note on the bedside cabinet. He kept the dead body warm by wrapping it in an electric blanket for about a day to stop the normal processes kicking in. That was something he had picked up from TV. No chance of rigor mortis while the body is still warm. Then, when the time was right, he put the body back in bed, made sure he was out and about and seen by everyone before returning home. Confronted by the sight of his dead wife, he phoned the police.

'The forensics people checked out the body without much joy. Then someone had a look at her fingernails, they're always good for trapped DNA. You know, a scratch or something, getting someone else's blood under the nails? The husband reckoned he had thought of everything. He actually clipped his wife's nails, making sure there was no sign of his DNA. Very smart, but that, too, provoked a response from the forensics people. Who could be bothered clipping their fingernails if they knew they were going to top themselves five minutes later? They searched the bins in his house. Lo and behold, they found the clippings in a bin in the kitchen. Unfortunately, for the husband, his fingerprints were on them. Miniscule particles of his skin were under them, too. The nails were about an inch long and the cops got enough off them to prosecute the bloke. He cracked up and told them everything. He was led away muttering, "Fuckin' fingernails."

'Aye, I remember that case now,' said Brock. 'In typical tabloid style, the News just used the word "NAILED!" as their headline on the front page. The Telegraph probably went for "HUSBAND FOUND GUILTY OF WIFE'S DREADFUL MURDER AFTER ALERT POLICE FORENSIC EVIDENCE SHOWS PRINTS FOUND ON FINGERNAILS AND SKIN UNDER FINGERNAILS." Something catchy like that.'

El Cid smiled. He continued, 'Mind you, there is a bloke out there who would boggle even the greatest minds of CSI. He's actually a Glaswegian hitman. We know his name, but we just can't get the bastard. We also know he has told accomplices he has "done in" at least twenty victims. To be fair, he's probably doing us a favour because every single one of the blokes he has put to sleep have been villains. However, I don't think Glasgow is quite ready yet to embrace a vigilante. That's okay for Charles Bronson in New

York, but we're not likely to welcome wee Willie McGlumpher taking the law into his own hands in our fair city.

'How clever is this? He goes around pubs and clubs and picks up cigarette stubs left outside in the bins. Then he'll go inside and help himself to cocktail leftovers, bits of lemon, cherries and so on. He also lifts clippings from various hair salons. He'll go in a place when he sees it is very busy. You know, people getting ready for the weekend. Fridays around lunchtime are not a time to go to a barbers if you are in a rush for a haircut, believe me. The suits are out and about getting prepared for functions at the weekend when they want to impress their boss. Doesn't look too good if you turn up looking like Screaming Lord Sutch for a swanky dinner party at the boss's gaffe. So, our guy will sit down, pretend to read a newspaper, drop a coin, go and retrieve it and, at the same time, pick up samples of hair, probably from about three of four different heads. He'll give it another minute and then walk out. No-one takes a blind bit of notice. Why would they? Just in case forensics can identify the type of mopping-up liquid, Mr Gleam or whatever, that has been used to clean the floor in a certain salon, he'll go to another hairdressing salon and go through the same routine.

'He will pick up leftovers outside chip shops or kebab shops. Chinese. Indian. Anything. Half-eaten burgers in the dustbins. Dog hairs, cat fur, feathers from a parakeet. He'll collect anything that has been chucked away. He's even been known to pick up discarded nappies. Honestly, nothing is overlooked by this guy. Then he takes them home, pops them into a liquidiser to create a dust from the concoction and then he will spray it all over a crime scene. The poor guys from forensics are left completely bamboozled. They scrape everything together and then wonder what on earth has been happening in that particular room. They can have something like a thousand DNA samples mixed together. That would fuck up even the blokes in Miami on the telly.'

'I could hire that guy,' said Brock. 'There could be a former editor I wouldn't mind being taken care of.'

'I'll have a word with him if you like, Charlie,' laughed El Cid. 'I can tell you he is expensive. Possibly not in the Jackal price range, but he does deliver. He does exactly what it says on the tin. He's very clever. He's not afraid to kill in crowded places. He's confident enough to know that there will be thousands of micro-samples around and that's when it becomes just about impossible to isolate one sample.'

R.I.P. laughed and said, 'I read a book recently about the Mafia. Good story. This particular mob decided to bump off one of the godfathers. They believed he was getting too old and too soft in his dotage. He refused to step down and a let a young Don take over. So it was time for him to go and meet Marlon Brando in the Sky. The hit squad knew the godfather was going to his favourite Italian restaurant in New York one evening and they planned to do the job there. One of the hit men came up with the cunning idea that they should all be roughly the same height, about six foot, and they should dress the same. There were about twelve of them outside the restaurant. It was winter and they were all wearing long black coats, their Astrakhan collars turned up with their faces barely visible. And, of course, they were all wearing huge Cossack hats. They were mingling around for a few minutes until the godfather arrived. Then they walked up and simply shot him as he got out of the car. Dead on the spot. The police arrived and they questioned the witnesses. They were baffled. Everyone of the shooters looked the same. They had to put out an APB searching for twelve guys who were all dressed identically. Very clever these murdering bastards, aren't they?'

'Aye and we've just to keep working away, looking for that little something that leads to their arrest,' said El Cid. 'On this one, we've just got to keep knocking on doors. Literally as well as metaphorically. You never know, something might turn up either tonight or tomorrow. We'll keep probing away. Then, again, if this Wild Bill Hickok bloke was shot at, say, eight o'clock, whoever pulled the trigger could have got round the island in time for the 8.30 crossing to Largs. Jumped into a fast car when he arrived before 8.45 and could have been having a pint with his pals and playing dominoes in a pub in Sauchiehall Street by about ten, even before the body had been found. If that's the case, there's every probability that we're well and truly fucked.

'Old Man Briggs wants a good job done on this one. And he's sending over another column of constables tonight. If he keeps this up there are going to be more cops on the island than cows. Fuck knows where they're all going to sleep. The police cells only hold two at a pinch and I don't see the beat cop - what's her name?

Fiona? - sharing her bed with half of Strathclyde CID. All the hotels and guest houses are packed, too. But I'm sure Charlie here will find me a chair at his place.' The Detective Inspector lapsed into deep thought again. He looked at Charlie Brock.

'BROCK!' he bellowed above the general din of a busy pub. 'BROCK'S LAST CASE! I remember it now. It was an American TV movie made in the early seventies and it starred Henry Fonda. It was about a New York cop who retired to a Californian citrus ranch. He got caught up in a murder. It was the pilot movie for the series they later renamed Madigan, a tough New York cop, played, by Richard Wydmark. Good movie. Written by a bloke called Alex Gordon. Good Scottish name. Wonder if he was Scottish?'

'Never heard of him,' said Brock.

CHAPTER TWENTY-THREE

1.47pm SUNDAY

'You're always telling us how good you are at whodunits, Brock. Told us you got the murderer in The Mousetrap long before the interval. You might just have a hidden talent. Mind you, we only have your word for cracking The Mousetrap, haven't we?'

'Are you that desperate, El Cid, that you are trying to enlist the help of a freelance sports journalist whose only aim over the next couple of days is to enjoy himself, thunder a couple of gallons of lager towards his overworked bladder and, if he's extremely lucky, get into bed with a female at least half his age?' Brock thought he had put up a convincing argument for being left in peace by the Detective Inspector from Strathclyde CID.

'Think about it, Charlie,' said El Cid. 'Look at all the oddball cops we've had on the telly...'

'Thanks. So now I'm an oddball?'

'But think about it. We've had the wee one-eyed guy with the rumpled coat who goes around scratching his head and saying, "Oh and another thing" in every episode.'

'That would be Peter Falk in Columbo.'

'And we've got the baldy bloke with the shades who toddles about with a lollipop stuck in his face and says, "Who loves ya, baby?" all the time.'

'That's Telly Savalas in Kojak. By the way, El Cid, do you know there are only two types of people who wear sunglasses indoors?'

'Aye, you've told me this before. Blind people and arseholes. Then there's the bloke that's stuck in the wheelchair.'

'Ironside, the San Francisco Chief of Police, played by Raymond Burr.'

'And the interfering old dame that's always solving crime every-where she goes. I would arrest her right off. She visits some quiet, deserted wee spot in some remote village and suddenly there's a murder. Too much of a coincidence, I think. I'd clap her in irons. Take a rubber hosepipe to her and beat a fuckin' confession out of her.'

'That would be either Miss Marple, played by Margaret Rutherford and a whole load of others, or Murder She Wrote which starred Angela Lansbury.'

'Margaret Rutherford? Was that the old dame who looked like an ugly bloke? We would have had her screaming the place down if we had got the electrodes attached to her private parts. And what about that irritating cowboy who rides through the streets of New York? Does he even know the damage he is doing to a horse's joints by riding it on a hard surface? Someone should throw him in jail and send the RSPCA round to kick the crap out of him.'

'That's Dennis Weaver in McCloud and it was a TV spin-off of Clint Eastwood's character in the movie Coogan's Bluff.'

'Who said you only know about football? Quite impressive, Brock. What about the multi-billionaire bloke with the Polish name who kept solving the crimes none of the top insurance investigators could even get close to?'

'George Peppard in Banacek.'

'How about it? If that selection of buffoons can solve crime, you can give it a go,' challenged El Cid, mischievously. "You can talk the talk, Charlie, but can you walk the walk? Can you go out there onto those mean streets, the place where crime is rampant, the filthy, breeding ground for criminals, murderers, rapists, drug pushers, scumbags, pimps, lowlifes, paedos, arsonists?'

'In Millport?'

El Cid smiled. 'Look, there's a pint of lager in it for you right now.' They were both standing at the bar in the Nashville. 'Hughie, a couple of beers down here. Ta.' The bar owner motioned he would be with them in two ticks. He made some sort of motion with two fingers, anyway.

'A pint of lager?' said Brock, playfully joining in El Cid's wind up. 'You want me to go out there, risking life and limb, into the underbelly netherworld of the Isle of Cumbrae and help you find a murderer for the price of a pint of lager? Do you think Banacek took home a can of Extra Strong for saving a company from paying out billions in an insurance scam? Eh? Miss World's lying there stark naked on the bed, legs akimbo, in some fancy boudoir on his floating gin palace and he strides in and says, "Solved it again, darling." Turns and throws a can of Extra Strong on the bed and says, "Get stuck into that, Melinda. There's plenty more where that came from."'

'You drive a hard bargain, Charlie. How about a pint a lager AND a packet of smoky bacon?'

'Deal. I'll have my lawyers draw up a contract in the morning.'

'Hey! I hope you're not gambling over there.' Hughie Edwards noticed some cash mounting up on top of a table where six cowboys were sitting in a corner at the Nashville.

'You're okay, boss,' said one. 'No cards here. We're having a wee bet to see who can come up with the best song title for someone getting shot.'

'Sick bastards,' thought the bar owner. 'Poor Wild Bill's probably still warm.' He shouted across the bar that was already rapidly filling with cowboys determined not to be compos mentis by five o'clock. 'Okay, don't let it get out of hand.'

'What about that song from the big Scottish bloke with the chin the size of Brighton Pier?' said a cowboy. 'You know the guy I mean? He did that World Cup song.'

'*We're On The March With Ally's Army*?' ventured a pal. 'Naw, don't be daft. That was Andy Cameron. I bought that in 1978. Argentina. Whit a fuckin' disaster. Naw, it wisnae *Ole! Ola!* either because that was old Rod the Mod. *I Had A Dream*, that was another. Who did that?

'Was it BA somebody? BJ? No, it was BA Robertson, wasn't it? Aye, the chin the size of an aircraft carrier. Aye, he did that. And he did that other song, as well. What was it called? *Bang! Bang!* Something like that?'

'Don't forget Eric Clapton,' said another. '*I Shot The Sheriff But I Didnae Shoot The Deputy.*' That was brilliant. He started to sing, 'I shot the sheriff...'

'Give it a break, Sam. Wait until the karaoke tonight. Hey, that's a good idea. Why don't we have a themed night? You know, songs all about punters getting wasted, blown away? I think that's a great idea. I'll ask the bar guy. I'm sure he'll go for it. Aye, I like the sound of that. Probably fed up with Sinatra by now. Right, who's next?'

'I've got a cracker,' said another. '*Eton Rifles* by The Jam,' he said proudly. 'Can anyone top that?'

'Aye, good one, Ed. Like it. There must be millions of them out there. Fuckin' millions. What about Johnny Cash? He must have done millions himself. An old ex-con singing about murder and death...only in America,' he laughed and shook his head. 'Another six beers, gents? I'll get them in.' The cowboy battled his way to the bar. 'Six lagers, please,' he said to Hughie. 'Hey, I've got a great idea for tonight, boss. Why don't we have a karaoke all about guns, bullets, death, that sort of stuff? Would go down a storm, eh?'

'Sick bastards,' thought Hughie, looking over his shoulder at the Jewish Piano. He said, 'Great idea, mate. I'll see what we've got on the machine.'

'*Don't Take Your Gun To Town*. That was one of Johnny Cash's. Wonder if he took his own advice?'

'Elvis Costello did one, as well, didn't he? Aye, he did. What was it called?'

'*Watching The Detectives?*' mused a pal.

'Naw, I don't think there was anyone shot in that one. Nae shooting. Just a lot of watching. Ach, what was it called? It's on the tip of my tongue.'

'Put your tongue out and I'll see,' smiled another. His mate stuck out his tongue. His drinking partner pretended to read it. 'John?'

'Naw, that's no' the name o' the song. That's the name o' ma tongue.'

'Ah'm sure it was something like *Shot With His Own Gun*. Aye, that wis it. *Shot With His Own Gun*. Good number.'

'That Right Stoned Cowboy must have shot a few, going about pished and the like?'

'What the fuck are you talking about? Right Stoned Cowboy? It was *Rhinestone Cowboy*. A Glen Campbell song. It's got fuck all to do with people getting pished and shot to bits.'

'You sure? It's not called Right Stoned Cowboy? Christ, I've been going around singing that all my life. "I'm a Right Stoned Cowboy..." I prefer my version. Fuck Glen Campbell. Scottish bastard. What does he know?'

'How about *Call The Shots?*' asked one.

'Who the fuck did that?' chorused the other five.

'Girls Aloud,' came the answer.

'Girls A-Fuckin'-Loud? Get a grip, Andy.'

'Ach, you know how it is. The weans play it around the house...'

'Any more? Who wins the big cash prize? What's in the pot? Sixty quid? I'm well up for that.'

'I've got a cracker,' said Andy, struggling to get back into his mates' good books after his Girls Aloud gaffe. 'What about *Chitty Chitty Bang Bang*?'

'For fuck's sake, Andy. Are you taking this seriously? *Chitty Fuckin' Chitty Fuckin' Bang Fuckin' Bang*? Don't recall Dick Van Dyke running around the streets of London blowin' the bad guys away with an Uzi machine gun.'

'Are we forgetting The Beatles?' asked one. 'The *White Album* was littered with songs about guns.'

'Was it?' queried Andy, thankful the gaze of his mates had been deflected for the time being.

'Aye. There was *Happiness Is A Warm Gun*, for a start. What the fuck was that all about? *Happiness Is A Warm Gun*? Who thinks up songs like that?'

'What about the guy who wrote *Life Is Just A Bowl Of Cherries*?' Andy was getting his confidence back. 'What was that guy smoking when he wrote that?'

'Doris Day sang that,' said one. 'Old Calamity Jane herself. You know what they used to say about her in Hollywood, don't you? "I remember Doris Day before she was a virgin!" Aye, brilliant, eh?'

'And what about *Rocky Raccoon*? That was on the *White Album*, too, wasn't it? Did you know that was the last Beatles song where John Lennon played the harmonica? Aye, true.'

'You talk about people getting blown away. What about poor John Lennon? Shot in the fuckin' back.'

El Cid was at the bar replenishing the drinks after being joined by R.I.P. Professional to the end, the newspaperman had filed a sidebar piece on the Wild Bill Hickok murder, getting the reaction of the punters on the island, some local colour.

El Cid overheard the cowboys behind him talking loudly about John Lennon. Now that was a murder in which he wouldn't have minded being involved. Nothing at all to do with headlines, fame or glory. The guy, Mark Chapman, shoots Lennon outside the Dakota Buildings in New York and then stands around reading a book until the cops arrive to pick him up.

'Do you know what you've done?'

'Yes, I've just shot John Lennon.'

Just like that.

'And I've got a fuckin' murder here in Millport and I can't get anyone to own up.' El Cid thought life wasn't fair.

'Okay, is that us? Anyone mention the Stones? They must have done a few songs with people getting wasted, surely? Old Mick and the boys. Top stuff. They did Start Me Up, didn't they?'

'More like Finish Me Off!' said Andy. 'Okay, who's won the dosh?'

'No' you, anyway,' said his mates.

Andy realised it was a mistake mentioning Girls Aloud and Chitty Chitty Bang Bang.

CHAPTER TWENTY-FOUR

2.52pm SUNDAY

'You want your murderer? I've got the perfect solution.'

Charlie Brock was taking this sleuth thing seriously, thought El Cid, as he slid into a seat in the corner of the Nashville. 'Have you got your braces caught in the door?' asked Hughie Edwards. 'Popping in, popping out. I'm getting dizzy.'

'Do I want the murderer? I'm all ears,' said Harry Booth, Detective Inspector of Strathclyde CID, settling down out of sight with a small glass of whisky in his hand. 'I've got fifteen minutes. This better be good. So far we've dug up the square root of hee-haw. People remember seeing Wild Bill Hickok strolling around the town. However, it seems he was always on his own. No-one saw him out on the street with anyone else. A bit of a loner by all accounts. That doesn't help, believe me. I know he talked to you, Hughie and this lad Matthew Thompson. Tip-Toe Thompson? Has everyone on this island got a daft nickname?' asked El Cid.

A guy at the bar overheard the cop's question. 'I haven't,' answered Eddie No Bum, who didn't know he had a nickname.

'Right,' said Brock, 'here's how I would handle it. First, line up everyone who is still on the island all along the front. You can leave out the kids and the old grannies. But everyone else must line up. You got that?'

'I'm intrigued by your investigative process so far, Charlie. No, I really am,' El Cid added, though he really wasn't.

'Then we get an ocean of scopolamine...'

'Scopolowhat?'

'Scopolamine, El Cid. Have you never seen Where Eagles Dare? It's a truth drug. And the Gestapo were going to shoot it into the veins of American General Carnaby to get him to reveal all about the plans for the Second Front. Although the German High Command didn't know they actually didn't have a real high-ranking American General, but an American actor who looked like the real...'

'Aye, very funny. There's been a murder on this island and we

138

have nothing. The brass are getting a bit jumpy now. They had hoped that everything would have been done and dusted by now. Liked we'd come off the ferry and there'd be a guy standing there with his hands up in the air, shouting, "I did it! It was me!"'

Brock wasn't about to be derailed. 'Okay, I realise there can be side effects to scopolamine and it's not readily available over the counter at Boots. Okay, Millport might become an island of curiosities. Just like HG Wells' The Island of Doctor Moreau...'

'You should see a fuckin' doctor. R.I.P. always said you had a dangerous imagination. You stick to football, mate. Talking of our old pal, where is he?'

'Gilhooley phoned about an hour ago,' said Brock. 'He wants him to check and see if this is really the first murder on the island. Someone's called the office to say there was one a few years ago that has been kept quiet. So R.I.P. has donned the deerstalker and is off on pursuit of the truth. Good luck to him.'

'Don't you want to go and help him? You are a journalist, after all.'

'Aye, I'll go and assist R.I.P. as soon as he comes along to the Scottish Cup Final and tries to help me get aftermatch quotes from some grumpy old managers complaining about dodgy penalty-kicks, outrageous offside decisions, stupid red cards, the price of milk. No, he's happy in his field and I'm happy in my mine. Seriously, are you really hitting your head off a brick wall?'

'You better believe it, Charlie. It's hard to accept we are on such a small island and no-one appears to have seen anything. Most of them didn't see or hear anything beyond nine o'clock, anyway, because they were out of their box. Look at this place. Hughie was saying it's been packed since he opened the doors a couple of days ago. As someone has fallen out, someone has fallen in. The punters are down here for a good time. And then they don't remember much about it. Don't think too many came onto the island with murder on their mind. Mind you, some of the wives I've seen...'
The cop let the sentence drift off.

'Sounds a bit like Wembley before that game was torpedoed by the authorities, El Cid. Remember those good old days? You, R.I.P. and me down at the White House Hotel? Christ, did we do a serious bit of shagging in those days, did we not? Couldn't fail. As soon as the English birds heard the Scottish accent that was you in. Didn't matter if you had a face like a half-chewed caramel. You were in. Those were the days, my friend. Now I can't get a nod off a rocking horse.'

The door opened and R.I.P. entered. 'Case solved, Sherlock?' asked El Cid. 'Has there been a previous murder on the island already? Charlie was telling me your editor's had a phone call.'

'A lot of crap,' said the newspaperman, heading straight for the bar, showing a neat piece of footwork to sidestep a dancing cowboy. 'What're you having, guys? Pint, Brock? Half, El Cid?' He didn't wait for an answer. Calamity Jane was behind the bar. 'Calamity, when you've got a minute, please, a wee round down here. Where's Hughie?'

'Downstairs changing a barrel,' answered Calamity who didn't like answering to Calamity. 'You want me to give him a shout?'

'No, I'll speak to him later. Stick a brandy and port on the tab for him and one for yourself, please. Okay?'

'No problem.' Seconds later there was the sound of breaking glass.

Hughie returned and met up with the Three Amigos at the bottom of the bar. He passed over the drinks and said, 'Cheers to whoever bought me the drink.' R.I.P. waved.

'So what was the big story, seeing as we haven't had a sniff ourselves on this one?' asked El Cid.

'Oh, there was a bit of trouble about five years ago and a guy was found dead in his flat. Someone thought it was a bit of gay bashing, but that hasn't arrived in Millport yet. Give it time and it'll catch up with the Twenty-first Century...'

'People have been saying that for centuries,' chipped in Brock.

'Aye, so it would appear. I checked it out with the woman who owns the florists. She told me there had been an argument at the bloke's flat on Glasgow Street. Nothing serious, just two guys shouting and bawling at each other, both drunk. One staggered off into the night and, hours later, one keeled over with a heart attack. Dead before he hit the carpet. Only thirty-five-years-old. No foul play suspected. A genuine, one hundred per cent, good, old-fashioned cardiac arrest. So, no murder back then, gents.'

'And we're still waiting for our first drive-by shooting,' pointed out Hughie.

'Aye, but we do have a murder now,' said El Cid.' He drained his glass. 'Thanks, guys, I'm off for a wee walkabout. Maybe the murderer will return to the scene of the crime. I'll go and have a look and see if there are any ghouls out there who want a swatch at where Wild Bill Hickok was shot down. Freaks, creeps and geeks. Wish me luck.'

He headed for the door to a chorus of 'Good luck.'

'Seriously, maybe we could do El Cid a turn,' said Brock to Hughie and R.I.P.. 'But where on earth would we start? I do like a good murder mystery, but preferably when there's no chance of someone coming at me with a gun.'

'Brock, have you thought this through?' asked R.I.P. 'Wild Bill probably spent as much time on this island with you as anyone else.'

'Tell me about it,' said Brock, ruefully. 'My ears are still ringing. If there's anything you want to know about Wild fuckin' Bill Hickok, I'm your man. I might never watch another western. God knows who he was talking to when he wasn't in here. One thing's for sure - he would have been talking. In any case, he was chatting to Hughie, too. He was yittering away to Hughie when I came in on Friday afternoon.'

'Aye, that's true,' said the bar owner. 'It wasn't just the usual small talk you get with a punter. The weather, the economy, the price of a pint. Pulled out a pile of newspaper cuttings and started to tell me all about Wild Bill Hickok. And then you came in, my friend, and rescued me.'

'But he didn't just come walking into the pub and start talking about Wild Bill Hickok, did he?' asked Brock. 'There must have been some sort of preamble, surely?'

'Let me think,' said Hughie, pulling at an earlobe for inspiration. 'It was kind of busy, you know. He came in and came straight to the bar and leaned on it right beside me. I was pouring a few pints. What did he say?' Hughie looked pensive. 'I do remember calling him "mate" and he corrected me, telling me to call him Wild Bill Hickok. I wondered if he had already been drinking. Barking mad, but sober as a judge. He did say he'd been over at the Kentuckian. Aye, that's right. And he asked me when the bar brawl was due to start.'

'So was he looking for a fight?' asked Brock.

'Anything but,' answered Hughie, pouring another couple of pints of Guinness for some thirsty cowboys. 'No, he said he had already acted out one of those daft brawls in the Kentuckian earlier. No, he wasn't interested in another fight.'

'Could the one in the Kentuckian maybe have got a wee bit out of hand?' pressed R.I.P. 'These things can happen, can't they?'

'No, not if you have them early enough, before the booze takes over,' answered Hughie, continuing to think hard. 'They're just a bit of harmless fun. The cowboys flip a coin to see who gets to batter the other one over the head with the candy bottle. It's just a bit of nonsense. No, you saw him, Charlie. He wasn't a troublemaker.'

'Aye, Wild Bill was a nice enough guy...who liked to talk,' conceded Brock.

'Maybe we should have matched him up with Boring Brian. That would have been interesting,' said Hughie, passing over two immaculately-poured pints of Guinness. 'I can put a wee shamrock on that if you want,' he offered.

'Naw, chief, you're okay,' said one. 'We're Rangers fans.'

'Do we know if he went into any other pubs? That would be helpful,' said Brock.

'Honestly, don't know, Charlie,' said Hughie. 'Would take me two minutes to find out, though. I've got all the numbers here by the phone.'

'The cops will have visited everywhere, surely?' said Brock. 'It's not easy keeping cops out of pubs, is it? Any excuse and they're in.'

'This is a murder enquiry, remember, Brock,' said R.I.P. 'They've just taken a stiff off the island. The cops are lucky this is Sunday.'

Hughie, still looking a bit puzzled over the shamrock knock-back, talked to himself. 'We're Rangers fans? What does that mean? Do you want a shamrock on the head of your Guinness? No, thanks, we're Rangers fans? I'll work that one out some day,' he mused.

He asked R.I.P. 'Sunday? Why are they lucky it's Sunday?'

'There are only two quick bulletins on television tonight. Blink and you'll miss them,' answered the newspaperman. 'You'll get the national news on BBC and STV and, if you're lucky, they'll fit in about a minute of news from Scotland before the weather forecasts. They'll probably not even mention a death in Millport. Fuck, Scotland could be attacked by Switzerland tonight and it probably wouldn't get a mention.'

'Why would Switzerland want to ...'

142

'So, there will be no immediate pressure on the cops to come up with answers. Different story tomorrow, though. Lunchtime bulletins and two half-hour programmes on either channel at tea-time and there is no doubt at all that this murder will get mentioned. I would guess it would be in the first ten items, maybe top five. Possibly, lead item on a slow day. I would put money on it. That's when old Maverick is whisked out in front of the TV cameras to give the nation an update. And it's never very clever that he is still asking for witnesses to come forward for a murder that took place on Saturday on a tiny, wee island and then, suddenly, it's six o'clock on a Monday. Doesn't look good on anyone's CV. Maverick will want this one tidied up tonight or tomorrow morning, at the latest. Then he can put on his best smile, assemble the press corps and give himself a pat on the back while a country looks on.'

'So that's how it works?' pondered Hughie. 'You learn something new every day, don't you?'

The Man in Black at the opposite end of the bar nodded in agreement.

CHAPTER TWENTY-FIVE

3.45pm SUNDAY

'Howdy, stranger, what brings you to these here parts?' Hamish McNulty, veteran host of the Mitre, aka the Kentuckian for the next few days, greeted Charlie Brock as he squeezed in the front door, the pub still doing a roaring trade as hangovers were being topped up. There were a few shaky hands among the customers. 'Quick Draw McGraw, they ain't,' mused Brock.

'Oh, just thought I would see how the other half live, Hamish,' replied Brock. 'Slum it for a wee while.'

'You mean try the best pint on the island? Lager?' asked the bar owner as he stepped up to the pump.

Brock smiled and nodded. 'You better not let Hughie hear you saying that. He'll have the trades description people on you in a flash. You know what he says? "Try the rest, come back to the best."'

'Aye, good one, that. Wish I had thought of it,' said McNulty. 'One perfectly poured pint of lager. On the house. Cheers.'

Brock echoed, 'Cheers. Are you trying to seduce me? Get into my wallet?'

'Of course,' laughed McNulty, a small, wiry individual whose sharp features matched his business acumen. Here was someone born to deal with the public, an easy-going manner disguising an excellent and astute commercial brain. McNulty would never see seventy again, but he was as bright as a button. He realised Brock wouldn't about-turn after just one pint. He was a 'four or five man'. Hamish knew a few sports journalists and he welcomed them to his establishment during the quieter months. They would come onto the island, four or five of them, for a game of golf on a perfect course that, sadly, would normally be deserted during the autumn and winter months. As a bonus, the newspapermen would normally bring a few 'celebrities' with them and that helped rouse the locals to use the Mitre and listen in to some football talk among the so-called experts. So many newspapers had ex-footballers writing columns these days that it hardly left space in the sports sections for bona fide journalists.

Brock also realised how hypercritical a lot of these 'star columnists' were. They wouldn't utter two words - or, if they did, they normally ended in 'off' - to the press during their playing and managerial days. Then they retired or got the bump and you couldn't get them away from the media, their agents banging on doors at newspapers, television and radio. Brock actually liked most of them, but there were a few he would quite happily drop off the Empire State Building just to see how high they bounced. 'Mind you, with all that hot air,' he mused more than once, 'they would probably just take off and head for Staten Island.'

Brock accepted the pint from Hamish. 'Cheers,' he said again as he lifted the glass of ale to his lips. 'Aye,' he said as he tasted the brew, 'that's not bad at all. I'll tell Hughie he's got to buck up his ideas.'

'Busy over there?' asked McNulty. Brock smiled again. On this small and wonderful island he knew there were spies everywhere. Hamish would send out a local to do a wee walkabout to see what was happening in the other pubs, the opposition. Hughie did the same. All the bar owners followed the same practice.

'Aye, it's been chaotic,' answered Brock, still smiling. 'Here?'

'Aye, chaotic here, too,' replied Hamish. 'Can't complain. Getting my share.' The bar owner laughed.

'I'm sure you are,' said Brock, 'I'm sure you are.'

McNulty then asked, 'What's happening over at the west end? A dead cowboy? I've never seen so many police on this island. They were in here earlier this morning, disturbed my beauty sleep. Questioned me for about half-an-hour. What the fuck would I know about a dead cowboy over the other side of the island? Told them I didn't know anything. But they kept asking questions. "Where was I between the hours of 8pm and 10pm last night?" Where'd they think I would be? The busiest weekend of the year, the place packed out? Where'd they think I would be? Asked me if I had any witnesses to my whereabouts. Fuckin' hell, Brock. I told them to ask half the island. The place was stowed. I haven't even had time to check the till yet, but I can tell you it's groaning.'

'You do know the guy who was shot was in here?' asked Brock.

'Aye, I remember him,' said McNulty. 'Hard to forget him. A

lot of these weekend cowboys simply go through the routine like yourself. A checked shirt, a pair of denims, a belt with a big buckle, that sort of stuff. But he had the full bhoona. A real cowboy. And he was in early enough to get his name down for the Bar Brawl. Told me his pals had told him it was good for a laugh. He was quite insistent about getting a slot. Told me he would pay for it. I told him that wasn't necessary. I put him in the book for one o'clock.'

'Does Jimmy still film the fights in here?' asked Brock.

'Try and stop him,' smiled McNulty. 'He'll film anything that moves. Calls himself Jimmy B de Mille. Some eejit bought him a camcorder a few years ago and it goes everywhere with him. Man With A Camera, I call him. Aye, he's filmed everything so far over the past couple of days.'

'What does he do with the tape, Hamish? Does he keep it? Or just film over it?'

'Fuck me, Brock, have you joined MI5? You're asking more questions than the cops.'

'Old instincts die hard. There might be a scoop here, Hamish. Besides, you know I like a whodunnit. And you've have got a handle on everything that goes on in Millport.'

'Aye, I suppose so,' nodded the bar owner. 'Your business is my business. To answer your question, Jimmy files everything, absolutely everything. I'll bet he has kept everything he has ever filmed. It could be a dog having a pee up against a lamppost. That'll be filed under something. Probably "P".' Hamish laughed again, a full throaty job. 'Why are you asking?'

'I wouldn't mind having a look at some of that film. Do the cops know about the film? I'm sure they'd want to view it.'

'Now you're asking, Brock,' McNulty swept his hand over his full head of white hair. 'Don't know. Jimmy's not been in yet. He's due in about five o'clock. He'll have been out on the boat today. He always does a spot of fishing on a Sunday. I've offered him double wages to come in and help out this afternoon, but he's not interested. Tells me, "Never come between a man and his fish." Off his fuckin' rocker. Mind you, not that daft that he doesn't send in his wife to film the bar brawls when he's not here. He won't pass up easy money.' Hamish paused, scratched his chin and added, 'I suppose, then, that the cops haven't got to him yet. Unless they hire a boat and catch up with him over at Skate Point.'

'Hamish, have you heard the expression, "A cowboy can't walk on one leg alone?"'

'Can't says I have,' answered McNulty. 'What the fuck does that mean?'

'Wild Bill Hickok used those words when he was ordering up a second drink on Friday. New one on me, too.'

'Aye, I heard he had been over at Hughie's. Had his bar brawl here and then had a natter at the bar with the guy he whacked over the head with the bottle. What was that guy's name? He drinks in here quite a lot at the Country and Western Festivals. I've seen him a few times. He dresses up, too, in the cowboy gear. Always wears a bright lime green shirt and a red leather waistcoat. Fancy sheriff badges as cufflinks. I've joked with him not to get into a real gunfight. You couldn't fuckin' miss him. Stands out a mile. Wears that shirt every year. Never any trouble. He had a couple of large Macallans with Wild Bill Hickok and they shook hands at the end of their wee chat and the Wild Bill guy left. Headed straight to Hughie's, I'm told.' McNulty smiled again. 'A guy's got to have spies, Brock.'

'Anyway, Hamish, a cowboy can't walk on one leg alone.'

'If you want a fuckin' pint just ask for a fuckin' pint,' smiled Hamish.

'Can I have a fuckin' pint, please?' grinned Brock. 'And a fuckin' gin and tonic for yourself.'

CHAPTER TWENTY-SIX

3.50 pm SUNDAY

'Right, let me get this straight, Mr. Harris,' said El Cid, elaborately producing his notebook and fishing out a pen from the top pocket of his jacket. 'You don't remember anything after you left this pub last night? Nothing? Is that right?'

John Harris, stockbroker, from Morningside, in Edinburgh, aka Sitting Bull, swallowed hard. 'I didn't kill anyone.'

'I'm sorry, Mr. Harris. When I asked if you didn't remember anything after leaving this pub last night did you think I asked you if you had killed anyone?'

'No,' said a flustered Sitting Bull. 'I just assumed...'

'Please, just answer the question. Do you...'

'No,' said Sitting Bull. 'I don't remember anything. Nothing at all. I was drunk.'

'I see. So, in fact, you cannot account for your whereabouts between eight o'clock and ten o'clock last night?'

'The time when that bloke, Wild Bill Hickok, got shot?'

'Oh, so you know the time of the incident, do you? Interesting. I'll just take a note of that. "Suspect knows time..."'

'Suspect? What do you mean suspect? I'm a stockbroker. From Morningside. In Edinburgh.'

'Oh, now you are telling me stockbrokers don't commit murder?'

'You know what I mean,' Sitting Bull wasn't sitting comfortably. The cop had asked Vodka Joe to move to another table as he commandeered the area at the corner of the front window away from the rest of the cowboys. 'I'm a professional, you know.'

'Some sort of code? Do you take an oath? "I am a stockbroker and I pledge not to murder anyone." That sort of thing?'

'It's just that you don't expect a stockbroker or a professional to murder someone. That's what I'm trying to say, officer.'

'Did you know Adolf Hitler was a painter, Mr. Harris? Yes, he indulged in water colours. I don't suppose anyone thought a painter might one day want to rule the world. What do you think?'

'Hitler wasn't a stockbroker. I'm talking about stockbrokers.'

'Who did Adolf Hitler remind you of, Mr. Harris?'

'Charlie Chaplin.' Sitting Bull didn't even hesitate.

'Ah, yes, my point precisely. They looked alike, could have been twins. But one wanted to make us laugh and the other wanted to bomb our cities, take over our countries and commit unspeakable atrocities. Do you get my meaning, Mr. Harris? Appearances can be deceiving.'

'Charlie Chaplin wasn't a stockbroker, either.'

'Have you ever been angry enough to want to punch someone, Mr. Harris?'

'I'm not a violent man. I don't go around punching people.'

'Stockbrokers and professionals don't go around punching people, then?'

'I would think it would be highly unusual. Am I really a suspect?' asked Sitting Bull.

'We compile lists, Mr. Harris, and then we go through them very carefully. Process of elimination, Mr. Harris. At the moment you are merely helping the police with their enquiries. You've heard that expression before, I would expect?'

'Yes, of course, I have. I'll help as much as I can.'

'You also know that when we use the expression "helping the police with their enquiries" we often know the guy is guilty. Did you know that? It's just a polite way of us saying, "We've nailed the bastard and now we are going to get the truth." We then knock them about for a couple of days. We queue up to put the boot in. Guys will sign in to start their shift and the first thing they do is got down to the cells and kick shit out of the guy who "is helping the police with their enquiries." Gets the lads in the mood for the day ahead. We batter the suspects around the ribs, places that won't show all the bruising. We never touch the face. Wouldn't do for the guy turning up in court looking as though someone had taken a pneumatic drill to his face. Know what I mean, Mr. Harris?'

'I thought that only happened in films or in The Sweeney.' Sitting Bull was actually becoming concerned.

'Oh, no, Mr. Harris. You want to pop into the cop shop at Easterhouse any given Saturday or Sunday. There are a lot of mutilated testicles about the place. People who just don't know how to behave themselves. Now you're not going to be one of those blokes, are you, Mr. Harris? You don't want your plonker pulled, now do you?'

'I don't want my plonker pulled!' Sitting Bull's concern was growing.

'Too late, Chief,' smiled El Cid. 'Your plonker has just been well and truly pulled. Come on, get them in. Mine's a pint of heavy.'

'What...what do you mean? I'm not a suspect? You don't think I shot Wild Bill? I'm free to go?'

'Oh, for fuck's sake just get the pints in or I'll change my mind.'

Vodka Joe ambled over. 'Okay to get my spot back? Did you get your confession? He looked right fuckin' guilty to me.'

Sitting Bull walked to the bar. 'I knew he was kidding all along, Hughie. A beer for the copper and a large Bell's for me. Ha ha. I enjoyed that. I'm feeling better now. Nothing like a wee joke to help get rid of a hangover.'

'What's that unsightly damp spot at your groin?' asked Hughie as he poured a pint for El Cid.

CHAPTER TWENTY-SEVEN

'Brock! Twice in one day. Jings! Twice in two hours. I'm honoured. Has Hughie barred you?'

Charlie Brock had returned to the Kentuckian.

'All this sleuthing is thirsty work,' he rasped. 'Not barred yet, Hamish, but I'm working towards it. Only a matter of time and then I'm all yours.'

'Pint?' asked the pub owner.

'Aye, please, Hamish. Grab a G and T for yourself.' Brock looked around. 'Any sign of Jimmy?' he asked.

'Aye, he's on his way,' said Hamish. 'Happy as Larry. Caught a couple of big ones. He phoned in. I gave him an extra hour. The fish were biting. You reckon there might be something on these films? Jimmy said he would print out some stills for you. He sells them to the punters. Ten quid a throw. He's making a killing.'

'You might want to rephrase that, Hamish,' noted Brock. 'To be honest, I don't even know what I'm looking for. Maybe something will just jump out. There might be something that's so obvious that it's smack in front of your nose and you don't see it. Woods and trees, that sort of thing. You going to be quiet at any time tonight?' Brock looked around the bar that was still doing a brisk trade.

'Aye, it'll slow down around an other hour or so. People will want something to eat. We only do toasted sandwiches and that won't be substantial enough for some of the Billy Bunters we get in here. Jimmy'll be happy to help you. I'll have a break when he takes over and then I'll come back and give him an hour. That suit you?'

'Perfect, Hamish,' replied Brock. 'I'll give R.I.P. a buzz and let him know I'm here.'

'Who or what the hell's R.I.P.?' asked Hamish.

'It's Griff Stewart, Chief News Reporter of the News. An old pal of mine. One of the only sane guys left in the newspaper industry. He's only been down to Millport once before. Last year, in fact.'

'And you didn't think to bring him along and introduce him

to your Uncle Hamish? R.I.P.? Not sure I actually want to meet him.'

'Long story. Aye, shame on me, right enough. Actually, you won't like this, but we hardly stepped outside Hughie's for the whole of a long weekend. Spent a fortune.'

'And here's me saving up for a couple of weeks' retirement.' Hamish McNulty smiled. Brock knew he had enough stuffed away in mattresses to have retired twenty years ago. That was never going to happen. The bar owner would have to be lifted kicking and screaming out of his pub.

'Once all this is out of the way, we'll be back,' promised Brock. 'And this time we'll start off from here. Sound fair?'

'Couldn't ask for any more,' said Hamish. 'And, speaking of which, are you ready for any more?'

Brock nodded and called R.I.P. 'Hi, mate, I'm in Hamish's. The Mitre. Oh, The Kentuckian. I've nicked your deerstalker for a moment. You coming over? Aye, good. Bring El Cid if you can find him. He'll not be far away. I last saw him going into Hughie's. Aye, I want to have a look at Jimmy's films. You know, the fight scenes. Wild Bill's in one of them. You never know what you might spot. Worth a chance, eh?'

R.I.P. joined Brock at the bar in fifteen minutes. 'Maverick's just cancelled a press conference,' said the news reporter. 'Nothing fresh to tell an expectant nation. El Cid had five minutes with him in the backroom of the Tourist Information Centre. Told me he's going round the bend. The cops have talked to everyone on the island, I'm sure they've interviewed the Crocodile Rock a couple of times, too, but they're getting nowhere. Unless this is one great conspiracy, no-one has seen or heard anything. Anyway, where's this bloke Jimmy?'

'He's just arrived, down in the cellar just now. Hamish has set up a room upstairs for us to have a look at some film when it's quiet. Jimmy's got everything, and I mean *everything*, on film. He's transferred the lot onto his laptop. That's the good news. Do you want the bad news?'

'It's five pence dearer for a pint in here than it is in Hughie's?'

'Jimmy reckons he's got about three hours' worth of footage. The first fight every day takes place at High Noon. It normally lasts about ten minutes. Then there are another five at half-hourly intervals. So, that's six a day over three days. Eighteen bar room brawls coming to around a total of three hours. There's a bit of extra footage before and after the fights, so that'll stretch it a bit. Jimmy's already got it set and ready to go for the Wild Bill Hickok fight.'

'Three hours?' R.I.P. looked at his wristwatch. It was almost half past six. 'Can we fast forward through some of it?'

'Aye, I suppose we will have to. Our suspect, whoever the fuck he might be and if he's still here, can leave this island any time he wants and the cops will probably never get near him. We'll never know he was even here. Nobody asks for ID on this island. He could have stayed anywhere and paid cash.'

'What about Cal-Mac?' asked R.I.P. 'Do they keep a record of anyone coming onto the island?'

'Afraid not. They will ask for your car registration if you are buying a book of, say, five journeys, but if you're just popping over for the weekend, they don't bother. Don't suppose they've ever thought they might need border control over here.'

'Something's just dawned me, Brock,' said R.I.P. 'It's amazing there's never been serious crime over here before. Millport is the perfect place to commit a murder.'

CHAPTER TWENTY-EIGHT

6.05pm SUNDAY

'Thought you had him there, Sid,' said Vodka Joe, whispering out of the side of his mouth. 'Always thought he was a bit suspect, that guy. Dressing up as a fuckin' Indian on Country and Western Festival? Does he have a death wish or what?'

Vodka Joe reclaimed his place by the front window at the Nashville. 'You let him go. Why? I thought he was squirming, you were minutes away from a full confession, Sid.'

'We were minutes away from him shitting himself,' said El Cid. 'You're Vodka Joe, aren't you?' He offered his hand to the island's colourful character. 'Harry Booth, Detective Inspector of Strathclyde CID at your service. I bet you could tell a story or two, Joe, about the goings-on in Millport. You'll have a secret or two to tell, I would think. Right?'

Vodka Joe smiled his usual wee smile, touched the tip of his nose with the forefinger of his right hand and said nothing.

'As a matter of fact, Joe, where were you between the hours of eight o'clock and ten o'clock last night?' asked the cop returning the smile.

'Oh, am I going to get the same treatment as Sitting Bull?' he grinned. 'Am I "helping the police with their enquiries", too? Let's see now. Where was I between the hours of eight o'clock and ten o'clock last night? I'll tell you where I would *liked* to have been. I would have liked to have been snuggled up in bed with Gina Lollobrigida.'

'I thought she was great in Bueno Sera, Mrs Campbell myself,' said El Cid. 'Did you see that one, Vodka Joe?'

'Aye, I almost ripped my cock out of its socket at that one.'

'This doesn't answer the question, though, does it, Joe? What's your second name, anyway? Smirnoff? Cossack?'

'It's actually Smith,' said Vodka Joe. 'Fairly dull, eh? I prefer Vodka Joe.'

'Right, where were you...'

'Ach, I was in bed. On my own. Gina was washing her hair and couldn't make it.' He smiled his little smile again. 'Ask Hughie. He carried me home. One minute we were having a quiz about westerns and the next minute I'm off my seat and on the floor. Do you know how many times Yul Brynner took off his hat in the Magnificent Seven?'

'Aye, once, when he was digging the trenches outside the Mexican village before Eli Wallach and the Mexican bandidos turned up.'

'How the fuck did you know that?' Vodka Joe was clearly impressed.

El Cid smiled and touched the tip of his nose with the forefinger of his right hand and said nothing.

'You'll do for me,' said Vodka Joe. 'Not too many people know that. That's won me a vodka or two over the years, Sid.'

Vodka Joe then made a clumsy attempt to pick up his glass. He knocked it across the table. 'Oops, sorry, Sid. Thank Christ it was empty, eh?'

'Would you like a refill, by any chance, Vodka Joe?' grinned the cop.

'Well, if you're asking that would be very kind of you. I take back everything I've ever said about police. Large would be nice. Just to be sociable.'

El Cid ordered up a double vodka for his confidant and a pint of heavy for himself. 'One for yourself, Hughie,' he added.

'I bet you've been as sociable as a newt sometimes, Vodka Joe. Right?'

'You better ask Hughie. Cheers.' He raised his glass, looked at the clear liquid and put it to his lips. 'If only tap water tasted this good I would never leave my kitchen.'

'Aye, cheers,' returned the cop. 'So, you've got no recollection about Saturday night? None whatsoever?'

'Sorry,' Vodka Joe frowned. 'I would like to help, but I know nothing, Mr. Fawlty. One minute a quiz about westerns with your mate Brock and Bungalow Bob and the next - wham!, I'm out the game. Vodka can do that, you know. Okay one minute, fucked the next. Just creeps up behind you and hits you with a fuckin' sledgehammer.'

El Cid smiled, 'I think I'm going to have to remove you from our list of suspects, Vodka Joe. Hughie has already told me he gave you a Fireman's Lift home on Saturday afternoon. Said you were out your face. He's already vouched for your good character. You're free to go. Or stay here, if you prefer.'

'I'll stay here, if it's okay with you, Sid. By the way, what was Billy The Kid's real name? Bet you a pint you don't know.' Vodka Joe had just discovered he liked the company of the police. That was a first in his life.

'Aah, you think I'm going to say William H Bonney, don't you? A lot of people are suckered by that one. Nope, his real name was, in fact, William H McCarty Junior and, according to most records, he was born in New York City.'

'Okay, nice one,' conceded Vodka Joe. 'What did the 'H' stand for, then?'

'Henry. The name on his birth certificate was William Henry McCarty Junior. Strange that. You might expect his father to be named William Senior, wouldn't you? Nope, he was called Patrick. So, why he was called Junior we don't really know. His dad died quite early and the family moved to New Mexico. He also used the names Henry Antrim and Kid Antrim. Some folk thought that was some sort of tribute to his mother's Irish roots. County Antrim, that sort of thing. But, in fact, his stepfather was called William Antrim, so he used that name sometimes.'

'I don't suppose you could tell me which deodorant he used, too?'

'Probably Lynx Laramie,' said El Cid. 'Is that worth a pint of heavy?'

'I don't mind losing to the better man,' conceded Vodka Joe. 'I'll get them in. You fancy a vodka?'

'I'll stick to beer, thank you, Vodka Joe. I've got a long day ahead of me. I've got to find a murderer, you know.'

CHAPTER TWENTY-NINE

6.47pm SUNDAY

'This where Wild Bill Hickok punches the other guy.' Jimmy B de Mille moved his chair to the side as he adjusted his laptop on the table in front of him. Brock, R.I.P. and El Cid, who had just arrived after his chat with Vodka Joe, peered over his shoulder.

'Hey, that's not a bad punch,' exclaimed the cop. 'Could do with him in the Strathclyde Boxing Championships. Govan's cleaned up the last few years. He looks like he could fight at middleweight.'

'El Cid, the guy's dead,' said Brock. 'Remember?'

'How could I forget?' answered El Cid. 'Right, Jimmy, can you keep the action going, please?'

'Right, now here's where he hits the other bloke over the head with the bottle.'

'Hey, that's got to hurt,' said R.I.P.

Jimmy laughed, 'You never saw one of these bar brawls before? They're quite safe just so long as you remember to switch the glass bottles with the iced candy ones before someone gets walloped over the napper. Here's where the guy hits the deck. Realistic, eh? You'd be amazed how many punters want to buy pictures of themselves lying sprawled out on a bar room floor. They probably pop the photos into a frame and hang it over the fireplace at home. Might take some explaining if someone comes visiting and notices a photograph of someone spreadeagled on the floor of a pub. Takes all sorts, I suppose. I prefer naked ladies myself.'

'Can you just let it run for a wee while, Jimmy? Okay, there they are shaking hands, taking a bow and heading for the bar. All perfectly civilised. There they are having a drink. There's Wild Bill smiling. And there's the other guy - Two-Gun Jake, wasn't it? - scratching his head. What's Wild Bill doing now? Strumming an invisible guitar? He looks as though he is singing. Have you got sound on this, Jimmy? Can we hear what he's singing?'

Jimmy leaned forward and pressed a couple of buttons. Wild Bill's voice was drowned out completely by the noise of the punters in the pub. 'Sorry. That's the best I can do, lads. Maybe I'll get some sound booms set up next year. Sell the DVDs to the cowboys. Make a killing.'

'I wish you guys would stop using that expression,' said Brock. 'Right. Is there anything else that we should look at? Is that all there is of Wild Bill?'

'I normally leave the camera running for a wee while after the fight,' said Jimmy. 'There you are. They're still talking. Looks as though they're getting on well. I wish I could lip read. There's Two-Gun Jake buying a drink. There's Wild Bill shaking hands with Two-Gun Jake again. He's draining his glass and it looks as though he is preparing to leave. All looks perfectly amicable. Sorry, lads, I don't know what you were expecting.'

'Neither do we, unfortunately,' said Brock truthfully. 'Is that the end of the film? Jimmy, sorry to be a nuisance, but is there any way you could put it back to the start and I'll watch it again?'

'No problem. I hit this button and, zoom, we're back to the beginning. Okay to go?'

'Aye, if you don't mind. I'll buy you a beer later for your trouble.'

'Oh, no trouble at all. Great to have some excitement on the island. Maybe the police might want to buy the tape?'

'Hold onto it just now, Jimmy,' said El Cid. 'I think we can handle this on our own for the time being. No point in this place swarming with my colleagues. Somebody will hit the wrong button and erase the whole fuckin' thing.'

He looked at his wristwatch. It told him it was a minute before seven o'clock. 'Time I got back to Maverick,' said El Cid. 'Tell him nothing's happening here. See what else we can come up with. Maybe someone's already confessed?'

'And maybe I'll find sunken treasure at the bottom of my bath,' said R.I.P.

The newspaperman rose with his cop friend. 'Brock, you staying? I'll get along the road with El Cid and have a chat with Maverick. Might get something off the record.'

'Don't want to upset you, R.I.P.' said El Cid. 'But I don't think there is anything you don't already know. You probably know more than Maverick.'

'I'll hang on here for a bit,' said Brock, looking intensely at the screen on Jimmy's laptop. 'You go on without me, I'll catch up.'

'I've still got another half-an-hour before I've got to get back to work,' offered Jimmy helpfully. 'I'm happy to stay here with you, Brock. Help you fiddle with some nobs.'

'You married, Jimmy?' he asked.

'For my sins, yes,' replied Jimmy. 'Two boys, Jake and Zak. Why?'

'Just wondered,' replied Brock.

CHAPTER THIRTY

7.22pm SUNDAY

'Brock would quite happily have throttled him, especially when he produced that raft of newspaper cuttings from the old Wild West,' said Hughie Edwards, owner of the Nashville. 'Murder him? Don't think so. Too many witnesses.'

El Cid, had popped into the pub along with newspaperman, R.I.P., on their way along Stuart Street to meet DCI Bert Martin, aka Maverick, at the police HQ at the Cumbrae Tourist Information Centre. 'Very good. No, I'm talking about anything, however infinitesimal, you might have seen or heard the other night. And, yes, I'm doing some straw clutching here.'

'Honestly, El Cid, I would love to help you. Suddenly snap my fingers, like they do in the movies, and say, "Gee, I remember now." Unfortunately, I can't think of a single thing. Wild Bill came in on Friday afternoon after he had been to the Kentuckian, had a few beers right at this very spot, chatted to Brock, bored him rigid, prepared to leave the pub and told us he would be coming back in the evening. He returned about six o'clock and settled back at this very spot again with Brock and produced even more old newspaper cuttings. I left him to Brock. Quite happy to offload him, to be honest. I was busy enough.'

'Did he say anything before he left again? Any little thing?'

The bar owner slowly shook his head. 'No, don't think so. He was at the bar with myself, Brock and Tip-Toe. Oh, I asked him if he would be back on the Saturday, yesterday. Told me he had people to see and things to do. Yes, that's right, that's what he said. "People to see and things to do." His very words.'

'Did he say who he was going to see? What things he had to do?'

'No, definitely not. Didn't mention any names. Said he had a big day ahead. Told me he aimed to stop drinking by eight o'clock and get to his bed because he wanted a good night's rest before High Noon. He said he wanted to make Wild Bill Hickok proud of him by winning the Gary Cooper Cup. I asked him if he would be back in on Saturday and he said it was unlikely.'

'And that was all? You sure there weren't any names mentioned?'

'No, that was it. No names. We said farewell and he turned his back and made some sort of joke about the bottles on the bar.'

'What sort of joke?'

'Something about spirits. It wasn't very funny.' Hughie snapped his fingers, the way they do in the movies. 'He said he might get in some shooting practice. Aye, that's what he said. He was going to get in some shooting practice as he got ready for High Noon.'

'Fuckin' shooting practice? Where?'

'He didn't say. I know a lot of the cowboys practice at the back of West Bay, near the helipad.'

'I thought you said the gun marshals would take their guns off them if they saw them out of the holsters?'

'Aye, that's right, but that's normally just if the cowboys are in town. The gun marshals would never get near the cowboys at West Bay. They would see them coming for miles.'

'Did he say anything about anyone else getting in some shooting practice? Think, Hughie, this could be very important.'

'I'm afraid not. That was all. He would be in bed at an early hour as he got ready for High Noon. Wanted to make Wild Bill Hickok proud of him by winning the Gary Cooper Cup. And he probably wouldn't be in the pub on Saturday. You could ask Brock or Tip-Toe. But I'm certain there's nothing else. Sorry.'

El Cid looked at R.I.P. 'What does your famous newspaper intuition tell you?"

'Shooting practice? That's interesting,' R.I.P. said. 'Was he practising on his own? Or was he with someone else? Was there anyone around to time him or something like that? If there was, it would be nice to talk to that person.'

'My thoughts precisely,' said El Cid. 'So, the cowboys practised their quick draws on West Bay? Not far from the place where Wild Bill was found with a bullet between his eyes? Coincidence?' The Detective Inspector of Strathclyde CID rubbed a hand across his chin. 'You've given me something to think about, Hughie. Wish you had mentioned this earlier.'

'Sorry, El Cid, I didn't think it was important. How about a pint? Will that get me back into your good books?'

'And a wee hauf?'

'Good as done. R.I.P? Brandy? Gentleman's measure?'

'Perfectly acceptable offer, my good man.'

'Fuck's sake, lads. Keep this up and you'll drink me into house and home.'

CHAPTER THIRTY-ONE

7.48pm SUNDAY

'Sorry, Jimmy, can you go back right to the start? Before the Wild Bill Hickok fight? And then can we go to the other stuff after Wild Bill? Maybe fast forward through some of that. You never know, possibly something there.'

'No problem, Brock,' said Jimmy B de Mille, thoroughly enjoying every minute of viewing his masterpieces. 'Hamish used to laugh at me, but I knew that this camcorder would come in handy some day. Imagine if one of my films helped trap a murderer? Wow! Wouldn't that be something?'

'Aye,' said Brock, somewhat wearily. 'Maybe some Hollywood director might want to do the story.'

'Do you think Johnny Depp might want to play my role? Maybe Brad Pitt? Maybe George Clooney? How about James Bond? What's his name? Daniel Craig? He looks a bit like me.'

'Ailsa Craig looks more like you,' thought Brock. He said, 'Can we get back to the start, please?'

Reluctantly, Jimmy was transported back to Hamish McNulty's upstairs room at the Kentuckian after his brief flirtation with cinematic fame.

Brock looked round at Jimmy. 'We okay to go?'

Jimmy pushed a button and the screen on the laptop came to life. Brock looked at it. It was the same script as Wild Bill Hickok and Two-Gun Jake. Two cowboys meet at the bar, they have a wee chat, one throws a punch, the other falls on his arse, the other cowboy picks up a bottle off the bar, walks over and smashes it over his head. The stricken guy remains on the floor. The upright cowboy takes a bow. His victim gets to his feet and he takes a bow. They link hands and both take a bow. And then they go back to the bar and have a drink. Not exactly Dances With Wolves, thought Brock.

'I do all the scripting,' said Jimmy proudly. 'Good, eh? Took me hours to write that. Copied a wee bit from a John Wayne film, I admit. But worth my while, eh?'

'Aye, great,' said Brock. 'Who puts the set together?'

'Oh, the stuff on the walls? The flags and the guns? The old prints? That's me and Hamish. We do that together. Some pubs don't bother. They just change their signs outside and don't care what the inside looks like. Me and Hamish want to make it a bit more authentic. We reckon if the punters are going to get dressed up for the weekend, it's the least we can do. What does Hughie do at The Nashville?'

'Much the same,' said Brock. 'Stars and Stripes, Confederate flags, couple of toy guns, a picture of him and Maggie dressed up in old western gear. Sepia-coloured picture in a frame. Quite good, actually.'

'I wonder if Jeanie would be up for that? Wife's a bit strange about getting her photograph taken. Says they make her look fat. Won't even let me film her. I've told her film adds about ten pounds, but she still doesn't want to know.'

Jimmy handed Brock a pile of stills. 'These might be helpful,' Brock picked up a couple of prints. He said, 'How many of these pictures do you take? There looks about three or four hundred here.'

'Aye, that's just about right. You've got three full days there, Brock, six fights a day, eighteen in total. Probably about twenty snaps per fight. What's that? Three hundred and sixty. Aye, that's about right. The cowboys can't get enough of them.'

Brock lifted and looked through a pile. 'Are these photographs in any particular order, Jimmy?'

'Of course, they are. Let's see now. The top one will be the first fight at High Noon on Friday.' Jimmy picked up a snap and turned it over. 'There you are, perfectly filed. It says here, "Day One. High Noon. Fight No.1. Sam Wilson (left)." And there's the number 6 beside his name and a tick and the letters CA. The other guy is Tom Simpson and there's a number 4 beside his name, but no tick. And there's the date, September 3, tomorrow.'

'And what does that tell us, Jimmy?' asked Brock, slightly intrigued.

'The guy on the left, Sam Wilson, has ordered six prints and the tick with the letters CA tells me he's already paid. CA means cash. CH is cheque. The other bloke, Tom Simpson, has ordered four, but there's no tick so he hasn't paid yet.'

'What does the date mean?'

'Oh, that's when he is coming in to pick up his prints and settle the bill. A tenner each, forty quid in the bank. I'm getting paid for something I would do for nothing. Isn't life wonderful?'

'Aye. And there's no date beside the Wilson guy. That's because he's paid, right?'

'You catch on quick, Brock. I take cash or cheques. Haven't got round to plastic yet. Hamish doesn't trust plastic. Cash or a cheque with a name and address and a contact number on the back just in case it's rubber. Can't be too careful. Good wee system, eh? I make a point of trying to get everyone's address.'

'Why would you want all their addresses, Jimmy?'

'You'll never make it in business, Brock. I take snaps of the island all year round. Different views every year. Spring, winter, autumn, summer. Sun shining, snow falling. Snow is great for business. We don't get a lot of snow over here, what with the salt air and everything. But when it snows I'm out with my camera straight away. Honestly, some of the images are just brilliant. I'll select a few and post them off to all the addresses I've taken in at the Country and Western Festival. I stick in a wee note saying I'm compiling a calendar of Cumbrae if they're interested. Delighted to tell you, Brock, a lot of them are up for it. There's one old dear in Edinburgh who orders fifty calendars every year. Fifty! Every year! She's got relatives all over America, Canada, Australia, New Zealand. I sell them at £15 each and I'm guaranteed £750 from that old dear straight away. I think she's about eighty. Hope she's got a couple of years left in her. She pays for Jake and Zak's Christmas on her own, God bless her.'

'Aye, good luck with that, Jimmy,' said Brock, rifling through the prints. 'Wild Bill Hickok had his fight at one o'clock on Friday, so there were only two fights before him. He'll be near the top. Ah, that looks like our boy.' Brock selected a snap from the pile. 'Let's see now.' He flipped it over. He read Jimmy's carefully printed filing system. 'Thank the Lord the boy's meticulousness,' thought Brock. 'Okay, it's Day One and it's one o'clock. It's Fight No.3. We've got James Hitchcock on the left. We've got the number 10 beside his name, but no tick and no CA or CH and there's the date, September 2, today. That tells me he's ordered ten prints, right? He hasn't paid yet and he was expecting to pick them up today and settle his bill. Right?'

'Spot on, my friend,' said Jimmy.

'And this other guy, let's see, is Andy Boone. There the number 4 beside his name, a tick and the letters CH. He's ordered four and he's paid by cheque? Do the guys get their prints immediately, Jimmy?'

'Just about. I tell them to come back after the last fight of the day. It normally starts about two-thirty and I'll film that and then convert everything to stills. I can have everything ready by about three-thirty. Pop everything into their respective envelopes, stick their names on the front and Robert's your mother's brother. I offer a full money back guarantee if the punter's not fully satisfied. I let them inspect them before money changes hands. I've been doing this for ten years or so and you know how many dissatisfied customers I've had, Brock? Go on, take a guess.'

Brock decided the helpful barman deserved a compliment. 'Looking at the quality of your prints, Jimmy, I would say none. Correct?'

'Spot on again, Brock.'

'If I ever get in a bar brawl and I want my photo taken lying on a pub floor, you'll be the first guy I call for.'

Brock continued to examine the photographs with Wild Bill Hickok in action. 'You know, Jimmy, he did look the real deal, didn't he?'

'Aye,' said Jimmy forlornly. 'Pity he's dead. Ten pictures at £10 a pop. He's just cost me a hunner quid. I suppose that's the world of big business for you. Peaks and troughs.'

'Aye,' said Brock, 'I'm sure Wild Bill's gutted at letting you down.'

CHAPTER THIRTY-TWO

8.06pm SUNDAY

'I don't mind telling you I'm getting a bit of grief, lads.' Detective Chief Inspector Bert Martin, aka Maverick, gazed wearily through the ceiling-to-floor front window of the Cumbrae Tourist Information Centre.

Darkness's grey cloak was descending upon the island. The Firth of Clyde was inky blue. There was still hardly a breeze worthy of note. 'Paradise out there,' he said, 'and hell in here.'

Harry Booth, his loyal Detective Inspector, and Griff Stewart, the newspaperman he trusted completely, shared in his misery. Maverick stood at the window, admiring an island he knew nothing about. 'First time I've ever set foot on this place,' he said, wistfully. 'I'm an Arran man myself. But just look at this place. Breathtaking. Those old Victorian buildings. Fabulous, wonderful architecture. Built to last when builders had pride in their work. Bet you people come onto this island and don't even notice what's all around them. A guy could retire to a spot like this. And, yes, before either of you say it, I realise that might only be about a week away. But it's little wonder this place is called one of the gems of the Clyde. It's so peaceful, so tranquil.'

He sighed and added, 'Pity there's been a fuckin' murder.'

El Cid told his boss about James Hitchcock's parting shot in the Nashville on Friday night. 'He was going to get some shooting practice on Saturday. He was preparing to take part in High Noon at the Newton Beach today.'

'Shooting practice?' asked Maverick. 'Did he go off with someone else? Did he test himself against another cowboy?'

'We don't know yet, Boss,' said El Cid. 'He was seen in the Confederate HQ, the Georgics Hotel, over at Quayhead Street early on Saturday. Place was busy. He was on his own. The barman talked to him briefly and was told he wanted to be called Wild Bill Hickok. He then went walkabout and was seen in various parts of the town. Was spotted heading up towards Glaidstane Point. Do you know that's the highest point on the island? Didn't appear to have a care in the world. Strolling along in all his gear, big coat, the lot, despite the sun blazing out of the sky. A bloke doing a bit of sightseeing. And always on his own.'

Maverick, stretched to his full 5ft 11in as he turned back from the window. 'What do the newspapers think, Griff? Are they going to crucify me tomorrow? There are a few guttersnipes out there who wouldn't mind sinking their size tens into my exposed bollocks. I've already seen a few of your mates on the island. That bloke, what do you guys call him? Sniper? Aye, Ken Cameron of the Gazette has already paid me a visit. He wanted to know when I was going to call a Press Conference. I told him I would do that as soon as I had anything to add to the statement we've already put out. He grunted something and left. Well named - Sniper.'

'Aye, gets guys like me a bad name, Bert,' replied R.I.P. who had more than a few run-ins with a thoroughly despicable rival. 'He would sell his grannie for a story. You can be sure he'll be looking under every rock for a line on this story. He won't lose any sleep in running a story that would make every cop in the land look like Noddy.'

Maverick held up a hand, 'Ach, you're only telling me what I already know, Griff. Sniper smells blood on a wounded animal and he'll go and give it a good kicking just to make sure it's in pain. I've seen him in action.'

Maverick dragged a hand across his bald pate. 'Christ,' he exclaimed, 'I'm sure I had hair when I first came onto this island.' He managed to smile for a moment. Then back to seriousness. 'Actually, I can't blame anyone for giving me a doing,' he admitted somewhat candidly. 'The scrambled-egg brigade back in Glasgow just won't understand why we cannot apprehend a criminal on a toaty, wee island. Honestly, you would believe it would be an open-and-shut job, wouldn't you? Where can you hide on Millport? We don't even know if our guy is still here. He could be in fuckin' Venezuela.'

Another deep sigh. 'Everybody has been interviewed, all the bloody toy guns have been checked, doors have been knocked, tents have been visited, every landlord on the island has been virtually interrogated. Nothing. Absolutely nothing. I'm not having a bad dream, am I?'

At that moment R.I.P's mobile phone shrieked to life.

CHAPTER THIRTY-THREE

8.11pm SUNDAY

'Get your arse over here, R.I.P. I think I've got something. Bring El Cid.' There was an excitement about Charlie Brock's urgent tones.

The sportswriter, with his heart pounding in his chest, turned to Jimmy B de Mille once again. The barman looked at his wristwatch. 'Brock,' he said, 'I've only got another five minutes. Hamish will be sending out the SAS to look for me.'

'Don't worry about that,' said Brock with a sweep of his right hand. 'This is a lot more important. You want to see your name in lights, don't you?'

Jimmy didn't hesitate. 'Aye, you're right.' An image of the barman and Jennifer Lopez sharing a black pudding supper at the Crocodile Rock snapped into his mind. 'Hamish can go fuck himself.'

'Right. Can you go back, let's see, to the third fight on Saturday? The one o'clock fight. Can we run through that again?'

'We've already looked at it about three thousand times, Brock,' protested Jimmy, restarting his laptop.

'Let's look at it three thousand and one times, Jimmy. Let's see if I'm not hallucinating. Okay to go? Right work your magic, Spielberg.'

Even the barman seemed to be tiring of watching the same piece of film time after time. But he did like the nickname Spielberg. And he did have the hots for Jennifer Lopez. He set up the laptop in front of Brock and pressed the button. 'When I say "freeze" stop the action, Jimmy. Okay?'

'Fine,' he said.

Brock looked at the screen. 'I see you've changed angles for the fights on Saturday, Jimmy. Any reason for that?'

'Aye, the stuff I took on Friday was from the table at the TV in the corner. It's a good angle and you get a good view along the bar. But the punters wanted to see the horse racing on Saturday, so I was shifted to a more central place. Does it make a big difference?'

'If I'm right, it will make the world of a difference, Jimmy.

Right, there are the two cowboys meeting and greeting. They're flipping a coin to see who gets the go-ahead to smack the other over the head with the bottle. So far so good. Now they come away from the bar and...FREEZE!'

Brock positively roared giving Jimmy a start. 'Christ, Brock, I wish you wouldn't shout, there's nothing wrong with my hearing.' He clicked on his mouse and the picture came to an abrupt halt.

'Can you see what I see, Jimmy?' asked Brock.

Jimmy, slightly puzzled, looked at the screen. 'I see two cowboys setting up for...'

'Forget the cowboys,' said Brock. 'Look at the mirror behind the bar.'

Jimmy squinted once again. 'I can see the mirror, so what?'

'Look at the reflection, Jimmy. What do you see now? What do you see in the mirror?'

Jimmy peered at the laptop. 'Maybe it would be better if I brought it up a bit, Brock.' He tapped on the mouse a couple of times to enhance the image. 'What's that, Brock?' he asked.

'That, my young friend, could be the biggest clue in the case, if I am not mistaken.'

'Christ!' exclaimed the barman. 'Who's that?' He double-clicked the mouse, bringing up the image until it began to pixelate.

'Go back a bit, Jimmy. Right stop there. What can you see?'

Jimmy adopted an earnest expression. 'Someone's taking a rifle off the fuckin' wall,' he practically shouted. 'Someone's stealing one of Hamish's rifles. Why the fuck would they do that?'

Brock ignored the question. 'Right, Jimmy, can we fast forward to, say, one o'clock this afternoon?'

'Aye, not a problem,' said the barman. Within a minute the action had moved on twenty-four hours. Brock concentrated on the screen. 'Right, Jimmy, your missus took this film at the same angle as yesterday? Okay?'

'Aye, the football would have been on earlier. Jeannie wouldn't have got near the TV.'

'Let's roll some film and when I shout "freeze..."'

'Just say "freeze", please. My eardrums are still ringing.'

'Right, Jimmy. Let's see what we've got today.' The film rolled and Brock couldn't stop himself. 'FREEZE!' he shouted.

'Fuck's sake, Brock, you've just done in two perfectly good lugs.' He stopped the action.

'Look at that,' said Brock. 'The rifle's back on the wall. I didn't notice it when I first came into the bar, but I'll bet it's still on the wall right now. Nip downstairs, Jimmy, and have a quick look to see if it's still there. Don't touch it. Please don't touch it. Tell Hamish we'll be finished in a few minutes. Tell him I'll buy him a large G and T for hiring his barman.'

'And I want a pint. I don't come cheap,' said Jimmy as he swiftly descended the backstairs that took him down to the lounge next door to the bar.

'What's keeping you?' Hamish required bar assistance as the Kentuckian began filling with cowboys anxious to make absolutely certain they didn't remember anything about the journey home.

Jimmy peered over Hamish's shoulder. 'Aye,' he said, 'it's still there, right enough.'

Perplexed, Hamish looked in the direction of Jimmy's gaze. 'That wall? Aye, it's been there for about two hundred years.' Jimmy wasn't listening.

The door opened and in stepped R.I.P. and El Cid. Hamish greeted them. 'Hi, lads, you look out of breath. What're you having?'

'A nervous breakdown, I think,' said R.I.P.

'A heart attack,' added El Cid. 'Okay, to go upstairs, Hamish? Brock thinks he's got something.' 'Knock yourself out,' said Hamish.

The cop and the news reporter arrived a few seconds behind Jimmy. 'We've just broken the two-minute mile, Charlie, this better be good,' wheezed El Cid, still trying to get his breath back.

'This might just be better than good, El Cid,' said Brock. 'Jimmy, can we go back to one o'clock yesterday, please? Let's run through it one more time for my two friends here.'

El Cid and R.I.P. watched the film, looked at the frozen images and were trying desperately to look impressed. 'What's the exact significance of this, Brock?' asked R.I.P. 'What can you see that we can't?

'Look carefully at the reflection in the mirror behind the bar. There's someone taking down that rifle off Hamish's wall on

Saturday afternoon,' said Brock. 'And, twenty-four hours later it's back on the wall.'

'So?' asked El Cid. 'I'm failing to pick up the thread here, Charlie. Someone takes a rifle off the wall on the Saturday and returns it on the Sunday. So what?'

'When something is out of the ordinary it becomes extraordinary,' said Brock.

'What the fuck are you talking about, mate?' queried R.I.P.

'It's something old Agatha once wrote. Or was it Conan Doyle? Anyway, humour me, I'm working on a hunch here. You still got forensics on the island El Cid? Get them over here right now. I think you'll find that rifle is the murder weapon. And the hand in the picture belongs to the murderer.'

CHAPTER THIRTY-FOUR

9.57pm SUNDAY

'So Wild Bill Hickok was shot and killed because he called Two-Gun Jake a cowboy?'

Harry Booth, aka as El Cid, Detective Inspector of the Strathclyde CID, shook his head. 'I've heard it all now. He was shot and killed because he called the other guy a cowboy? At the Country and Western Festival in Millport? Who would believe it?'

'I figured something happened with Wild Bill in the Kentuckian,' said Charlie Brock, sipping a pint of lager at the bar of The Nashville. 'Maybe it was just the way he said a couple of things before he left us on Friday night. "People to see. Things to do." I knew he had come down to the island early on Friday. He told me he was on his own, his first time on the island. I was working on the hunch that the only other place where he had spent any time was the Kentuckian before he arrived at Hughie's. So it stands to reason that he wouldn't have had the opportunity to meet too many people. He was involved in the one o'clock bar room brawl over at Hamish's. Jimmy's film showed us that he had a couple of drinks with the guy he walloped with the bottle. Then there is no sign of him when Jimmy filmed the half-past-one fight. He was probably on his way here.'

'Aye, that's about right,' said Hughie. 'He got in just about half-past-one, in fact. I was waiting for the coach to arrive with some more punters. It was about fifteen minutes before you arrived, Brock.'

'Was he acting odd when you spoke to him, Charlie?' El Cid was anxious to get a clearer picture.

'Odd? Ach, not really,' replied Brock. 'A wee bit off the wall with all his cuttings about Wild Bill Hickok and the like, but I wouldn't have pegged him as seriously odd. I thought at the time he might be a bit squirrely. But he fitted right into the scheme of things in the bar that day. Although he could talk the hind legs off a mule, I found him strangely entertaining. If I ever go on "Who Wants To Be A Millionaire?" and I get to the last question I've got to hope Chris Tarrant asks me something about Wild Bill Hickok. There's nothing I don't know about that boy.'

Brock lifted his pint pot and slurped lustily. 'I deserve this,' he smiled.

'Right, carry on, Brock,' said R.I.P. 'You sure you don't want to switch to news? Gilhooley could make you my assistant.'

'I'll pass on that, thanks, R.I.P.' laughed Brock, leaning on the bar while taking centre stage. 'Right. Where were we? Aye, that's why I believed anything we could find on Jimmy's films might point us in the right direction. The fight he had with Andy Boone, Two-Gun Jake, looked harmless enough. They were obviously fooling around at the bar. It looked as though Wild Bill was singing to Two-Gun Jake and was even strumming an invisible guitar. Wild Bill had stuck up a drink. Then they were chatting. And at one stage it looked to be a wee bit serious. Wild Bill was smiling, but his drinking companion didn't look too happy.'

'That must have been when Wild Bill called him a cowboy,' said El Cid.

'That's right,' said Brock. 'He ruffled a few feathers with that comment. Nothing too serious, obviously. Boone even bought him another drink. They continued talking and that's when they struck the deal to have a gunfight. Sure of it. That's what the other handshake was all about. It wasn't a farewell handshake. They were sealing the bet. They were agreeing to a duel. And they knew they would have to do it away from the prying eyes of the gun marshals. So, they settled on a corner at West Bay when they knew the place would be quiet. Nine o'clock on the dot on Saturday night. They would have the place to themselves. Everyone would be getting out of their faces in the pubs. They would have their own private shoot-out to see who was the top gun. According to Boone, they had bet a large Macallan on the outcome.'

'But Wild Bill told us he would be in his bunk by about eight o'clock on Saturday night,' said Hughie. 'Remember?'

'Ach, probably a little bit of subterfuge,' said Brock. 'At that time he knew he would be having his gunfight with Boone at nine o'clock at the West Bay. He wasn't about to invite us over to see his prowess with the equalisers.'

'The equalisers?' queried R.I.P.

'Aye, that's what he called his guns,' answered Hughie. 'He

showed them to Brock and me. He looked at them in much the same way a mother looks at her newborn child. Honest. They were his babies. Anyway, I'm sure he would have loved an audience at West Bay, but he couldn't take the chance of someone dropping it in the ear of a gun marshal. That would have ruined everything. He also said he might get in some shooting practice. Now we know exactly what he meant. He would warm up for High Noon with a gunfight with Two-Gun Jake. Quickest draw wins – just like at school.'

El Cid took over. 'Two-Gun Jake, Andy Boone, is now spilling the beans to Maverick as we speak. He took the rifle off the wall at the Kentuckian and hid it inside his waistcoat. He didn't have a clue that it was a real rifle and it had one bullet in the spout.'

'Why did he even bother taking the rifle off the wall?' queried Hughie, allowing Maggie to take charge of the bar as the cowboys thundered their alcohol levels to a dangerous high. 'He had two guns in his holsters, hadn't he? What was the matter with them?'

'I think I can answer that one, Hughie,' said Brock. 'I'll bet Two-Gun Jake actually believed Wild Bill would be too fast for him in a conventional draw for their guns. He aimed to surprise Wild Bill by whipping out the rifle from underneath his waistcoat and firing that at him. My Christ, he must have got some fright when the bloody thing went off.'

'I think Wild Bill would've got an even bigger fright,' said Hughie. 'Poor soul. Imagine that rifle being loaded all those years? Hamish told me he found it lying around his pub after a Country and Western Festival about ten years ago. Didn't think anything about it. Just thought it was a toy. Didn't even bother to tell the police. Why would he? Just chucked it in with the rest of the Wild West stuff when he was clearing up and dusted it down and put it on his wall every year. Could've blown his head off while he was cleaning it. Jeezus. You never know the minute. So, there was a bloody loaded rifle in clear view of everyone for about a decade? Any cowboy could've taken it off the wall for a joke and shot someone.'

'Well, that's exactly what happened, Hughie,' said Brock.

'Aye, our forensics are now looking at that rifle very closely,' said El Cid. 'Apparently, it's quite unusual, according to the experts. It's a model of an 1892 Winchester with lever action and a modified stock. The barrel has been cut down to nine inches. Quite rare, I'm told. Known in the trade as "Mare's Leg", apparently.'

'Was it worth a few quid? Hamish will go bonkers if he discovers he's been sitting on a valuable antique,' quipped Hughie.

'Don't know about it being valuable, Hughie, but we would like to know where it came from in the first place. Who brought a loaded rifle onto this island for a Country and Western Festival? Why would anyone do such a thing? Did they even know it was loaded? Did they know it was a real weapon? Did they leave it here on purpose? Was that their main aim? To lose it among a pile of toys? Why not drop it into the Firth? Has it been used in other crimes? Forensics are going to have a field day with this. Could you even start to guess the amount of fingerprints that will be on it? There's everyone Hamish has employed for the past decade, for a start. It's been on a wall all those years and any punter could've touched it. How many cowboys on the island this weekend? Twelve thousand, according to Cal-Mac. Multiply twelve thousand by ten years and we've got one hundred and twenty thousand possible fingerprints. Looks like forensics might need to enlist the help of the Miami guys to give them a hand with this one.'

'I've got to ask you, Brock,' said R.I.P. 'Did you have an inkling that it was this guy Andy Boone?'

'I could come over all Sherlock and say, "Elementary, my dear Stewart," but that wouldn't be quite true. I thought Boone might be involved somehow because Wild Bill hadn't actually bumped into too many people on the island. And he had spent a wee bit of time with him in Hamish's. But I didn't really think it was possible for someone to come over here for a bit of fun during the Country and Western Festival and then actually shoot and kill someone. And, after watching the film of the two guys, there didn't seem to be any animosity.'

'You were sure when we were in Hamish's earlier, though. You pointed El Cid in his direction. What changed?' asked R.I.P., secretly impressed by his old mate's powers of deduction.

'That's easy,' grinned Brock. 'There aren't too many lime green shirts with huge sheriff badges as cufflinks on this island. You could see a fair bit of his cuff on Jimmy's film in the reflection on the mirror when he stole the rifle. Had to be him. Maybe if he had a better fashion sense we might still be searching. Either way, we would have got the fingerprints off the rifle. And if he was in the system...'

'El Cid would have had him bang to rights,' smiled Hughie, still doing his damndest to make it as a stand-up comedian. 'Get it, lads? Bang to rights?'

R.I.P. sighed. 'My God, isn't life cheap? Shot dead for calling someone a cowboy?'

'There was something else we should have noticed,' said Brock. 'Those photographs Hughie took of Wild Bill. His guns were the right way round in their holsters. Wild Bill always wore them the way his hero did with the handles the wrong way round. So, he went for his guns and Two-Gun Jake produced the rifle and popped him. Right between the eyes. Two-Gun Jake was so startled he tried to clean up the crime scene. Couldn't believe he had actually shot someone. Was probably in some sort of state of shock. Wasn't really thinking when he put Wild Bill's guns back in their holsters the wrong way round. Or the right way, as he would have thought. His fingerprints will be on those ivory handles, too. The guns had obviously dropped to the ground. That blown-up picture from Hughie's mobile showed some mud on the nozzles of both revolvers. Wild Bill kept those guns immaculate. That was another clue that we missed. Aye, it's right. Whenever something is out of the ordinary it becomes extraordinary. Those gun handles should have been pointing out the way and the revolvers would never have had any dirt on them.'

Bert Martin, Detective Chief Inspector of Strathclyde CID, shoved open the door to the pub and made straight for Brock. He extended his right hand. 'Great work,' he said. 'I was heading for the gallows there. Could feel the noose tightening around my neck. Or my testicles.' He smiled. 'You're a genius, Brock. Right up there with the guy who invented the wheel.'

'Actually, that guy wasn't a genius,' interrupted Hughie. 'It was the guy who invented the other three. No applause? I think I'll stick to pouring pints.'

Maverick continued, 'Andy Boone is over at the cop shop. He's helping us with our enquiries, as they say. Seems happy enough to tell the entire story. Actually feel a bit sorry for him. I've told him to get a lawyer. He thinks we're going to charge him with murder.

We won't, of course. It was hardly premeditated, but I'll let the Procurator Fiscal sort that out.'

Hughie stuck up a large glass of Cutty Sark for the DCI. 'Cheers, Hughie,' said Maverick, lifting the drink swiftly to his lips. 'I asked Boone why he didn't just own up. He told me he didn't think we would believe it had been an accident. I also asked him why he didn't get off the island on Saturday night. He had plenty of time to get the last ferry. He said he didn't want to attract attention to himself. He had made arrangements to meet people in the Kentuckian after High Noon and thought it might arouse suspicions if he was suddenly missing. He could have been long gone on the Saturday and we would have been none the wiser.'

'Actually, that's not the case,' said Brock. 'We would still have nabbed him. Once we had identified the lime green shirt and sheriff badge cufflinks in Jimmy's film, we would have got his name and address from the back of the cheque he wrote when he was buying the pictures of his brawl with Wild Bill. Jimmy doesn't trust anyone. If your cheque bounces, he'll hunt you down to the end of the earth. Of course, Two-Gun Jake didn't realise how helpful he was being when he signed his name and address and, for good measure, added his mobile phone number. That was before he shot someone.'

Maverick swallowed another mouthful of whisky. 'Aah, lovely. You know I asked Boone why he didn't just dump the rifle in the Firth. He told me that would have been theft. He had to return it to its owner. He had just shot someone between the eyes and he was worrying about theft.' He sipped again. 'We're going to have a word with Hamish McNulty, too, I'm afraid. He's had a loaded weapon on his premises and doesn't own a gun permit.'

'I'm sure he'll talk his way out of that,' smiled Hughie.

Another gulp of neat whisky. Another sigh from Maverick. 'We've got right out of jail here. My officers checked every single weapon on this island apart from the ones that are on the walls of the pubs. As a matter of interest, how many have you got in here, Hughie?'

'Five,' answered the bar owner. 'You want me to check them to see if any's loaded?'

'Might not be a bad idea,' said Maverick, winking. 'Actually, I can't blame my troops for overlooking those guns. They do look like toys, don't they?' The cop checked his wristwatch. It was just going beyond 10pm. He turned to R.I.P. 'Have you filed your story yet, Griff?' The newspaperman said, 'Aye, it's gone. Gilhooley's worked on it and the first editions will be just about to hit the streets as we speak. Front page splash. Nice wee exclusive. Stuck it right up Sniper's arse.'

'Good for you,' said Maverick. 'I think I better call a Press Conference for your colleagues and give them the good news. But, before I do that, I think I'll have another large Cutty Sark and whatever you gentlemen are having. Agreed?' There wasn't a single dissenting voice.

Maverick grinned. 'Wild Bill Hickok shot between the eyes by Two-Gun Jake here on Millport? Amazing. Isn't life amazing?'

'Aye,' said Brock. 'And death's quite amazing, too.'

CHAPTER THIRTY-FIVE

9.36am MONDAY, SEPTEMBER 3

'Poor Wild Bill Hickok, his life too soon to surrender,
  Should have stayed in the Nashville and gone on a bender.'

Hughie Edwards stepped forward and took a bow. There was a ripple of applause from the audience in the Nashville. Brock, R.I.P., El Cid, Vodka Joe, Sitting Bull, Tip-Toe Thompson, Boring Brian and Bungalow Bob were among those in attendance for a pre-opening pint at 9.30am.

'Is that it?' asked Brock. 'When we said last night that we would all pen a fitting ode to Wild Bill Hickok, that was the best you could come up with? Christ, Hughie, you really put your heart and soul into that, didn't you?'

'It rhymes, doesn't it? What more do you want?' said the bar owner, adding somewhat defensively, 'I wasn't very good at poems at school.' Inspirationally, he offered, off the top of his head, 'Rub a dub dub, I now own a pub.'

'Aye, very good,' said R.I.P. 'What's the top prize, anyway? What did we agree last night?'

'A tenner a head,' said Hughie. 'The money's as good as mine. Can anyone better that?'

Vodka Joe stepped up to the bar. He produced a sheet of paper from a pocket of his black leather jacket. 'Ahem,' he said. 'Gentlemen, I think I have a winner right here in my hands. If I may be permitted, I'll begin.' He peered at the foolscap paper.

'Too slow to shoot,
  Noo his tea's oot,
  He lost the race,
  Took one in the face,
  Would've been better off in Bute.'

Vodka Joe took a bow. 'I thank you,' he said. 'Did I hear someone shouting for an encore now? Or will we wait until the end when I accept my prize? You know, like they do in the Eurovision Song Contest?'

'Aye, that's what to do,' said El Cid. 'Right, who's next?'

Bungalow Bob took centre stage in front of the bar. 'I was up all night with this one,' he said earnestly. 'This, gents, is my best shot. Here goes.' He, too, unraveled a crumpled piece of paper.

'*Here lies Wild Bill,*
See, I told you he was ill.'

Before he could take a bow, there was a loud throaty raspberry sound from Tip-Toe Thompson. 'Thief!' he exclaimed.

'What do you mean? Thief?' Bungalow Bob looked mortified. But, at the same time, he knew he had been rumbled.

'Spike Milligan did that,' said Tip-Toe. 'You've ripped off Spike Milligan. You've plagarised a legend.'

Hughie Edwards growled, 'If we did plagiarism it would probably be the best plagiarism in the world.'

'You look more like Orson Welles than you sound like him,' observed Vodka Joe.

'He's dead,' said Hughie.

'Exactly,' said Vodka Joe.

Bungalow Bob returned to his seat amid a chorus of derision from the audience. 'Och, I didnae hae the time to write anythin',' he said by way of explanation. 'I wash downstair windaes for a livin'. Fuck the lot of you.' He had a fair inkling he wouldn't be winning the top prize.

'Okay, R.I.P. Let's see what you've got to offer,' said Hughie. 'You are a wordsmith, or so you kept telling us last night, so this should be good. The floor is yours.'

The Chief News Reporter of the Daily News walked forward, ready for his moment in the spotlight. 'I can assure everyone that I have not nicked this from anyone,' he said looking sideways at Bungalow Bob. 'This is all my own work. Here goes and if you could please hold your applause until I get to the end, that would be greatly appreciated.' He fished out a piece of paper.

'*There was a young man called Wild Bill,*
Had an itchy arse, would never sit still,
And then one day,
He fancied some gun play,
Now you'll find him buried in Boot Hill.'

R.I.P. took an extravagant bow. Another mild round of applause. He looked at the audience. 'Come on, don't be shy,' he said. 'Let your emotions wash over you. You loved it, didn't you?'

'My turn,' said El Cid. 'If I can't do better than that, then I'll buy the entire bar a drink. I think you will recognise a winner when you hear it, gentlemen.' He, too, produced a piece of paper and began reading.

'*Briefly, we got to know Wild Bill,*
A gun-totin' cowboy from Maryhill,
It wasn't his day,
When he got blown away,
But his memory lives with us still.'

The detective inspector punched the air footballer-style. 'Good, eh? A winner, right enough. Cough up, gentlemen. I don't think we need to hear any other entrants. I thank you. Money in the pint pot, please. Hughie, if you could do the honours.'

'Hold on, paleface. Me got heap better words.' Sitting Bull strode forward. John Harris, stockbroker from Edinburgh, was in full Red Indian chief mode for his last day of the Country and Western Festival. 'Me think that has stench of buffalo fart. Me have winner right here.' He cleared his throat.

'*Cowboy no friend of mine,*
Wild Bill last in line,
Bang! He was dead,
Shot in the head,
That suit me, mighty fine.'

'Did Hughie write that shite for you?' asked R.I.P. 'That sounds like something Hughie would write.'

'Sitting Bull, keep the day job,' was the advice from Vodka Joe.

'Me heap no pleased with paleface,' said the Indian. 'That very good offering. It rhyme, too. Me believe I win. Palefaces cheat. Steal our land. Rape our women. Kill our buffalo.'

'Okay, Sitting Bull,' said Hughie. 'It was very good. I would have been happy to have penned that. Excellent.'

'All white squaws are pigs with knickers,' said Sitting Bull under his breath as he took his seat at the table and chucked a large Bell's down his throat.

'Right, who's up next?' said the bar owner. 'Brock? Tip-Toe? Boring Brian? You haven't had your say yet. Remember, folks, you have got to be in it to win it. There's ninety crisp pounds waiting for someone. Go on, give it your best shot, lads.'

Tip-Toe didn't need a piece of paper. He had rehearsed for this moment. He cleared his throat and began.

'Up there on yonder hill,
There once stood Wild Bill,
To his guns he was slow,
And he took a mortal blow,
Alas, he was just too easy to kill.'

Tip-Toe, like his rivals, stepped forward with a flourish and took a bow. He said, 'Gentlemen, I think we have a winner. Yes?'

Bungalow Bob, still upset at his Spike Milligan deception being so easily discovered by the chef, made a rude sound.

'Is this a "men only" thing or are mere females allowed to join in?' Maggie, long-suffering wife of Hughie and barmaid extraordinaire, carried through a bundle of empties from the snooker room. 'Does Calamity Jane do nothing about this place? What do we pay her for? These've been lying through there all night. Fuckin' waste of skin.'

Hughie looked startled. He had never heard his wife swear before.

'Okay, lads, I've penned a small ditty myself. There's my ten pounds, Hughie.' She flourished a brand new tenner and placed it on the bar. 'Here we go,' she said as she unraveled a napkin.

'There was a young lad called Wild Bill,
Who was known by his triumphant shrill,
Then one day,
His voice faded away,
And...'

The bar room was quiet for fully five seconds. Boring Brian broke the silence. 'You've missed a line, Maggie. I think that's you disqualified.'

'Go and make yourself useful, woman, and get the drinks in for this lot,' said Hughie. He was positive he heard his wife say, 'Suck loo.'

Boring Brian seized his opportunity. Now was the time for some much-awaited acclaim. From anyone. He started to read.

'Wild Bill got shot,
Er, that's the lot.'

More silence.

'And you wonder why we call you Boring Brian?' said Hughie.

'And then there was one,' said the pub owner. 'I've seen you shying away, Brock. Look, mate, we know you're only a sportswriter...'

'A sportswriter/sleuth, if you don't mind,' corrected Brock.

'...aye, that as well. You're only a sportswriter and you're only good for telling us the big full-back bashed the ball from twenty-five yards past the goalkeeper and into the onion bag. Fair enough, that's your job. So, we don't expect much. We promise not to boo, don't we gentlemen?'

'NO!' they barked back in loud unison.

Brock made his way to the front of the bar. 'I wrote this, good people, while I was getting on the outside of a nice bottle of JP Chenet, so I beg your indulgence. Here goes.' Brock produced two wrinkled pieces of foolscap.

'Hey! He's cheating,' said Bungalow Bob. 'He's got TWO pieces of paper.'

'That just means it will be twice as shite,' Vodka Joe smiled his wee smile. 'Right, carry on, Brock, give it your worst shot,' he added.

'Okay, here goes.' Brock looked at the first page and read.

'Oh, Lord, the Gates of Heaven please open this day,
To welcome a brave cowboy who is coming your way,
'Tis a time to cry, 'Tis a time to weep,
For an innocent's soul for you to keep.

Oh, Lord, please listen to his plea and his prayer,
Make him feel special in Your loving care,
Please let him see happiness through Thine own glorious eyes,
Allow him to join the angels in Your Paradise.
Embrace him with Your love, smile upon him with a sigh,
Wrap him in Your warmth, his life too swift to pass by,
So, now I serenade poor James Hitchock with this sweet lullaby,
As he goes to meet Wild Bill Hickok, in the prairie up on high.'
Silence.

'Fuck me, what was that?' cried Bungalow Bob eventually.

'Did you nick that out of a greetings card?' shouted Vodka Joe.

'What was the stuff you were drinking last night? Jeezus, does that stuff fuck with your head.' Tip-Toe made his observation.

'Heap no' bad for paleface,' said Sitting Bull.

'Aye, no' too bad for a whitey,' chipped in Hughie.

'Sportswriters don't write guff like that,' said R.I.P.

'All that and he knows the offside law,' added El Cid. 'Is there no end to this man's talent?'

'I thought it was too long,' said Boring Brian.

CHAPTER THIRTY-SIX

MIDDAY MONDAY

'What I don't understand,' queried Vodka Joe, 'is why Wild Bill Hickok was smiling when he got shot. Hardly a laughing matter, a bullet thudding between your eyes. I don't think I would have seen the funny side and I'm well-known for my sense of humour.'

'Actually, you would be surprised at the amount of people who die with what looks like a big, bright beaming smile on their face,' said Bert Martin, Chief Detective Inspector of the CID, aka Maverick. 'It's a nervous reaction. It's more of a grimace than a grin. You should see some of the folk we've had down at the morgue once rigor mortis has set in. They look positively delighted to be have met up with the Grim Reaper.'

Maverick lifted a large glass of Cutty Sark to his lips. 'First of the day,' he lied. The occupants of the Nashville were sure he had had at least another four after joining them an hour ago. Maverick checked his wristwatch. 'One more Press Conference in half-an-hour and then I'll be off your island, gentlemen and lady.' He toasted Hughie, Maggie, Vodka Joe, Tip-Toe Thompson, Boring Brian and Bungalow Bob. 'Thank you one and all for your hospitality. I think I'll give my fishing trip to Arran a miss in November. I will return to your island, I promise. In happier circumstances, hopefully.'

The cop sipped his whisky.

'Oh, I've got another question for you, chief,' said Vodka Joe, the seeker of all knowledge. 'I've heard stories about blokes having ejaculations when they've just been hung, is that right?'

'Hanged,' corrected Brock, without thinking. 'Only pictures are hung.'

'Aye, whatever,' said Vodka Joe. 'Is that true, Sid? Do they have hard-ons when they plunge to the end of the rope?'

'Can't says I've ever seen evidence first hand, Vodka Joe,' smiled Maverick. 'It's been a wee while since anyone was hanged in this country. But, yes, we do know there are a few weirdos out there who do all sort of things to help them get an erection. What about that Tory MP in London a few years ago? He was found in his hallway dangling from a rope. He was dressed in a black, silky basque, had the suspenders and stockings, the lipstick, the wig, the banana, the lot. "Death by misadventure," was the coroner's verdict.'

Vodka Joe, in an instant, realised there was a world out there he knew nothing about. He would keep it that way.

Maverick checked his wristwatch again. 'Time to go,' he said placing his empty glass on the surface of the bar. 'What about you, Sitting Bull? You leaving soon?'

John Harris, stockbroker from Morningside, in Edinburgh, decided to give up the Red Indian act. He looked at the clock on the wall of the pub. 'Aye, I'll not be far behind you,' he said. 'Back to work tomorrow. Sitting Bull will be put back in the wardrobe for another year.' He paused, smiled and said, 'Me return to Millport in many months. Me try not to make complete fuckin' arse of myself next time.'

'You say that every year,' smiled Hughie.

EPILOGUE

EARLY MONDAY EVENING, SEPTEMBER 17

'Hey! Worzel! Eight banana daiquiris right noo. And we want they wee umbrellas, tae.'

Hughie Edwards, an ice-cold shiver tap-dancing down his spine, turned slowly from pouring a pint of lager for Tip-Toe Thompson. He looked to the opposite end of the bar. He was face-to-face with Spice Witches, The Sequel. Not the original cast, but pretty damn close. Uncannily, they had parked their ample backsides at the top end of the bar, the exact same spot as Paisley's finest beauty consultants on the last day of August. Remarkable.

'Pardon, ma'am?' said Hughie, handing Tip-Toe his pint and then walking in their direction as they still piled in from the side-door. All shapes and sizes. Fat, skinny, tall, short. Ugly and uglier. They were all wearing tasteful fluorescent orange T-shirts emblazoned with the six-inch high words in red letters, 'BLOW JOBS R US'.

'Ur ye deef as well as blind? Listen, Milky Bar Kid, we want eight banana daiquiris and we want them right noo.'

Hughie composed himself. 'Certainly, ma'am. May I know the name of the lovely lady to whom I am addressing?'

'Eh?'

'Can ye tell me your name, please?'

'It'll no' dae ye any good, grandad, cos Ah don't dae charity work. Ah don't shag ancient geezers. No' even a wee BJ for you, Ah'm afraid. Yer right oot o' luck, Engelbert. But if ye must know it's Lola. Dae ye hae a problem wi' that?'

'No, no, of course, not. It's a lovely name. Well, Lola, can you answer me one more little question?'

'Don't even think aboot asking fur a phone number. Ah might have to come ower that bar and skelp ye good lookin'.'

'No. Would I ever dream of making such a request? Could I ever be that optimistic? Be still my beating heart. No, Lola, all I want to know is how long you and your extremely fine companions will be staying on the island? Is this a day trip?'

"Nuh! It's Lucy's hen week. Whit's today? Monday? We go back hame on Sunday night. And we aim to rip the arse aff it. If ye see me sober, point me in the direction of a pub or an offy. We've saved up three months for this week. And we are goin' tae party, party, party. Aren't we, girls?'

A wall of sound, in varying decibel levels, shrieked agreement with that very sentiment.

'Six full days, eh?' mused Hughie. 'Eight banana daiquiris coming right up, my lovely. Would you like ice with them?'

Hughie smiled and began pouring. 'And I won't forget the umbrellas, my little ray of sunshine.'

'Hey, weasel-features! Ye better make them large cos it's gonnae be a long night and we a' aim to get oot oor fuckin' faces.'

Beaming broadly, the bar owner whispered to Tip-Toe, 'Music to my ears. Six days and six nights, eh? That's the deposit for next year's cruise in the bank. There is a God in heaven, after all.'

Hughie Edwards was already looking forward to giving the Loathsome Eightsome the appropriate send-off on Sunday night. He began humming very softly to himself.

'Nellie the elephant packed her trunk and said goodbye to the circus...'